author managed to weave in several real-life xenophobic/ bigotry issues which just made the characters feel like they were operating in real life without detracting from the story. In fact, I'd say it enhanced the story because we need to call more attention to these things. I've never been on Route 66, but based on the descriptions and the adventure it's on my bucket list moving forward.

-C-Spot Reviews

Beacon of Love

This is a well-written book about love, loss, redemption, and parenthood. Roberts intertwines her characters like a helix and slowly unveils the truth about each one... This is one of those books that sneaks up on the reader. There aren't a lot of bells and whistles, it doesn't shout at you, nor does it hit you over the head. It is, however, well written and in a quiet way, the characters and their story will stay with you long after you finish the book and put it aside.

-LambdaLiterary.org

D1561378

Praise for the works of Ann Roberts

Dying on the Vine

The story is well-paced, with revelations coming bit by bit, whetting the appetite. The writing shows skill and a love of language. Ms. Roberts is extremely skilled at bringing her characters to life. It was a joy to read and is the kind of book to savour, like a large glass of your favourite wine.

-*The Lesbian Review*

I've read many Ann Roberts books, but this was my first Ari Adams Mystery. There is an excellent ensemble cast of characters, all of whom are nuanced, fully drawn, and intriguing. It's hard to say which is more interesting—the cast of characters and their relationships, the swift pace of the investigation, or the details of the art and science of winemaking. The relationships portrayed are genuinely adult and therefore complex and engaging. The culture around vineyards and winemaking is a passionate one and that passion is reflected in the characters and situations in the book. Highly recommended. I look forward to starting with the very first Ari Adams mystery and finding out everything I've missed.

-Anja S., *NetGalley*

Justice Calls

I must admit that I was sucked in from the first sentence because Ann Roberts has a way of crafting a story to keep her readers captivated. I definitely got a realistic portrayal of the gutwrenching pain, frustration, and anger that Ari and her father felt as they worked tirelessly to find out who killed Richie. I can't believe that I went through a gamut of emotions with every word I read and I just couldn't let Ari, Molly, or Jack go even when the story ended. If you're looking for heartfelt moments, character growth, timeless love coupled with an understanding that knows no boundaries and a compelling mystery, then this story is certainly for you!

-The Lesbian Review

A Secret to Tell

This is surely one story you should not miss out on reading. I can assure you, this story has the right amount of angst, mystery, comedy, and romance to keep you up way past your bedtime. From the first page I was completely sucked into the story due to the nonstop action and the steady flow of angst and excitement. The characters were realistic and the dialogue between them was fantastic!

-The Lesbian Review

Deadly Intersections

June, 2011, RLynne - Roberts has given her reader a wild roller coaster ride in a plot filled with dead bodies, intrigue, lies, and corruption. Her characters are very real with flaws and baggage, and very likeable. Set in Phoenix, Arizona, juxtaposes the bright sunlight with the very dark underbelly of the city. This is a book full of surprises with an exciting cliff-hanger of an ending.

-Just About Write

Vagabond Heart

The story starts off with a bang and kept my interest all the way through. It's been forever since I picked up a book that I had trouble putting down. This one could easily make it into my read-again pile. Both Quinn and Suda are interesting characters and their interactions didn't feel scripted or overplayed. The

THE
CONVINCING
HOUR

Other Bella Books by Ann Roberts

The Ari Adams Mystery Series
Paid in Full
White Offerings
Deadly Intersections
Point of Betrayal
A Grand Plan
A Secret to Tell
Justice Calls
Dying on the Vine

Romances
Brilliant
Beach Town
Petra's Canvas
Root of Passion
Beacon of Love
Hidden Hearts
The Complete Package
Pleasure of the Chase
Vagabond Heart
Screen Kiss

General Fiction
Furthest from the Gate
Keeping Up Appearances

THE CONVINCING HOUR

Ann Roberts

BELLA
BOOKS
2021

Bella Books, Inc.
P.O. Box 10543
Tallahassee, FL 32302

Printed in the United States of America on acid-free paper.

First Edition - 2021

Editor: Katherine V. Forrest
Cover Designer: Heather Honeywell

ISBN: 978-1-64247-252-3

PUBLISHER'S NOTE

For Dr. Janice Johnson

Compassionate soul
Kindest human
Relentless climate advocate
Passionate educator
Outstanding leader
Ocean lover
Eternal optimist
Trusted colleague
Attentive listener
Fierce child advocate
Life-long learner
Talented teacher
Brave fighter
Excellent mentor
Dearest friend

Thank you for believing in me and giving me the
opportunities that made this book possible.

PROLOGUE

Culver City, California

Whap!
When I shoved Paige's scrawny, bulimic body against the gym locker, it felt good. I won't deny it. Just givin' her a little taste of Newton's First Law, the one about goin' along until you meet a force. She'd been goin' in her little straight line of bullying and harassing me, and my Xena-warrior body compelled her to change course—right into the locker.

Like I said, it felt good and I saw purple, my color of rage. In school they tell you RED is the color of rage—and anger. But I've never seen red. Just purple. Ms. Olsen, the school counselor, told me it didn't matter what color I saw. Only thing that mattered is that I knew I was gettin' mad.

"I ain't no ho!" I shouted over the yells of the other P.E. students. "And don't you be talkin' about my mama!"

"Fuck you," she spat.

I twisted her spindly arm behind her back and yanked her ponytail. "Take it back."

"Let go!" she wailed.

"Punch her!" someone yelled.

"Kick her!"

Easy for them to say. I'd learned how much suspension each of those hits was worth. Easy for somebody else to tell you what to do when they wouldn't ever do it themselves.

"What the hell is going on?" boomed Lardass, the P.E. teacher. The only thing bigger than his voice was his body. Ex-football player and ex-Marine, who still wore a flattop. He wedged between Paige and me and wrapped his tree-like arm around my neck. He was givin' me his own spin on Newton's First Law.

"I can't breathe," I squeaked.

His sickeningly sweet cologne mixed with sweat made me gag. He had a sneer on his face. He was enjoying this. He'd hated me since the first day when I refused to do the climbing wall. I couldn't think about it anymore. The only thing I could think about was *air*. He was growling at me and for a split second I wondered what color his rage was.

"Let go, John!"

Thank God for Ms. Barnaby, the principal. Hearing his boss's voice, he let go. I crumpled onto the bench—gasping and grabbing my throat—and the rest of the class dispersed. Everybody knew the closer you are to the trouble, the more trouble you get. Except for Paige's sycophants. They huddled around her like a force field. They kept throwing me shade, so I looked away.

I practiced my breathing and stared at the graffiti carved into the bench—an infinity symbol. I almost laughed. I agreed. P.E. never seemed to end.

Across the room Lardass leaned against the lockers, looking away while Ms. Barnaby laid into him. She waved her radio, the antenna like a pointer. She wasn't trying to be quiet and he didn't seem to care until she said, "...involuntary suspension without pay."

I smiled. I knew I was in it deep but so was he. *Hello, Lardass, meet Mr. Newton.*

Finally, three other members of the Hoover High security team rushed in. I rolled my eyes. I knew they'd been off campus at the Quik Stop, either getting a lousy burrito for lunch or taking a smoke. As a regular Hoover troublemaker, I was on a first-name basis with each of them. Goomba, the youngest, scowled at me and immediately went to Paige and her Barbie doll friends. He'd graduated from Hoover two years before and he still acted like he was a student. He let the popular kids get away with anything. Kinda funny because Goomba was never popular. His real name was Herman Flinch. Seriously.

Troy, one of the only decent security guards, went straight to Ms. Barnaby looking for direction, while Extra Sauce Mike trudged in last, wheezing. I laughed, picturing his sixty-year-old body trying to hustle across the street so he didn't miss the action. He bent over to catch his breath but he didn't care what was going down. He was just making an appearance to keep his job.

Except for Troy and a guy named Promo, security didn't do shit. That's why Ms. Barnaby seemed to be everywhere. She had to if she didn't want a riot at her school.

Of course, none of them talked to me. And that was fine. It didn't matter. Nobody ever believed me anyway. I bit my lip. That wasn't true. Ms. Barnaby and Ms. Coyne, her fine-looking assistant, always gave me the benefit of the doubt. And I'd never lied to them. Not once.

I closed my eyes and thought of the ocean, changing that purple to the deep blue of the sea. Only good thing about Culver City was I could get to the shore on the bus. My rage receded like a wave spent on the beach. I was in control again. I wasn't angry anymore but I was ashamed. Ms. Barnaby, Ms. Coyne and Ms. Olsen would be disappointed.

"Breanna, I need you to come with me," Ms. B said quietly.

I grabbed my backpack and followed her, the rest of the class staring at me. Now, the old Breanna would see the purple again and wipe those smirks off their faces, even in front of the security guards. Even if I got hurt. But the new Breanna just swallowed it and sauntered out of the gym with Ms. Barnaby.

Once it was just the two of us, my shoulders slumped when the shame returned. *So much for the new Breanna. You're like a Project Runway model who just fell off the runway!* "You want to tell me what set you off in there?" Ms. B asked gently.

"Paige is talking shit. Callin' me a ho. And my mama. She might be a lot but she ain't a ho."

I knew it was ironic that I got in trouble defending a woman who hated me and wished I was dead.

"And that's when you threw Paige against the locker?"

"Yeah. Am I goin' home?" I snuck a glance at her but she ignored the question. *She doesn't need to answer, dummy. You know the play.*

I looked around. I had Ms. B all to myself. Usually half a dozen people were running up to talk to her but now everybody was back in class. *Ask her!*

"Why are you still here?"

Ms. B blinked. I'd surprised her. She didn't answer and I wasn't sure she would. I snuck another look. Her blond hair was shiny and fell to her shoulders. It was pretty and didn't come out of a bottle. She had the longest eyelashes I'd ever seen, and since I'd been in her office a lot, I'd had plenty of chances to look at them—and her pretty green eyes. Her lips were puffy and I'd imagined kissing her...

"I'm here because I want to be," she finally said.

"Why? If it'd been me that won the lottery, I woulda bailed right away. Said, 'sorry, chumps. You can take Herbert Hoover High and shove it up your ass!'" I coughed and added, "Sorry about swearing."

She laughed. "I thought about doing that."

"You did?"

"Of course I thought about leaving, but then I'd miss these stellar opportunities to converse with the student body."

I looked at her sideways and saw she was smiling. Even though I was in deep trouble, I smiled back. "That's jacked."

Everybody knew that Charlotte Barnaby, principal of Hoover High School, had won the largest lottery *ever.* Like anywhere. One and a half billion dollars! She wouldn't talk about it at all, except at the ceremony when they presented her with the big, fake check. That was the law. If she wanted the money, she had to do the dance. I knew all this because I'd been in the office for an in-school suspension when the lottery guy showed up to talk with her about the deets.

He didn't understand her either. Why was she still working? Why didn't she want to celebrate? He sounded jealous of her. But she was just…herself. Told him she wasn't leaving the school hangin' in the middle of the year and she'd use the money to help people in some way. That part didn't surprise me at all. And a billion dollars could help a lot of people.

She convinced them to do the check presentation at Spring Break, thinking that maybe everybody would forget by the time they got back to school. Hard to forget when there's a bunch of TV news crews out in the parking lot.

Mama certainly wasn't gonna forget. When she saw it on TV, she threw her beer at the screen. "Are you fucking kidding me! Her? She's the last person who should win anything! This is so jacked!"

I tried to calm her down. "Maybe she'll leave now and Mr. Newman'll be the principal?" Newman was the other assistant principal in charge of athletics. All he did was hang out in the weight room with the jocks.

Her eyes widened and she nodded. "Well, that would be something. He knows how to stay the hell out of our business."

But she'd stayed.

"So, is your mother home these days?" Ms. B asked as she swung open the door to the admin building.

"Yeah, but she said not to bother her anymore."

She snorted, "Not how it works."

"You're gonna be sorry," I warned. "She hates you even more since you got rich. You really will be sorry."

Ms. B sighed. "Yeah, I probably will."

I knew it'd be a few hours before Mama bothered to show up at the school to take me home and it was guaranteed she'd make a scene. Not because she'd be defending me or talking about the bullying that happened. No, she'd be mad that she'd had to take three buses to the school, probably interrupting the remainder of her high from the score she'd made the morning before.

I'd convinced her to let me switch schools because my old school, Edison, was worthless. And she'd let me go but she wouldn't move out of our 'hood. She said it was 'cause her friends were there, but I knew she wanted to stay close to her dealer.

"Take this one, please," Ms. B said, pointing to a student desk in the hallway that sat next to the conference room.

I slid into the chair and buried my head. The worst part of being sent to the office was the boredom and the constant ringing of the phones. Nothing worthwhile ever happened and none of the staff gossiped about each other or the students. It had been more entertaining at Edison because the principal was a do-nothing slob who never left his office except to talk to the policemen who regularly arrested members of the student body—usually the Black kids. There was always something going down there and I didn't feel safe. But Hoover was different.

Why! Why do I get so angry? I'm stupid. Stupid. Stupid. I stared at my balled fists and felt the anger rising, saw the purple. But this time I was mad at my mom, not Paige. I hated her even though I was in trouble for defending her. I could say anything about her but nobody else got to dis her.

See, I'm bipolar, but Mama won't fill my meds regularly. If it's between her meth or my prescriptions, guess what wins? She's never understood I need them to stay even. To stay safe. To stay above the waves. But most of the time I felt like I was drowning…in the sea of purple.

I wouldn't have whooped on Paige if I'd had my meds.

"What are you doing here?"

I looked up at Ms. Coyne, the assistant principal. She was a tall, incredibly beautiful Black woman. I knew her first name was Elle, like the fashion magazine. Maybe her mama had suspected she'd be as beautiful as a model. She always wore classy business suits, large earrings and a necklace with a diamond teardrop.

She was as cool as she looked and she was a fabulous athlete, played basketball at UCLA. Me and her talked sports, especially softball, my fave. Ms. Coyne thought I could get a scholarship and be a Bruin just like she had. I wanted to believe it could happen but every time I wound up sitting outside Ms. Barnaby's office, I believed Ms. Coyne a little less.

"Was it Paige again?" Ms. Coyne asked in a low voice.

I nodded. "I just couldn't...I couldn't stop."

Ms. Coyne only offered a hard stare. I hated disappointing her. I dropped my gaze. I didn't deserve to look at someone as fine as Ms. Elle Coyne.

"Did your mother ever refill your meds?"

I closed my eyes. When I got a whiff of her expensive perfume I knew she was squatting beside me.

"Why didn't you come and tell me?"

Why? It's fucking embarrassing! I HATE being on them but I would for you! "I didn't want to bother you."

"Breanna, sit up and look at me, please."

I did as she asked and gazed into her kind, brown eyes.

"You're never a bother. I know you have your pride, and I know the meds make you feel loopy. But still, you need them now. At least for a while." She took a breath and looked down the hall. "I don't know what's gonna go down on this thing with Paige. You'll probably be suspended but..." I opened my mouth to protest but she pointed at me. "...it won't be for long. I promise you that. Now, do you have any homework I can get from your teachers?"

I shook my head. "I did it all."

Ms. Coyne chuckled. "Of course you did. It's all too damn easy, isn't it?"

I shrugged and felt my cheeks burn. That was the truth. School was easy. I was on the list to do "enrichment projects," which were challenging and fun, but supposedly all the spaces in the special class were filled. I knew that was bullshit. Mrs. O'Dell, the oldest and *whitest* teacher, didn't want me there. I couldn't blame her. Who'd want a front row seat to one of my shit shows?

I cleared my throat. "Is Paige okay?"

"Yeah. She's got a few bruises and a cut on her forehead. But her lovely personality remains exactly the same."

I looked away and stifled a laugh.

"Okay," Ms. Coyne continued, "I'm going to get you some paper and a pencil so you can draw or write some poetry."

"Can I ask you a question?"

"Of course."

"Do you think Ms. B's gonna stay as principal now that she's rich?"

"Um, I don't know." Ms. Coyne smiled.

Liar. Ms. Coyne and Ms. Barnaby were close and I'd wondered if they were a couple. The look on Ms. Coyne's face told me Ms. B was leaving. That sucked. If Ms. Barnaby left, then Ms. Coyne would probably leave too.

"I'll be back in a minute," Ms. Coyne said.

She turned away and I called, "Thank you."

Ms. Coyne looked over her shoulder and winked. I felt all fuzzy inside and grinned.

"Get my daughter, lady!"

I jumped at the sound of Mama's voice.

"Now!" she barked at Ms. Rodriguez, the super-kind woman who always spoke sweetly to the kids even when they didn't deserve it.

I couldn't hear Ms. Rodriguez's reply, but I heard Ms. Barnaby say, "Shaneesha, you need to come into the conference room. We have to talk before Breanna leaves with you."

"Like hell you do!"

"We do. The police are involved."

"For shit's sake! This school is the worst one yet!"

I turned over the page with the poem I'd been working on so Mama wouldn't snatch it away when they went into the conference room.

She came around the corner still in her ratty pajama bottoms and a worn T-shirt, her large breasts jiggling free underneath the sheer fabric. When she saw me, she came at me. "I oughta slap you senseless, girl!"

Promo, the only other good security guy, quickly grabbed Mama's arm and pulled it behind her back.

"Assault! Assault! Get your hands off me, asshole! This guy's assaulting me! Call the cops!" she cried as he forced her into the conference room and tried to close the door behind him.

I stuck out my foot and caught the corner of the door before it clicked shut. I wanted to hear this but I didn't need to see it. I knew Mama's moves, her expressions, all of it. She'd been mad at me my whole life. Our lives were like a bad TV show that kept repeating.

"I'm gonna sue all of ya, exspecially you, Principal. You goin' down! I'll take those millions from you."

"Ms. Waits, you need to sit and discuss this matter calmly," Ms. Barnaby said, "or I'll end this meeting, go to my office and call your parole officer. He'd probably be very interested to learn that you're using again."

"You can't do that!"

"I most certainly can. Look at yourself. You're in no shape to parent Breanna."

"*Parent* Breanna?" she snorted. "Nobody *parents* Breanna. That girl does whatever she wants."

"Do you even know your daughter?"

"What the hell you talkin 'bout?"

"Do you know how intelligent she is? How successful she could be if—"

"Shut up, lady! I don't give a fuck! Don't you see that? You missin' my message? How dumb are you?" When Ms. B didn't say anything, she added, "You think you're so damn smart, you take her."

"Excuse me?"

"I saw you on TV holdin' up that huge check. I don't want her anymore. I ain't goin' to jail for that little bitch. She's a hot mess and I can't control her. I've been telling you people that for the last two years! I got my own shit to solve. You're a rich woman now. You take her."

I leaned closer to the door. Nobody said anything. I guessed Ms. B was shocked. I wasn't.

"I'll make it easy for you," Mama blurted.

There was a commotion. A crash. Mama screamed. Promo's heavy footsteps grew closer and I slid the desk away from the door just as it flew open, propelled by Mama's dirty orange kicks. Promo had her in a bear hug, carrying her down the empty hallway toward the security office. Troy appeared and as he attempted to grab one of her flailing feet, she popped him in the face. She laughed but it turned into a whimper—then a cry. I guessed Promo had tightened his grip.

They disappeared into the security office and the door slammed shut. I looked down. *What happens to me now!*

Ms. B came to the doorway, dabbing her cheek with a paper towel.

"You're bleeding," I said.

"Yeah, your mom got me with that ring she wears."

"Her high school class ring. Only thing she owns from her old life. And yeah, it leaves a mark."

"Did she finish high school?"

I nodded. Mama loved talking about high school, the only memories that made her smile. *It wasn't high school that made her smile. What made her smile was Grandma Esther. Then she died...*

Ms. B said, "Breanna, is there anyone you can call, an adult that you trust?"

You're the only adult I trust—most of the time. I shook my head.

"What's on the paper? Is that the poem I saw you working on earlier?"

I nodded.

"Would you read it to me?"

I hesitated. *What if she hates it?*

"Go ahead. It's okay."

I glanced up. She looked like she really wanted to hear it. "It's about you winnin' the lottery."

She rolled her eyes. "Yes, that seems to be all anyone talks about." She thrust her chin toward the paper. "I'm ready. I can take it."

I chuckled and cleared my throat. "I call it 'Filthy Lucre.'"

Ms. B snorted. "Great."

I took a deep breath.

"Greed, greed, that's all I see,
You won it big,
Are you better than me?
You may not change
But everybody else will,
They'll try to put their hand
In your till.
They got their own dreams,
Expect you to flip a switch,
If you ignore 'em,
Then you're just a bitch.
Get outta here,
It's the only way.
Otherwise they'll make you pay."

I couldn't look up at Ms. B. She was probably mad.

"Thank you," she said. "I appreciate this, Breanna. I really do. May I keep it?"

I held it out and she accepted it gently, like it was valuable.

"I have to make some phone calls, Breanna. I won't lie to you. Your mother is going to jail and you won't be going home with her." She touched my shoulder. "Just wait here while I go talk with Ms. Coyne."

Before she walked away, I had to know. "Ms. Barnaby, could you ever do it?"

"Do what?"

"Take me. Keep me?"

"Oh, I didn't know you heard your mother say that. I'm sure she didn't mean it."

"She meant it," I said quickly. "And if you adopted me, I'd be glad. And I wouldn't give you any trouble. Could you do it?"

She only gave me this sad look. I knew it was a no. What else could it be? That happy ending, fairy tale crap only happened on TV or in the movies.

Mama went to jail for thirty days, long enough to get sober, and I stayed with a friend as a Foster. Then I went back to Mama. Her next boyfriend, Johnny, who needed meds as much as I did, punched me hard enough to kill me. He'd been an amateur boxer so he knew how to hit. And as I lay dying on the floor, I wondered about the color of his rage. I ain't got no idea what color he saw but right before I died, I finally figured out why I saw purple when I got so mad. It was the color of the bruises I got from the people who supposedly loved me.

CHAPTER ONE

Five Years Later

Lakeview, Michigan
4ᵗʰ of July

    "Story, that's the most insane plan I've ever heard," my girlfriend Bertie announced.

    I shrugged. "I don't see any other way."

    We were lying on her bed, taking a break from kissing and touching, our shirts unbuttoned. We'd been going out for three months, but Bertie knew she was my first real girlfriend so we were keeping it PG.

    I glanced at the far wall and her display of softball trophies. Softball was her ticket out of Lakeview, all the way to the University of North Carolina. She'd just graduated and would start there in the fall. We'd already decided that our romance ended when she went off to college. I still had two years of high school left but if my plan worked, hopefully I'd be going somewhere else too. We would each start a new adventure.

    The rest of Bertie's room was like a shrine to sports and the history of sports. Her mother was African-American and her father was Puerto Rican. Her mom made sure she knew about Althea Gibson, the Williams sisters, Flo-Jo, and Lisa Leslie, while her dad shared his love of baseball and Roberto Clemente. They'd thought Bertie would be a boy, so when she came out a girl, she became Roberta and her dad made sure she learned all about softball. Bertie was most proud of a jersey signed by softball Hall of Famer Dot Wilkinson.

She sat up and raked her dark curly hair away from her face. I stared into the warm brown eyes I adored. I knew her concern was because she liked (*loved?*) me. "I wish you'd let this go," she said pleadingly. "You can get a scholarship to a great school. You're the smartest person I know."

I took her hand. "It's not about college. It's about right now. It's about spending two more years bored out of my mind."

"What if something goes wrong? What if Marvin has a gun? What if he shoots you?"

I pulled her to me for a kiss. "He's not going to shoot me. He knows me. Besides, Ivy's going to be there. She's the mastermind behind all of this."

Bertie snorted. "You just said Ivy and mastermind in the same sentence."

I threw up my hands. "She knows the system. She—"

"Yeah, 'cause she's been to detention like eight times."

"No," I scoffed.

"And what about detention? A lot of those kids are dangerous."

I looked away. It was the one part of my plan I tried not to think about too much. When I glanced at Bertie again, she was staring at me. She knew I was worried. She also knew I wasn't going to change my mind.

She sighed. "This is so jacked, Story. You're deliberately going to jail just so you might get a chance to go to a better school. A school that might not even exist."

"No, I know it exists. And yeah," I said, trying to sound determined. "That's exactly what I'm going to do."

"Do what I say and I won't cut you," Ivy said, leaning over the counter at Marvin's Mini-Mart. She pointed the filet knife in the general direction of Marvin's left eyeball. She glanced at me and said, "Story, hold up your pipe. Show him you mean business."

I stayed next to her, a scowl on my face, my right hand gripping a foot-long, rusty pipe she'd given me. I tried to look dangerous, settling on a sneer that my mother had perfected and used on me regularly.

Marvin shook his head like we were idiots. It was hard to take Ivy seriously while she was wearing a red, white and blue headband with blinking stars that looked like they'd sprouted out of her scalp.

I'd shown up at Ivy's grandmother's house with a brick I found along the way but she'd taken one look at it and said, "Story Black, what the hell are you gonna do with that? You throw it through his front window and this could go from misdemeanor to felony in a second. I said I'd help you but I'm not doing hard time."

She crossed her rail-thin arms and leaned against the doorway, one equally stick-like leg propped up against the threshold. She'd recently hacked her brown hair super short, a mistake I thought. Her hairstyle just made her sallow cheeks obvious. If there was anyone left at Franklin High who didn't know Ivy was bulimic, they did now.

She studied the brick and said, "Okay, maybe you should bring it. But we might not need it. If I say to chuck it, you know what to do."

"Got it."

"C'mon, I've got something else in the back."

The "something" was the filthy pipe I now held in my right hand. It smelled like the foul water that had passed through it for a few decades and I kept it away from my face.

When Ivy barked at Marvin, he automatically stepped back against the cigarette case, his hands behind him. His ridiculous top hat covered in American flags fell to the floor, exposing his nearly bald head. He always wore the same thing—jeans and a bowling shirt with his name stitched above his heart. Today's shirt was red, white and blue in honor of the holiday, and across from his name was a patch that said HIGH ROLLERS, most likely the name of one of his bowling teams. Bowling was big in Lakeview. Marvin loved to bowl and the area behind the counter was covered with trophies, photos of his teams, and bowling stuff—pins, bags, even a bright red ball.

When I'd shopped at the store, I always tried to read the little silver plates at the bottom of each trophy. In my fifteen years I'd never gotten a trophy for anything. I'd never wanted to be on a sports team and they didn't give trophies for reading books. When I'd stared at Marvin's collection, I thought it might be nice to have one. But I knew Mom would say, "Story, you don't need some shiny thing with a fake marble bottom. Trust me. Underneath that silver paint is cheap plastic! You might as well display a crappy toilet brush since they're probably made at the same factory."

Standing against the cigarette case, I couldn't read Marvin's expression. It was buried beneath his bushy gray beard. You'd have thought with all the hair on his face that his head would be the same. Nope. Spaghetti-like strands crossed his scalp in the worst comb-over I'd ever seen. If he was frightened, he didn't show it. His store had been in the 'hood for decades so I guessed he routinely dealt with *real* criminals, which Ivy and I certainly were not.

"We just want the money in the register!" Ivy barked.

Marvin's large, blue eyes shifted from her to me and his face softened. He looked sad. I looked away. *Maybe Bertie's right. Maybe this is crazy!* Marvin had always been nice to me. I'd tried to convince Ivy that we really should hit up a franchise since we should always support Lakeview's neighborhood businesses. Robbing a local wasn't very supportive.

She'd disagreed saying if I wanted to get arrested, only the locals pressed charges. She said the franchises had so much money that it was a waste of time to call their lawyers for little robberies.

"The money! Now!" Ivy poked the knife toward him and he nodded.

Then it all happened so fast. He pushed off the cigarette case like he was going to the register, but his left hand went sideways, grabbing the bowling pin. He smacked the butt of the pin against Ivy's hand. The knife went flying and she screamed.

"You fucking shit! You broke my hand!" She cradled it and backed toward the door. "Why'd you do that?"

I heard a siren and realized that at some point before disarming Ivy, Marvin had pressed a silent alarm. He came around the counter still holding the bowling pin and hissed at me, "Drop it, Story."

I let go of the pipe, remembering too late that my choice of footwear had been flip-flops. When the pipe landed on my big toe, I gasped. "Ow, ow, ow," I cried, jumping around on my good foot.

Marvin just shook his head at Ivy and me—two moaning girls. He was totally calm and I guessed he might've had daughters judging from his reaction. He picked up our sorry weapons and set them on a high shelf. Then he helped me sit down on a stack of dogfood bags next to his picked-over display of fireworks. The door buzzer sounded as Ivy bolted through the door. She yelled over her shoulder, "Chuck it!"

The siren was coming closer and he pointed at the door and said, "Story, you want to make a run for it too?"

I shook my head. "Can't run," I mumbled.

He looked at me knowingly. "Can't or *won't?*"

"Both." I gave him a sympathetic look and pulled the brick out of my shoulder bag. "Sorry."

His eyes grew wide and he shouted, "No!" just as I heaved it through the front window.

No way I'm running. This is MY Independence Day.

CHAPTER TWO

When the cops showed up, one had run after Ivy who, like me, was in flip-flops. What else was there to wear in the middle of summer?

"Just keep your head down and do as they say," Ivy whispered after they put us in the police car. "Follow my lead."

I squirmed, unable to sit back because of the handcuffs. And they were too tight. "What happens next?"

"They'll take us downtown. Some of it'll seem like TV but mostly it's just boring."

"Great. Couldn't we have done this on a day that wasn't the Fourth of July?" I'd wanted to sit in the park with Bertie and watch the fireworks, courtesy of Charlotte Barnaby, former school principal and now the town bigwig.

"No, we had to do it today because Judge Dickhead is running family court. He does it on all the holidays. And you want him."

"I do?"

"Yeah. And work on your attitude. It needs to get a lot worse. Think surly."

Surly. I can do surly.

"How many times exactly have you been arrested?"

"Three…no, four," she said emphatically. "Yeah, four. But Grandma's worked for the courts, geez…twenty years. I got all the gossip."

"Respect," I said, nodding.

When I'd first told her my plan, she didn't think it would work.

"Story, you've never committed a crime so they'll probably want to give you probation or put you in a diversion program and rehabilitate you," Ivy explained.

"But I need to go to detention."

She'd said she'd think on it and two days later she had a plan. Now we were living it. I was hoping my attempt at armed robbery, along with Marvin's statement, might sway the judge to send me to jail. When I threw the brick through his window, he went from sympathetic to super pissed.

The good thing was that we stayed together and they kept us away from the adult criminals. Everything was so different and unknown, completely overwhelming. The worse thing was the smell. "Ew," I said as we sat down on a bench in a tiny holding cell.

"It's the smell of fear," Ivy commented. "And urine."

Eventually a police officer appeared and said, "Which one of you is Story Black?"

I raised my hand and he said, "You live in Trailer Town?"

"Yep."

He narrowed his eyes. "That's, 'Yes, sir.'"

I rolled my eyes. "Yes, sir."

"We can't find your mother. She won't answer the phone number you gave us and she's not at your house…er, your trailer."

I shrugged. "Not surprising."

"Any ideas?"

"Maybe the library?"

"Does she work there?"

"Sort of."

He smirked. "Black, if you're messing with me…"

He stormed off and Ivy nodded. "That was good," she said, patting my arm. "Excellent attitude." Then she leaned closer and whispered, "I think this is so cool what you're doing."

"Thanks. And please don't say that out loud."

She winked. "Gotcha."

Ivy's mom showed up eventually after she got home from her overnight shift at the Gas 'n Go. They came and got Ivy but before she left she whispered, "Just hang in there and don't act like you're sorry about it."

After she left I took some deep breaths. My right foot was bouncing like crazy. I was nervous and anxious like I've never been. I guessed Ivy got to go home since she didn't throw the brick.

A young lawyer named William Krentz arrived and said he'd been assigned to my case. He asked a bunch of questions and I could've won an award for my performance as an apathetic teenager. I'd certainly seen enough of them. I'm not sure he totally bought it since I didn't have a record. A few times he offered these long stares at me like he wasn't believing what I was saying.

"So you don't have any remorse for what you did?"

"No, it was fun seeing how scared Marvin was. And throwing that brick through the window…" I laughed and asked, "Have you found my mom yet?"

He coughed. "Not yet. And we're due in court in an hour. If she doesn't show up, they'll probably send you to detention." His jaw set and he looked down at a paper. "This is Marvin's statement. He said he was afraid for his life and you deliberately threw the brick after you heard the sirens."

I stared at my fingernails. "'Bout right."

After another hard stare he shoved his papers into a briefcase. "I'll see you in a little while."

After he left I cracked a smile. I owed Marvin big-time.

Judge Richard Schoenfeld was old. Really old. Across the room I could see the liver spots on his face. His head was shaped like an egg and only a puff of white hair remained on his head.

He looked bored with all of the judicial stuff happening around him. I guessed he'd wanted to be on the Supreme Court or something and wound up stuck in family court. Not a great career move, Dick.

Mr. Krentz went back and forth with the judge until he looked at me and said, "Ms. Black, do you understand why you're here."

"I think I got it."

"Do not be obstreperous, young lady."

"Octopus, what?"

He frowned and I almost laughed. Of course I knew that obstreperous meant unruly. My gran had taught me that word in fourth grade.

Then the door burst open and I had to hang my head to keep from smiling. *Mom's here!*

"What the hell is going on?" my mother shouted.

Mom in all her glory. Her blond hair was everywhere and she wore a tank top and cargo shorts. Even across the room I could see her missing tooth—the obvious sign that she was a meth addict.

She scanned the room and when her gaze landed on me, her eyes grew wide. "What the hell, Story?"

The judge pounded his gavel. "Order, ma'am. Order!"

Mom froze and focused on me. Although she'd broken the law most days of her adult life, she'd never spent a day in jail. The fact that I was sitting in a courtroom was probably freaking her out.

"I apologize, Judge," she said.

"Do you know why your daughter is here?"

"The officers who came and got me said Story had committed armed robbery."

"*Attempted* armed robbery."

"I stand corrected," Mom said sweetly.

"And she threw a brick through the establishment's front window to the tune of twenty-five hundred dollars."

Mom's shoulders sagged and I knew she was quietly growling under her breath.

"I also understand that you've been unreachable for many hours. We've called, sent patrol officers to your home. Do you not care about your child? Where have you been, Ms. Black?"

Mom bit down on her lip, probably to stop the growling. It was her go-to move when she was about to explode.

"I repeat, Ms. Black, where have you been?"

"Out!" she bellowed. She took a deep breath. "The rest is not your business…Your Honor."

The judge seemed to back up in his chair. They stared at each other until he finally looked at me. He seemed to soften a bit, like he felt sorry that I was stuck with Mom. "Younger Ms. Black, other than not knowing the meaning of the word obstreperous, do you have anything—"

"Are you kidding?" Mom shouted. "She knows the meaning of that word. Story, what are you playing here?"

Judge Schoenfeld turned to Mom, his face beet red. "Ms. Black, do not interrupt the court!"

"But Your Honor, something's going on here! You're being suckered and so am I."

"Really? Are you implying this court is gullible?"

"Uh, maybe?" She pointed at me and said, "You better tell us what's going on right now, Story!"

A prickle of fear crept up my back but I held it together and just looked blankly at her, which only made her madder.

"I swear to God, Story—"

"Enough!" Judge Schoenfeld banged his gavel three more times. "Ms. Black, the court is inclined to send your daughter home with you since it is her first offense. Are you agreeable?"

Mom curled her lip up, looking as though she'd bested me. It was the same look she gave me when she beat me at chess, which was all the time. *C'mon, Mom. Say it.*

"No," Mom said, her head held high. "You keep her. Give her a sentence she deserves."

"Fine," Judge Schoenfeld said. "Three weeks at county detention."

I bowed my head to hide my grin.

Checkmate.

CHAPTER THREE

The worst thing to do in jail is count your days. Some kids have the number memorized and if you ask, "How much longer?" they can tell you in a second, but usually the number is wrong. Getting out depends on receiving services and the services always take longer than expected. My roommate Flor used to count her days. She was told three months max. Six months later she was still here. Then she stopped counting.

I'd never counted my days until now. I'd been here for twelve days, following Ivy's advice and keeping my head down, doing my absolute best in "jail school" and looking forward to Bertie's Sunday visits. We'd only had two and I'd spent the first one trying to get her to stop being mad at me.

"I had to do this," I said.

"I get it, but it's just time that we're losing, you know?"

I nodded. Bertie was so sweet and I'd miss her when she left for North Carolina.

"Has anything happened? Did you learn anything? Please tell me this was worth it."

I looked around the visitors' room before I whispered, "So I took this test called the SPOT. I'm thinking that if I do well enough, I'll get an interview. That's how it works."

SPOT was the Student Potential Opportunity Test and was given to kids in jail who proved they were literate and had more than street smarts. I'd heard stories about kids who'd aced the SPOT and left Lakeview. I'd seen proof that at least one had gone to college. Maybe it was mostly smoke but when I heard it, I figured out a way to get arrested.

"So if you do well during the interview, you get invited to go to the school," Bertie concluded.

"I think so. But one guy told me just getting to take the test is a big deal."

"Who gave it to you?"

"My teacher. She's super cool. You'd really like her."

Bertie nodded but I could tell she was upset. I squeezed her hand quickly when the guard looked away. We were supposed to refrain from touching and some Correction Officers, COs, gave the detainees a strike for touching their loved ones. "Hey, it's less than two weeks left," I said cheerfully. "Have you heard or seen my mom?"

Bertie shook her head.

Mom hadn't bothered to call or visit since I'd been in jail. It was probably for the best.

Bertie shuffled out and I felt bad.

That's when I started counting days. I'd already visited with my probation officer, Charity, the required number of times and completed a program about making better choices. She signed the forms while she sang my praises. Really she was singing her own praises, thinking she'd done such a good job of rehabilitating me.

Most of the kids in jail lacked maturity and couldn't resist temptation. They blew up over little things like the awful food. Many were like Flor and struggled in school. They weren't very smart, which explained why they routinely got caught, and my mother, a twenty-year meth user, had never seen the inside of a cell.

"Story," she said, "everyone's addicted to something. Your addiction will *not* be drugs. I'll see to that. But you'll crave something—maybe money, maybe power. The trick is not to let it run your life. That's how I've stayed out of jail."

Weekday mornings started at six thirty. We headed for chow around seven. Most of us were still half asleep so breakfast was the easiest time for the staff. Kids took their meds and they kicked in quickly. Nobody talked to anybody beyond a grunt. One CO, Officer Maxwell, loved to offer a sugary, "Good morning!" to each kid and he expected a response. If you failed to respond, you'd get a strike. Three strikes and you went to seg—segregation. So everyone looked up at him as they passed, pulled their faces into a smile for a split second and replied, "Good morning," before their gaze dropped to the linoleum again.

Breakfast was usually oatmeal or cereal with a banana or apple. Milk was available but so was coffee. The adults must've realized that street kids drink a lot of coffee and they're just as pissed as adults when they miss their caffeine fix. My mom had hooked me on the stuff around my twelfth birthday. It was the best way to stay awake in school after a long night of fighting with her or listening to her rant as she came down from a high.

After breakfast each unit walked to the education wing. Since only one unit arrived at a time, it took thirty minutes for every class to assemble. While we waited, the rules were simple: face forward and no talking. A lot of kids used this time to nap at their computer stations but I liked to check out what my teacher, Ms. Sutton, had written on the board. She always posted an interesting quotation for us to discuss once everyone got to class.

Today's quotation read, *Do I dare disturb the universe?* I stole a glance at Jelly and Samuel. Jelly, who looked like he had a bowl of jelly around his middle, made circles on the workstation table with his finger. Samuel slept sitting up, his arms crossed. Not the types to disturb the universe. Ever.

When the last student arrived, Ms. Sutton quickly finished her attendance and pointed at the quotation. "It's up there like always. Take two minutes on your own to think about it and then I want you to talk with your partner. What does it mean and how does it apply to you? And remember, no ACES."

ACES was the rule of the school. You weren't allowed to talk about faces, cases, chases or places—who you knew from the 'hood, your situation in jail, any car chases you'd seen or been in or which 'hood you lived in. It was the personal stuff that led to the fights. On my second day a kid named Gomez got beat up by a new guy because he learned Gomez had dated his girlfriend. He went to seg for two weeks and then got transferred to a different class.

"Okay, talk to your partner," Ms. Sutton said.

The rules said students had to have same sex partners for classwork. They said it prevented distractions between the guys and the girls. For whatever reason, the one other girl in the class, Lynette Colfax, wasn't here, so Ms. Sutton had to fill in. This partner thing was still new and the COs hated it, but I heard the principal thought it was important.

Ms. Sutton squatted next to my desk. I automatically smiled and she smiled back, showing a cute dimple in her chin. Her face was round and her short brown hair framed her face. She wasn't beautiful but she was adorable. "What do you think the quotation means, Story?"

"Uh, I think it's asking if it's worth it to stand up for what you believe in."

She leaned forward. "Tell me more."

"Well, the universe is this big place and we're little specks. In the universe we're nothing. Sometimes when you're standing up for yourself, you feel like nothing. So is it worth it to stand up for yourself when you're probably going to lose?"

"And what's your answer?"

I looked into her bright blue eyes and secretly prayed Lynette never came back. She was kinda odd, and I wanted Ms. Sutton to be my partner forever. "I say yes. I think you should always stand up for yourself even if you don't think you'll win. Maybe you'll be surprised."

She nodded. "As usual, great answer. I especially appreciate your optimistic attitude and belief in trying even in the face of adversity." Her eyes darted around the room, checking on the other kids, making sure they were actually talking to each other. Then she whispered, "You did really well on the SPOT."

I nearly gasped. "I did?"

"You did. You're going to get an interview. I don't exactly know when, but just start thinking about what you want out of life. Okay?"

I smiled. "Okay."

Yes!

She winked and stood before I could ask her more questions. Once she'd circled the room she returned to the quotation. "Let's hear from three people before we start our computer work. Mr. Copeland, what do you think?"

"Uh, that it's messed up to take on the universe. Why would anybody do that? *How* would anybody do that? It's the universe."

I rolled my eyes. Copeland was dumb and literal. Not a good combination.

"I think it's symbolic," Ms. Sutton said patiently. "Think of it as your own universe. Another word for this is schema. It's our own reality, the way we see the world."

"So it's like taking on the government," a new guy blurted.

"Ackland, no shouting out!" a CO directed. "Next time's a strike."

I didn't know this new guy. He was B-grade, meaning he was with us for only twenty-four hours, enough time to get him processed and sent to where he belonged: the tower where they kept the juveniles to be tried as adults. Whatever Ackland had done was really bad and dangerous.

Ms. Sutton ignored the CO. "Yes, Mr. Ackland, that's one way of looking at it." She scanned the room. "Mr. Santoni, your thoughts?"

Santoni shook his head. "Nope."

"Can you please elaborate? Nope, you don't have an answer, or nope, you wouldn't disturb the universe?"

"The second one."

"Why?"

Santoni sighed loudly, like Ms. Sutton annoyed him. "Because there's no point."

Ms. Sutton strolled down the aisle toward him. "Please explain."

"The boss always wins. It's about money and who has it. Even when you think you're disturbin' the universe, you really ain't."

"Can you give me an example?"

He looked away and his face got soft. "Okay, so, like cancer. All those charities raise money and everybody's wearin' pink and doin' the walks. It's been goin' on forever, but no cure. I heard there's a cure but the government doesn't want anybody to know about it because all the researchers, the hospitals, the doctors and thousands of people would lose their jobs because there wouldn't be cancer. It'd be over. So even when you're fightin' for a cause, it's not gonna to do any good if the government don't like it."

His eyes locked with Ms. Sutton's and I could see the tears. I'd heard that his mom was dead and I guessed cancer killed her. Maybe Santoni watched her die or had to help her every day. I could tell he was silently pleading with Ms. Sutton to call on someone else.

Jelly raised his hand and Ms. Sutton turned away from Santoni. "Mr. Rodriguez, would you care to add to Mr. Santoni's comment?"

"He's totally right. Like electric cars. I heard they had those back in the seventies but the oil guys kept them from being made so everybody would still need gas."

"But we have electric cars now, right?" Ms. Sutton asked.

"Yeah," Jelly agreed. "But it took like fifty years to get 'em."

"But it still happened," Ms. Sutton insisted. "The truth got out."

I raised my hand to defend Ms. Sutton's position. When she acknowledged me I said, "That's why it's good to disturb the universe. If everybody's disturbing it, eventually things change. You just need to be patient."

Santoni coughed and said, "Bullshit."

"That's a strike, Santoni!" the CO shouted. "One more time and you're back on unit."

Santoni slunk down in his chair. Ms. Sutton directed the class to get to work on their computers and went to him. She spoke until he nodded slightly and started to work. I felt bad for him. I felt bad for anyone who tried to disturb the universe in Lakeview.

The town of Lakeview had a view of Lake Michigan but not much else. Every time we walked past the closed factories on Lakeview Avenue, Mom told a story about how it was when she was a little girl. Drivers avoided the street during a shift change because everyone was going to or coming from work at the two huge plants. One made car parts and the other made shoes. The city counted on those jobs and a lot of parents told their kids that someday they'd work there just like them. Then the plants closed in the eighties and half the town lost their jobs.

A lot of families moved away, out of Lakeview or out of Michigan. Some abandoned their homes since they couldn't afford the mortgage anymore. The drug lords took over the empty houses and entire blocks filled with junkies, which drove more people out of Lakeview. The only ones who stayed were the people who ran Lakeview and the poor. And they couldn't do anything except survive. It's a strange thing: people boast about helping the poor in one breath and in the next say that the poor need to help themselves. When I'd hooked up with Ivy I was helping myself, and I didn't feel guilty about it.

All that changed when Charlotte Barnaby came to town. Suddenly there was a new technology company moved in. New apartments were built and the downtown, which used to be disgusting, had nightclubs and restaurants. About three years later Lakeview was a changed place and everybody knew the name Charlotte Barnaby. Then the rumors about a secret school started. That's when I started paying attention.

We powered up our computers and started working on our online classes. I was taking Geometry—again. I'd failed it the year before on purpose. The teacher had been a mean SOB who thought he was better than all the kids. He told us at least three times a week that we were the dumbest group of fucks he'd ever seen and he was only teaching to get his pension and we needed to stay out of his way. Every time he said shit like that, I thought, what's the point? I'd be so mad I'd skip school the next day. Eventually the truancy officer came to the trailer to talk to Mom, but she didn't answer the door. She never did.

"Story," she said, "nothin' good ever happens when somebody knocks on your door. The Publisher's Clearing House is never gonna show up with a million dollars for us. If anyone's at the door it means somebody died, somebody's in trouble, or somebody wants our money."

After I'd opened the door a few times, I realized she was right.

I started a problem on vertices when I felt a nudge at my elbow. I looked down and saw a question on a notepad. *Are you getting an interview?* The author was the kid next to me, A.C. Davis. A tall Black guy, A.C. played basketball on his high school team. He probably could've had a full scholarship to college, but I heard he'd broken into a house with his brother and now he was here.

I nodded at A.C. and looked back at my vertices. I didn't want to talk about it. I didn't want to screw up and miss my chance. When he nudged me again, I kept my eyes glued to the screen.

"Mr. Davis, please start your work," Ms. Sutton said.

My mom taught me this line from *Romeo and Juliet*. "Three can keep a secret if two are dead." Mom was right about that too. I'd never met a teenager who could keep a secret. Even if I just told A.C. because he seemed like a nice enough person, he'd tell one person and so on. Eventually everybody would know because you add up all those one persons and you got the whole school.

Within a few minutes everybody settled in and started to work while three COs wandered around the room. Usually only two COs were there but because Ackland was with us, he got his own CO. It was never completely quiet because their radios chattered constantly. They also didn't care if they ate in front of us or told jokes to each other while we tried to study. Ms. Sutton sometimes brought in treats for them so if she asked them to be a little quieter, they'd do it for her. Some of the officers in other classes didn't have any respect for the teachers and they misbehaved more than the kids.

If it weren't for the COs and the crappy clothes we wore, you would've thought we were a class at any high school in America—until you knew the stories. Jelly was delusional and told everybody he was a famous DJ who made forty thousand a year. Santoni had killed nine cats and was on his way to becoming a psychopath. Then there was Copeland. After Auckland he was the worst of all. I'd heard he'd stabbed his mother and left her for dead. They'd thought about trying him as an adult but he was mentally ill and they were still deciding where he should go. We all steered clear of him. He was bad in a way that made us all look good.

About half of the kids were returnees. A few actually admitted they liked jail better than the streets. They had a bed, food, and focus. It was easier to study in jail and do well in school. How messed up was that?

I knew all their stories but Ms. Sutton didn't. Once in a while she reminded us that she never read our files until she needed to. This was her way of saying, "If I read your file I'd probably hate you." Who wouldn't hate somebody who killed cats?

"Story, will you come to my desk, please?" Ms. Sutton asked. "And bring your book."

I gathered my book and notes and started for her desk until CO Shepard came to the door and said, "Black. Time for rec."

I made an immediate U-turn, deposited my stuff back at my computer station and dropped my tiny pencil in the correct hole of the pencil box. Since there were so few girls in jail, I had recreation with a different class that had more girls.

"We'll chat when you get back, Story," Ms. Sutton said.

I nodded and she gave me this empathetic look. She knew I hated rec. All anybody wanted to do was play dodge ball. Trying to peg somebody with a ball was a great way to get out your frustrations but it seemed pointless to me. Sometimes the games got out of hand if something bad had happened between two people on a unit. Most of the time it was just funny. You'd think the COs would've had a problem with dodge ball because it caused fights, but they just stood there laughing.

I led CO Shepard down the hallway with my hands behind my back. An alarm sounded and I immediately headed to the wall and sat down with my head between my knees. We were in lockdown. I smiled but she couldn't see it. Maybe I'd miss rec entirely.

When an all-call happened, everything stopped. Since I was in a hallway, I had to hit the floor. If I'd still been in the classroom, my head would be on my desk and if I looked up, I'd get a strike. Everything had to stop because most of the COs and supervisors went to the all-call room, leaving each teacher with only one officer. It took a lot of people to search an entire class.

I listened to the radio chatter and heard, "Sharp missing."

Somebody's pencil, a "sharp," was unaccounted for and a class needed to be searched. Most of the time when a pencil went missing it was just stupidity. A kid hadn't been paying attention and it rolled onto the floor or behind his books in a carrel.

I knew it wasn't my class because Ms. Sutton never lost anything. She was careful and most of the students respected her too much to try any shit. I guessed it was Mr. DeBruno's class. He had the worst rep of any teacher. His students hated him. He'd lost more than one pencil since I'd been in jail.

I hoped it took them a while to find it. I didn't want to go to rec. I could see CO Shepard pacing in front of me through my legs. I guessed she was frustrated that she was missing the search. The COs got off on that stuff. They loved action and sometimes I thought they initiated the problems. They wanted some excitement so they'd press a kid's buttons and make something happen. Then somebody would wind up in seg or lose privileges. I'd never been to seg and I never wanted to go.

"Is it true you're getting an interview?"

I realized Shepard was talking to me. "Permission to look up?" I asked.

"Permission granted."

I glanced up at her. She was a butch dyke with a short cut. She never smiled and rarely spoke to anyone. She seemed to separate herself from the other COs. Most of them didn't care if they rudely interrupted class, but she always remained respectful to the teachers.

"Yeah, I got an interview."

"Do you know when?"

I shrugged.

"Good," she said but her face showed no emotion. "You need to get out of here, Black. This place isn't for you."

"Yes, ma'am. I agree."

She looked up and down the hallway and then fiddled with her radio before she whispered, "I've heard there might be a fight at chow time. Not sure if it's lunch or dinner. Don't get caught up in it, you hear?"

"Yes, ma'am," I said with a nod.

She stepped closer and said, "I'm not supposed to know these things but I've heard that Ms. Money is coming on Thursday. Be ready."

"Thank you."

She nodded. "And if you have any trouble between now and release, you let me know. Write a note on your tablet during class and I'll find a way for us to talk. You got that?"

"Yes, thanks."

Her radio squawked. "Sharp found. End all-call."

I started to rise but she held out her hand. "Stay down for another minute, Black," she said slyly. "I know how much you hate rec."

CHAPTER FOUR

"What's your name?"

"Story. Story Black."

"How old are you?"

"Fifteen. Sixteen soon."

"And why are you in jail?"

"I held up a convenience store with another girl."

The woman interviewing me called herself Margaret but I knew that wasn't her real name. She'd looked slightly to the right when she introduced herself, like she was scrolling through her contacts, picking a name just for this interview. She glanced at an open folder in front of her, confirming what I said was true. While she debated her next question, I listened to the muffled kabooms of the hallway door clanging shut every time someone entered or exited the visitors' room. I re-crossed my legs and accidentally kicked one of the table's plastic legs.

"Sorry," I said quickly.

"No worries," Margaret replied without looking up from her notes. "First time offender. Sounds like you might've avoided detention but you went before Judge Schoenfeld."

"Yeah." I could tell from her tone that she didn't approve of Judge Dick.

"Decent grades in school, although teachers say you could do better. It says your probation officer is Charity Aguilera." She paused and added, "Great name for a P.O."

"Yeah. She always makes fun of her name."

Margaret scanned the P.O. log that Charity filled out when we met each week. "Says you're doing great."

I nodded and my knee bumped the table leg again. "Again, sorry."

Margaret looked up and smiled warmly. "It's okay. Take a deep breath. These rooms are the size of a shoebox."

She wasn't kidding. The tiny interview room was barely big enough for two people and we had three counting the videographer, plus a camera on a tripod. I pictured myself frozen so I'd stop flailing around like a baby. Wilkey, a kid who'd been interviewed a few weeks before, told me to chill while I waited for each question. He thought his nervousness fucked up his chances.

Margaret's brown eyes sucked me in. "What's the worst part about being in jail, Story?"

"The little pencils," I said automatically.

"Why?"

I sat up straight. "They're symbols, like symbols in literature. Outside in regular schools nobody ever keeps a short pencil. You throw it out and get a new one from the teacher. But in here it's the best we'll get and it's really hard to write with a tiny pencil. My hand starts to cramp. And I like to write. Sometimes I think about the teachers sitting at home, breaking perfectly good pencils in half while they watch their favorite shows. Then before they go to bed they sharpen them down to practically nothing. Such a waste."

"You understand why the detention teachers only supply short pencils, right? It's a safety issue."

"I get it. Nobody's gonna shank somebody with a tiny stub."

Her eyes narrowed as if she were studying a speck. "Why do you do that?"

"Do what?"

"You talk about literary symbols like a college professor and then you revert to colloquial street language. Why?"

I couldn't hide my surprise. "Well," I mumbled, "there's a way to act in here. A way to talk so you don't sound stuck up and people don't give you shit. That's really how it is in life." I shrugged. "I don't know."

When I looked up, she was staring at me. "That's not true. We've been watching you, Story. There isn't much you *don't* know."

She smiled and I felt a tug at the corners of my mouth. She was pretty. Her skin was much darker than mine and she had soft brown eyes and raven-colored hair. She was tall, so tall she had to sit sideways because her legs wouldn't fit under the cheap plastic table with the high heels she wore. The red leather pumps matched the silk blouse underneath her black suit. She probably ate at trendy restaurants and sipped champagne with a group of female friends who possessed equally fabulous smiles.

Her stylus flew across the face of her tablet as she took notes—about me. I wanted to say something unique to her, something that would make me stand out so she'd remember me.

Nobody is memorable in jail. That's the point. Everybody wears the same blue pants and Vans rip-off slippers. The T-shirts are different colors depending on your behavior. I wore red and that meant I'd never gotten a strike from a CO. I knew Margaret talked to a lot of kids and I imagined they rolled into one crazy juvenile delinquent with a really sad wardrobe.

I glanced at the camera in the corner. Like the blinking green light, I needed to be ON. My hands sweated and I rubbed them on my thighs while I waited for the next question. My leg bounced nervously and I pressed my heels to the floor to stop it. I didn't want to bump the table again.

Margaret looked over her shoulder at the videographer crammed in the corner playing with her phone. She was Margaret's opposite—short, blond, and white. Her hair flipped to one side and scrambled in a few directions from the product she'd applied. She wore a T-shirt underneath an old corduroy jacket with leather patches on the elbows, and the cuffs of her jeans were tucked into sleek black boots. Sleek was definitely the right word for her.

She'd arrived first and stuck a microphone on my T-shirt to test it. "Are you nervous?" she'd asked.

"Yeah," I admitted. "What kind of questions will she ask me?"

She leaned closer and glanced around the room, as if she was about to betray a secret. Then she said, "You'll be asked to recite the Declaration of Independence."

My eyes bugged out. "Seriously?"

She laughed and shook her head.

I let out a deep breath and laughed with her. "I'm glad you're kidding. I know it's an important document to the founding of our country but I couldn't recite it." I noticed a copy of George Eliot's *Middlemarch* sticking out of her camera bag. "I really liked that book." I figured it couldn't hurt to be pleasant with her. Maybe she'd put in a good word for me.

"What other books have you read?"

"Everything by Jane Austen. And I love Kurt Vonnegut and Willa Cather and Mary Oliver. Just lots of people." I didn't want to name the hundreds of authors I'd read and sound stuck up.

She smiled and said, "All great ones. Just be yourself. I'm Jill." We made small talk until Margaret arrived. Then Jill snuck behind the camera and turned it on. I stared at the light and willed myself to stop being nervous.

Margaret set her tablet down and leaned back. "You have an interesting name. How'd you get it?"

"It's a long story."

She chuckled. "I'd like to hear it."

"It really would take too long to explain. I shouldn't have been born. What happened made the local newspapers and my mother still carries the clipping from the paper around. So, I'm a story."

I'd never told anybody that much but Wilkey said I needed to impress this lady if I wanted anything to happen. He called her the key to getting out—out of jail and out of Lakeview. Ms. Sutton had told me to be honest and respectful. I was trying.

"Tell me about your family."

"I live with my mom now."

"Any brothers and sisters?"

"Nope. I lived with my grandma but she died two years ago and I went back to my mom."

"Is your father in the picture?"

I shook my head. She didn't write down my answer so I could tell she already knew. "It's just me and Mom now that Gran's dead."

She glanced at the folder. "Her name was Matilda Black, right?"

"Yes."

"And your mother is Patience."

"Yes, but she goes by Patty. Patience doesn't really fit her." I tried not to make it sound sarcastic but I snorted at the end of the comment.

She grinned but kept her eyes glued to the tablet. I waited for her to ask me about Mom's six trips to rehab and why my home life was so screwed up or how I'd wound up in jail, but she didn't ask those questions like the other fourteen adults who'd interviewed me. Instead she leaned forward and rested her chin on her upturned palm.

"Story, what are your dreams?"

I took a deep breath and sat up straighter. I was ready for this one. "I've been thinking about some different career paths and weighing my options. I'm a voracious reader but I also enjoy mathematics, specifically algebra. I could see myself becoming a journalist or an engineer."

She nodded. "Those are excellent career choices." She paused and asked, "What are you passionate about?"

My face dropped into a frown and I looked away. I'd thought of every question I could imagine but I never thought about passion. Of course I knew what the word meant, but it wasn't like I had time to paint, or sculpt, or write. Surviving filled my day planner. I glanced at her razor-sharp gaze. She was watching me stumble around the answer. I shook my head. "I…I don't know."

She set down the iPad and stylus and crossed her arms. She looked shocked. "You can't answer the question?"

I should've seen this coming and planned an answer even if it was a lie. I licked my lips, searching, thinking. I wasn't good under pressure.

"It's a dumb question," I spat.

"I'm disappointed."

I glared at her. "Disappointed? What were you expecting? Some kind of a show? Maybe I'd start reciting the Declaration of Independence for you?" I glanced at Jill but she was focused on her viewfinder. "Or was I supposed to just kiss your ass and act grateful that you asked to talk to me. Is that why you're disappointed or did I miss something?"

She stuck her iPad and stylus in the messenger bag next to her. I sat back and closed my eyes. I'd screwed up and missed my chance, a chance I'd spent weeks planning for. I thought about what I'd just said. It wasn't me. It was my mom talking. Even jail couldn't keep us apart. I sunk lower in the chair and buried my face in my hands.

"Can I go back now?"

"Do you mean back to the unit or back to the street?"

"Both."

"Absolutely. Ms. Sutton gave you too much credit. I'll need to tell her she's losing her touch."

My head shot up. Ms. Sutton was the best teacher I'd ever known. Every day I was struck by the irony: I had to go to jail to get a great teacher. "What does she have to do with this?"

"Who do you think recommended you for the SPOT?"

I stared at Margaret. I knew what she was doing. She was judging Ms. Sutton based on my behavior. If I didn't do well in this interview, Ms. Sutton would probably lose a bonus or a promotion. That's how adults worked. They were the cruelest to each other. Normally I wouldn't care but Ms. Sutton was different from all the other adults I knew. I inhaled, visualizing the oxygen tingling my brain and suffocating the image of my mother.

"Your question is irrelevant."

Her eyes darted toward Jill so I looked over at Jill too. Her finger rested on the on/off button but she hadn't pushed it and the green light remained on. Margaret was waiting to see what Jill wanted to do—and not the other way around. Something was weird.

"Who's running this show?" I asked.

They looked surprised. Neither said anything and my nervous leg bounced like crazy. I was in real trouble now. I'd figured out their game.

Jill stepped away from the camera. "You're very perceptive, Story." She slid into the chair between Margaret and me and asked, "Why would I allow Margaret to ask you the questions?"

I thought about my earlier conversation with Jill. *Middlemarch*. The fact that Margaret was supposedly late. "You wanted to watch me answer questions but you also wanted to talk to me before we started. I wasn't as nervous then."

"Exactly," she said.

Margaret and Jill exchanged a nod. Margaret stepped behind the camera and Jill leaned on the table. "Now, let's go back. Tell me why having passion is irrelevant."

How could I explain? "Have you been to Walmart?"

"Once or twice, but I usually try to avoid it. I'm not much for obnoxious crowds."

"Me neither, but it's where you shop if you don't have much money."

"What does that have to do with pursuing your passions?"

"So one day I turned in to the baby aisle by accident and these three women were there. They came from the other direction, so I could see their faces. The oldest was probably in her fifties. She's holding a can of off-brand baby food and lecturing the youngest one, who's a little older than me. She's got on these teeny shorts and a string tank top. She's pretending to listen but she's getting tired of standing there. She shifts her weight from one foot to the other and slides this toddler from her right hip to her left. I guess that it's a grandma and granddaughter. Grandma's talking about how it's her disability check, and there's no way she's paying eighty cents more for the name brand. Every time she takes a breath, the granddaughter tries to tell her the name brand's better for the toddler because it's organic. They're getting louder and louder. Pretty soon the kid's crying. The girl lifts her shirt and shoves him to her breast to shut him up so they can keep fighting."

"What about the third woman?"

"She's the one I noticed the most. I'm guessing she's the granddaughter's mom."

"Four generations," Jill murmured.

"Yeah. She's leaning on the cart, not even paying attention to their fight over her head. She's there but she isn't there. She's checked out. It's the look on her face that I remember."

"What did you see?"

"At first I thought she might be stoned but there was a moment when the grandma said something really cruel and the mom closed her eyes, like she was trying to keep it together and not scream at her own mother."

Jill moved so close to me that I could smell the mint on her breath. "And what do you think that look meant?"

"She's helpless. Like she's realized this is her life. The grandma ranted on and the granddaughter is too young to know that her life is going be about fighting over eighty cents, day after day, week after week, and year after year. She doesn't see it yet but the mom gets it. She's completely stuck and she's made sure her daughter is stuck too. I think she felt bad."

Jill and Margaret exchanged a glance but I couldn't tell if they were happy or upset with my answer.

"What happened next?" Jill asked.

"I went three rows over and saw another grandma, mom, and daughter, only this daughter had two kids. So when you ask me about my dreams, that's what I see."

"You think that will be you."

"Won't it?"

"Where'd you get such an advanced vocabulary? Your teachers in school?"

I snorted, picturing my freshman year English teacher, Mrs. Shore, a woman who taught me nothing because she couldn't control her class. "No, it wasn't my teachers. When I was little and lived with Gran, she'd read the classics to me and we always had a word of the day. By the time I was in third grade I knew a ton of words and the teachers kept sending me to the library during reading time. They didn't know what to do with me. I just kept checking out books from the library." Something occurred to me and I looked at Jill quizzically. "I don't get it."

"Get what?"

"My gran did a great job with me but my mom's a mess. How come she didn't do such a great job with her?"

Jill glanced at Margaret again. It was like a private joke I didn't understand. I hoped I wasn't the joke. I thought I'd said something really stupid until she clutched my hand. I nearly jumped at her touch. "Story, you're amazing. I can't explain why your grandma did better by you than your mother, but the fact that you even recognize the significance is incredible. That's one reason why you're special. That's why we're having this conversation. I want you to have dreams. I want you to *achieve* them. What if I told you I could make sure you never have to worry about eighty cents *ever* again?"

For a moment I didn't breathe. My plan had worked! "You could really do that?" I asked.

Her green eyes grew darker and she smiled like she was proud of me. "Story, that's exactly what I'm going to do."

CHAPTER FIVE

I knew I'd made a good impression. Ms. Sutton would be proud of me. Before Jill left, she asked if I had any questions and I said I had lots of questions.

While Margaret packed up she said, "For now you can ask me one."

"Is it true that you can get kids out of here?"

"No, unfortunately, you're here for the full length of your stay. I can't do anything about the past, Story."

"I'm sorry for my poor decision."

"That's good, but it doesn't matter and you know it."

I couldn't look at her then. She was right. It didn't matter. And she probably wouldn't have liked hearing that I'd planned the whole thing.

"We'll be talking soon when you get out," Jill said. She squeezed my shoulder gently and motioned to the CO to escort her and Margaret to the lobby. "Stay out of trouble, Story," she whispered before she left.

As I walked the stripe back to my unit with my hands behind my back, following the painted line on the linoleum like a tightrope, I tried to make sense of the emotions knocking inside me. My heart pounded but I wasn't afraid. I was smiling. I was hopeful but it scared me. Mom always warned me that hope and disappointment were enemies who battled all the time. "Don't count on anything, Story. Then the disappointment won't hurt as much when nothing happens."

Still, hope crept around my brain. I stared at the university banners that lined the hallways. Most of the kids mocked them and the few who knew some of the schools only knew their basketball teams. I glanced up at the Claremont College banner and ran into the open door that separated the admin building from the units. I figured that was the universe handing me a reminder not to get too hopeful.

"Careful, Black."

I nodded at the CO. He was new and his nametag said *P. Kaufman*. It was the first time I'd heard him speak and his voice was deeper than I imagined.

"Black, Story, returning from administration," he said to the duty officer.

He signed me in and we waited for the door to open. We headed through the tunnel and our eyes met briefly before I turned away. I didn't know this guy. We were extra careful with the rookies in case they were on a power trip. I'd seen what happened to kids in the tunnel. They went in fine and came out twenty feet later with bruises or welts. Kaufman seemed okay. He hadn't said much, so that meant he was more afraid of me than I was of him. I wanted to tell him not to worry. I was going to be perfect for the next two weeks.

I kept my head down and stared at his shoes. Mom taught me I could learn a lot about people by looking at their shoes. Busy people had newer shoes but they didn't take care of them very well. They missed a lot of little details. The ones she called sticklers always kept their shoes shined. "You gotta watch out for them, Story. They pay attention to details. When you're going to scam somebody, first check the shoes. You don't want to scam a stickler."

Kaufman's black boots had been shined recently but several places were still smudged because he hadn't buffed them very well. He was the guy who followed the rules but wasn't going to make a fuss about following them, especially if it interfered with his social life. He was good looking so he probably had a lot of friends and partied on Saturday night. He forgot about shining his boots until Monday morning. While he sat at his breakfast bar in his tiny apartment eating a bowl of some sugary cereal, he'd suddenly remember, wolf down the cereal and run to find the boots and shoe polish.

"How'd it go?" he whispered.

"Fine," I said quietly. He was already violating the rule that said officers wouldn't chat with the youth.

When the solid metal door closed behind us with a reverberating bang, the second door opened and I hit the stripe again, headed for Unit Two.

"You know, I hear she's the big boss," he whispered.

"Really?"

"Yeah, that's the word. You just met Charlotte Barnaby, the richest lottery winner ever." He grinned but it wasn't a sick, lecherous grin. He just seemed happy for me.

"She told me her name was Jill," I replied, skipping the story of how she and Margaret tried to trick me.

"Probably just a cover. If you knew you were actually talking to the big boss you might screw up. She probably wanted to give you the best chance. I've heard she's pulled a whole lot of jail kids out of Lakeview."

"How?"

He shrugged. "Don't know for sure. Maybe she buys you a house in a different town. I've heard there's a special school and then maybe she offers to pay for college if you keep your grades up."

I tried to picture Mom moving out of the trailer park. She might go for it if the new place had a dishwasher. I thought about how hard I'd work at a different school. And there it was again. Hope sneaking inside again like a cat that wouldn't stay outdoors.

We turned down the empty west corridor. "Do you know who else she's talked to?" I asked quietly, not looking directly at him.

"Maybe one other girl. Do you know Lynette Colfax?"

"Uh-huh," I replied. "We're in the same class."

Colfax was a little weird. She rolled up into a tight ball whenever she was seated. The only time her back wasn't curved was standing in line. Then when she got to the lunchroom bench, her bunk, or a desk, she pulled her legs to her chin.

"Yeah, I heard she got an interview too," he said. "Maybe you'll both get picked? You know, Charlotte Barnaby owns most of the town now. She came to Lakeview five years ago with all her money and it was like she gave it away. She opened her own company but she saved a ton of small businesses and basically the town. She's a hero. You get in with her and you've got a ticket to ride."

He grinned and I grinned too at his Beatles reference.

"Maybe," I said, already feeling the light of hope dimming. It was probably a contest between me and Colfax and if the choice was about who needed the most help, it wouldn't be me.

"Stay out of trouble, Black," he whispered as we arrived at Wing A. He stopped at the top of the corridor and I continued my walk alone to my cell. I could feel eyes watching me and like magic, the door to A6 clicked open.

My roommate Flor sat on the edge of her bed with a magazine. We both knew she couldn't read but she liked the feel of the pages. I often read her homework to her but she didn't want anyone but me to know her secret. That's how it was in jail. Half the kids were stages of illiterate and the other half were stages of brilliant. All were fucked up somehow. In Flor's case, she'd messed around with her eight-year-old nephew. She showed him the only kind of love she'd ever known. She was waiting for placement in the sexual offenders' program and we both knew she'd be here awhile. It was that way for the sex offs. Way too many of them and not enough rehab programs.

When the door shut, Flor looked up. Her curly black hair fell over her eyes and she reminded me of Bertie. The coils shrouded her face like a mask. She said they made her feel more secure.

"What happened?"

Jill, or Charlotte, or whatever her name really was, had told me to say very little. She advised, "You'll have to tell your friends something. They'll expect it. We've helped too many kids. Word has reached the units. Be careful. Don't boast. Don't make it sound like it's a done deal. Don't give any specifics."

"They said I did well," I told Flor.

The magazine dropped into her lap. "What the hell does that mean? Are you getting out of here?"

I shook my head. She was concerned about getting a different bunkie. We got along really well and that was rare. "No, I have to do my time same as everyone else."

Flor looked confused. "Then why the fuck was that test so important? If they're not going to get you out, who cares?" She fell back onto the bunk and turned the pages of the magazine.

I shrugged. "Yeah."

I couldn't explain it to her. I glanced at the pictures above her cot. One was a pencil drawing of Medusa and her flowing hair of snakes. The new girl, Colfax, had drawn it for her. The other two pics were photos of her locked in an embrace with her boyfriend. She was smiling but he wasn't. Even though she'd diddled a little kid, he'd stood by her and agreed to marry her. She'd be knocked up in no time, and if the sex-off program didn't fix her, she was the granddaughter in the Walmart for sure—or worse.

I glanced at the clock on the wall, trying to read the numbers through the square steel cage around it. I still had three chapters to read of *I Know Why the Caged Bird Sings*. Ms. Sutton had assigned it to me and no one else. She wanted us to have a discussion about the main character, a girl named Maya. I grabbed the book and fell on my cot. I was still thinking and I wasn't ready to lose myself in someone else's story. I couldn't wait to tell Bertie. My plan had worked! It was all worth it. And I knew I could make it through the next several days, especially since I had Ms. Sutton for a teacher.

Living on the unit made you glad for school. That was probably the point. Lying on your bunk every night and weekend and staring at the ceiling was torture for most detainees. They missed their video games or messing around on the streets. Outside, everything was exciting except school. Here it was the opposite, but not so much for me. I liked books and I'd never hated school. I just wanted a better one.

Ms. Sutton was the best teacher I'd ever known so I didn't mind jail so much. I would've done anything for her. Some of the teachers were no different than the ones on the outside. Flor's teacher hated kids and constantly shook his finger at them and said they were damn lucky he showed up to work, like he was a gift to each of them. He didn't know the trouble he was stirring. If his COs ever ran out of his room for an all call, he'd get pummeled and somebody would break that wagging finger.

The Juvenile Department of Corrections got the rejects that couldn't find work anywhere else. Some, like Kaufman, seemed okay but every egomaniac in Lakeview applied to be a CO. Since there weren't a lot of jobs, the people doing the hiring on the outside were picky. The jails couldn't afford to be so picky because there were a lot of people in jail and somebody had to watch them.

The COs got off on their power whenever they could, telling you where to sit in the rec room, deciding who got to be in charge of the remote—always the biggest kiss ass—and ripping away privileges over nothing.

My first day in jail Flor told me I needed to keep my head down and never disobey an instruction. That was easy for me. I wasn't a troublemaker. In fact I never got in trouble. If my mom hadn't caused a scene when I went before the judge, I might've never gone to jail. It was the first time in my life where I was glad she embarrassed me. I figured the only way out of Lakeview was through jail.

A guy in the 'hood who went by Cluckie because he'd stolen thirty chicken sandwiches from a McDonald's, had come back from jail and said his bunkie, a guy named Tyrese, had left Lakeview. I didn't believe him. Anybody dumb enough to steal a bunch of sandwiches in front of the video cameras couldn't be trusted to know shit.

Then he showed me a postcard from Tyrese who wrote about how great it was to go to college. On the front was a picture of an old, clearly important building at Tulane University, and Tyrese had written, "Made it," across the backside.

That's when I knew I had to do something. Mom always said, "Story, the best way to handle your problems is to go through them. That's why tunnels exist."

I sighed and opened my book and listened for my heart's steady beat. The sound of hope. Once again, as much as I tried, I couldn't stop hoping that something good would happen and the woman who I'd thought was just running the video camera would change my life.

CHAPTER SIX

Ravaged. When I was nine, I came across that word in a novel. It accurately described my mother's appearance after years of drug abuse. My mom was ugly and her actions made her uglier. It hadn't always been that way but I only knew her as a drug addict who'd jumped in and out of rehab most of my life. She was thirty-eight but looked fifty, and no amount of expensive moisturizer was ever going to erase the deep lines on her face. She rarely laughed or smiled, believing she had little to laugh or smile about. When she did, her lips parted just wide enough to reveal two gaping holes, one on each side where an incisor should've been. Her filmy blue eyes reminded me of a dirty windshield in need of cleaning—even when she was sober.

She'd been pretty when she went to college and I'd seen the proof. She had one picture of herself with my father. I found it when I was ten and tall enough to see the top of the armoire. I pulled it down every few months, usually after we had a fight. I'd stare at the young college girl leaning against the shoulder of the man who was my father, a man I'd never met. Mom said he'd disappeared about two months after I was born.

The picture reminded me she wasn't always a shrew. She looked innocent, her blond hair thick and framing her face. While she was extremely thin now, then she had some curves. She was only five-foot-four and my dad wasn't much taller. He had curly dark hair that he wore long, hair that I had inherited. He looked like a wolf, with a thick mustache, dark eyes and sideburns that stretched down his jowls. His name was Rupert, but he went by Root, like the old baseball song that said, "Root, root, root for the home team." Apparently he'd played minor league baseball until he hurt his knee. According to Mom he'd been a drug dealer who frequented the college parties looking for new buyers. He'd found one in her.

She said she'd been young and naïve, which was why she actually encouraged me to have a lot of experiences rather than education. Anytime someone on TV mentioned the value of a college education, she'd guffaw like a donkey and shout, "Didn't do much for me!"

She was right. Root managed to hook her fast and she'd squandered her savings within a year and lost her scholarship. She told me this story often and the moral was always the same. "Story, smarts don't mean anything. I'm the dumbest smart person you'll ever know."

That was true.

What I'd told "Margaret" in the interview was also true. I wasn't supposed to be here. Mom got pregnant with me, and Root hung around long enough to throw her off a cliff—literally. About seven months into her pregnancy they took a trip to California, trying to make their relationship work. They drove down the coast in his little convertible MG and he fell asleep at the wheel. He woke up to a blaring car horn and swerved. He flipped the car and Mom flew over the seawall.

It should've been the end of both of us. Two hundred feet of jagged rock separated the highway from the shore but halfway down, tucked away on a natural ledge, was a five-foot La-Z-Boy loveseat. Surfers had placed it there to watch the waves. Mom landed on the loveseat. She didn't bounce off and it didn't cushion a fall on the rocks. She plopped down as if she'd dropped from the sky. No shit.

They rushed us to the hospital and we were all okay, although Root broke his arm. The miracle escape made the papers after a hospital volunteer told his friend who worked for the local newspaper. The national newswires picked it up and Mom carried the article in her wallet for years. The day I was born she pulled it out and showed it to the obstetrician. She was worried I might be suffering from brain damage. He read it and said, "Wow, she's quite a story!"

So Mom looked at me and said, "You're Story."

Mom loved to show that clipping to everyone but I'd realized it was more about her than me. It was the one time when she was a big deal even though it was probably the single moment in her life when she had no control over her choices. And it worked out for her. She'd managed to find the four feet of safety that existed over that seawall. I always wondered if that was supposed to have been some sort of sign of a second chance for her that she missed.

I often thought about the surfers hauling the loveseat up the side of the cliff. It must've taken them hours. The locals told the paper it had been there for a few years and the cops knew about it but did nothing. The surfers couldn't have realized all their energy would save two lives. Now I wanted to do something with mine, but Mom kept throwing hers away.

I was thinking about those surfers when a CO appeared at the door. "Visitor, Black."

Bertie!

I jumped off my bunk and hit the stripe on the hallway with a quick step.

"Slow down," the CO barked.

I couldn't wait to talk to Bertie. We still had a few weeks to ourselves before she left for school and I planned to make this up to her.

I turned in to the visitors' room and suddenly stopped. My shoulders sagged when I saw Mom sitting at one of the tables, chatting with CO Wood, the duty officer. I took a deep breath. I knew she was pissed as hell at me. By now she'd figured out that I had "life checkmated" her. That was our term for manipulating someone into doing what we—Mom—wanted. She hated being checkmated any time. At least she'd have to whisper-yell at me. The COs wouldn't allow her to blow up in the visitors' room.

She caught my look of disappointment but continued her conversation with CO Wood. The visitors' room stocked a few games and decks of cards so families had something to do other than talk about life in jail. Mom had checked out the chess set and arranged the board. She always let me be white and go first but she never let me win. She'd taught me to play when I was seven, during her longest period of sobriety. Chess was our thing and my middle name was Caïssa for the goddess of chess. Before I came along she and Root played a lot. She'd taught me lots of strategies but I'd never beaten her.

I joined her at the table and nearly gagged at her stink. Her button-down shirt reeked of cigarette smoke. It didn't seem to bother CO Wood, who listened attentively as Mom explained her rates for writing his daughter's senior research paper.

Mom's sole income was writing term papers for students. She made enough to keep us going—barely. She could read a sample of a student's work and assume their identity—their tone, their vocabulary, how they organized their thoughts. If they needed a paper for a subject she'd not yet studied, she could easily read two or three books on the topic and write the paper like an expert.

"It all depends on the paper's length," she explained to him. "And the amount of citations she needs or background research. What's her topic?"

He shrugged and said, "I'm not sure. Something about cloning, I think."

"Great topic. As a science geek, I've written a lot of those. Everybody got an A. Do you have a piece of paper and a pen so I can give you my number?"

"Cindy isn't an A student. More like B-minus," he said as he handed Mom a pen and a small notebook from the breast pocket of his uniform. "We'd make her do it but her cheer squad is going to nationals and she has to defend her senior thesis. This science teacher is a putz and a hard-ass. He won't give her an extension."

"I understand," Mom said as she wrote down her name and phone number. "Give me a call."

"Thanks, I will." He looked at me and said, "Hi, Story. I'll tack an extra few minutes on your hour since we were doin' business."

Mom offered her fake smile. "I'm sure Story is ecstatic to see me."

"I'm glad to see you," I argued weakly as I opened with pawn to e-four.

"Sure you are…"

She drummed her fingers on the table dramatically. I knew she was staring at me while I stared at the board. I realized she wasn't going to move a chess piece—or say anything—until I acknowledged her. I schooled a blank expression and met her gaze.

"So, I realized you'd life-checkmated me about two seconds after that judge banged his gavel. But I couldn't figure out why you *wanted* to go to jail. I wracked my brain searching for an answer," she said, her cigarette breath wafting over the chessboard.

She pursed her dry lips and brought her pawn to e-five. "Then I got a weird phone call yesterday."

"Who was it?" I asked casually, already picturing Char—or "Jill." It had been a week since she interviewed me, seven of the longest days in my life.

"Some woman named Elle said we're invited to a presentation after you get out of jail. It's about your future. Who the hell is she?"

I shrugged. "I don't know."

"Right. And what kind of name is that? Obviously her mom liked fashion magazines."

I felt her stare again. There are superpowers that certain humans possess, one of them being the combination of high intelligence and street smarts. Most people don't get both because their high intelligence keeps them off the streets. The streets had ruined my mom's life but she could read a person or a situation in a minute. Seeing through me was just too easy.

I brought out another pawn to d-four and instantly regretted it. "It might be because I took this test. It's called the SPOT."

"Like the dog?" she sneered.

"It stands for Student Potential Opportunity Test. They give it to all the kids who do well in school."

She snorted and crossed her arms. "Then why the hell would they give it to you? You're a C student."

"Not in here. I've done well. I have a great teacher—"

"That's BS, Story. This is *jail*. Who the hell are you trying to impress?"

Two tables over, Cesar Lucero's mother wailed. She clasped Cesar's hands and he tried to soothe her. Tears streamed down her face. It was like this sometimes during visitors' hours. Jail was harder on most of the parents than the kids but not my mom.

"I saw Theresa," she said, taking my pawn. Theresa was my oldest childhood friend. We'd been neighbors and gone to first grade together. She lived on the next block and my mom thought she was the person I should be. She never got in trouble because she spent most of her nights and weekends taking care of her siblings while her mom worked. She wasn't a junkie without a job. I didn't idolize Theresa. I idolized her *mom*.

"How's she doing?" I asked as I moved into position for the Danish Gambit.

"She's taking classes at the community college next year. She'll be a year ahead. Got a scholarship."

I nodded. "Great for her. Did you pay the electric bill?"

She looked away and I knew the answer. "Nah, I couldn't get down there." She took another pawn and pointed it at me. "The best way to refute a gambit is to accept it. And I see what you're doing. You're using Bird versus Lasker."

"Mom, you have to pay the bills on time. You'll get home one day and the lights won't come on. Remember last time?"

"It's just too much to do," she whined.

"You have to do it," I said. "You need to follow my system. Does that mean the water and the rent didn't get paid either? They're almost a month overdue." She shrugged and I sank against my chair, not caring if we finished the game.

My mother would only deal in cash, which was practically impossible in the age of technology. I was sure the government didn't know she existed. I doubted she'd ever paid taxes since almost all of her adult life had been spent dealing with drugs and rehab. She'd never had a real job that involved paperwork but she'd also never applied for food stamps or welfare. She claimed it was a fair trade. She didn't take anything so she didn't give anything.

But we had to have utilities so I had a little system I always followed on the first of the month. Mom either gave me her cash or put it in our savings account. On the first I'd take the cash Mom had earned from her writing business and get cashiers' checks for each of the utilities. I could take the streetcar to the city building to pay the water bill and then walk to the electric company. After I took the bus home, I'd stop at the manager's office and pay the trailer park rental fee. The whole thing took about five hours and my teachers came to realize I'd be gone at least one school day each month.

With her eyes on the board she asked, "Do you know that kid over there, the one with the crying mom?"

Cesar was a big gangster. I didn't see him often but everyone on the unit was afraid of him. "I know who he is."

"Good guy?" she asked, chewing on a nail.

"Not in the least."

"It's your move, Story," she prodded.

I ignored her. "Mom, you've got to get this done. Did anybody send you an overdue notice? Did you at least get the money in the account?"

She shot me a hard stare. "Don't lecture me. You and your damn system. Yes, I got the money in the account. Why the hell are you in jail?"

There was no point in discussing this with her. If I got out on time at the beginning of the month, I could rush around and pay everything so I'd come home to water and electricity. Otherwise the trailer would smell from the poop in the toilet because the water was shut off and by nightfall we'd be sitting in the dark burning the one candle we owned—pumpkin spice.

I continued moving chess pieces, not caring about the game. She'd already figured out my strategy. I'd gone online and learned the moves from several famous games, figuring I could beat her that way. What I hadn't realized was she'd already read up on all of them years before me. Her photographic memory was unfortunately one thing I hadn't inherited.

"So, what's this presentation we're going to see? Does it cost any money?"

"No," I said automatically but I had no idea. If I got to go to the secret school, Mom would probably be asked to contribute something. Maybe I could do some extra work for the principal since Mom had nothing to give.

"What day is the presentation?" I asked casually, masking my eagerness. If I wanted it too much, she'd do everything possible to screw it up for me.

"I can't remember," she mumbled, her gaze glued to the board. "When's the ninth?"

"In about two weeks. A week after I get out."

"Then I guess that's it."

"Did she give you a time?"

"I don't know. Ten. Maybe two."

"Which is it?" I pressed.

Her lip curled and her cold eyes met mine. "I'll have to check my date book."

I knew to let it go. I could tell she was curious but if I kept pushing, she'd find some reason for me to miss my chance. I studied the board and didn't say anything else.

It had been easier when Gran was still alive. She'd been a buffer between Mom and me but I'd never recognized it until after she died and I had to talk to Mom about everything.

Cesar's mom passed by us as she headed out. Her cheap perfume mixing with Mom's stale cigarettes made me gag. Mom motioned for CO Wood to come over.

"What are you doing?" I whispered.

"You'll see."

I held my breath, hoping she didn't say anything to ruin my chance or make my time in jail harder.

"Did you think of something else to tell me?" he asked.

"No," Mom said, shaking her head. "Totally unrelated. I'd like to report something to you regarding the lady who just left. I'm quite certain that in the midst of all the hugging and crying she did with her son, she slipped him some contraband and he stuffed it down the front of his pants. Just thought you should know."

He frowned and reached for his radio. "What was it?"

"Something in a baggie."

He called for a search of Lucero and we waited for a response. This was typical of my mother. She noticed details everyone else missed. Once when we were riding the bus, she leaned over and said, "Watch the driver's right hand. He's dealing." Sure enough, his palm swiped a passenger's palm as he boarded the bus.

Ten seconds later Lucero's escort radioed back, "Affirmative."

Wood nodded at Mom and said to me, "Don't worry, Story. I'll take the heat and tell Lucero I saw his mother give it to him." Then he returned to his post by the door.

She looked at me and shook her head. "I hope Lucero's got some other skills 'cause he ain't got quick hands."

"Don't forget that tomorrow's double coupon day at Walmart."

"I know. I'm so damn sick of doing everything. You need to get yourself the hell out of here." She glanced at the board and with a swirl of her hand dropped her queen at g-two. "Checkmate."

CHAPTER SEVEN

The scheduled day of my release had finally arrived. The last week had been torture, especially on the unit. I'd written twenty love letters and poems to Bertie. I'd sent a few of them but kept most of them, knowing I'd get out before snail mail ever delivered them. I'd just read them out loud to her.

School was bearable because of Ms. Sutton. I was reading *Macbeth* now and I kept picturing my mom as Lady Macbeth. I knew they didn't have meth back then but all of Lady Macbeth's weird paranoia sounded like a bad meth trip to me. I wasn't done with the play yet but Ms. Sutton said I could keep the copy she'd given me. I told her I could just check it out of the library and I didn't want her getting in trouble for giving me something that belonged to the school. But she said it was hers and all the books I'd read belonged to her. I told her I felt honored that she'd shared her personal library with me.

She even inscribed the copy for me. I almost cried. I wasn't used to getting gifts. Mom and I never celebrated Christmas or birthdays. Mom always said, "Story, we don't have money for gifts. You know that better than me since you pay the bills. Our mutual respect for each other's intelligence is gift enough."

So keeping the copy of *Macbeth* was the nicest thing anybody had done for me since Gran was alive.

Getting released wasn't a big deal to the detention staff because the COs knew half the kids would be back. In the past they'd had a party for the kid who was leaving but then a lot of kids bragged about it and some fights started. Now they just pulled you out of class as if you were going to clinic or to visit with your parole officer. A CO brought your things to the visitors' room and added your Terms of Probation, a list of everything you couldn't do or you'd wind up back in jail. They didn't even let you change clothes. You left wearing the colored T-shirt, blue cotton pants and ridiculous slippers. It was one last way of humiliating you. You walked out the second set of doors and into the lobby carrying a box. Sometimes there were caseworkers, parole officers, and family members sitting in the lobby waiting to be escorted into detention. All these strangers watched you do the walk of shame across the lobby and past security. Everybody had to have a ride but I knew Mom wouldn't come get me, and Bertie wasn't old enough, so Charity, my P.O., said she'd pick me up.

As I gathered my stuff in the small cardboard box they'd given me, I prepared myself for disappointment. A lot of kids were told it was their day and then something happened with the paperwork. A million pieces of paper sent kids to jail and a million more let them out. You could wrap someone like a mummy with all the paper involved. And if one form wasn't signed in the right place or if somebody hadn't checked a box, I'd be stuck here for at least another day.

Flor stayed by my side through chow. She was bummed I was leaving but she was happy for me. She'd found out they were sending her to a special group home for kids with her problem so that made my departure easier for her. Otherwise we wouldn't have been talking. Everybody resented the kid who got to leave.

After chow we started the march to class, unit by unit. I was surprised when my class detoured to the large study room.

That meant somebody was graduating. Graduation was another thing nobody talked about. Once every few months a detainee earned enough credits to graduate since our jail school was a real school. We had graduations year-round and the graduate's class got to be the audience. It was a way to inspire everybody else to do well. We lined up behind the white chairs that faced the makeshift stage. The graduate this time was Rodriguez, the kid who loved conspiracy theories. At the front an older couple talked with Ms. Sutton.

The CO barked, "Sit!" We all pulled out our chairs, sat down and folded our hands in front of us, just like little dogs trying to please our master.

A few minutes later the graduation music started. Rodriguez marched in wearing a maroon gown and mortarboard. It even had a tassel. The principal said a few words and then the superintendent spoke about the importance of an education. Most of the kids in the room seemed unimpressed. A few had been in jail two or three times. If they came through the system again, they'd go to juvenile prison in Kalamazoo. I looked over at Ms. Sutton. She winked and my face softened into a smile.

I had a chance because of her. She got up and spoke after the superintendent, stating how proud she was of Rodriguez and how much she wanted us all to graduate. I saw a couple of the guys wiping their eyes. She'd made them cry. Then Rodriguez spoke. He thanked Ms. Sutton and his grandparents for not giving up on him. Then they gave him a diploma and that was it.

They had a cake for his family and a few of his friends. Since he and I weren't tight, I knew I wasn't getting any cake. That was okay. I was getting *out*.

They called for me during rec. I grabbed my sweatshirt and met the CO at the door. He was a mean, dumb fuck named Luker. He hassled the detainees just because he could.

"Let's go," he said.

I remembered the copy of *Macbeth*. It was still in the classroom. With my head down I said, "Sir, I've left a personal belonging in the classroom. Can we stop there before I go out? Please, sir?" It was my best kiss ass voice but he didn't care.

"No, we're not going all the way back to the classrooms when the exit is twenty feet away. You should've taken it with you."

I bit down so hard on my lip I could feel the blood in my mouth. I wanted to scream at him. I wanted to call him a piece of shit human being. We weren't allowed to take anything to rec except our sweatshirts. He knew that. I followed him into the visitors' center. I saw CO Kaufman standing there with my box. I remembered he was the nice guy who escorted me back to the unit after the interview. He smiled when he saw me. Maybe Luker would just drop me off and I could plead with Kaufman to walk me back to the classroom. But when Luker saw Kaufman smile like he knew me, he grabbed the box from him, handed it to me and said, "I'll get this bitch out of here."

I nearly swallowed my tongue. Luker knew a lot of the COs hated him but they had to be respectful or they'd get in trouble. I was thirty seconds from freedom and he knew he could say anything and I wouldn't respond. And he probably knew I'd been interviewed. In that moment I swore to myself that I'd never mess up again—no matter what—and I wouldn't treat anyone like shit if I ever had power or became a CEO of a company.

Kaufman nodded and offered me a look that said he was sorry. As we headed to the tunnel and the lobby, I looked inside the box. In addition to the few things I'd packed that morning with Flor, they'd added the clothes I'd worn into detention and my release papers.

Dumbfuck Luker was still saying shit to me as the first door closed behind me. The second door clicked and I walked to freedom. I looked around for Charity but she wasn't in the lobby.

"Hey, Story," a voice said. Standing there was Jill. She looked great in a knitted sweater, jeans, and her excellent boots. "You don't look very happy for someone who just got out of jail."

I threw my chin at Luker, who was still watching us through the glass in the visitors' room, his hands on his hips. He was obviously curious about why the billionaire was picking me up.

"He wouldn't let me go back to the classroom and get the copy of *Macbeth* that Ms. Sutton inscribed to me."

She glanced through the glass at him and asked, "So, if you didn't think you'd get in any trouble right now, how would you like to respond to Officer Luker?"

"I'd flip him off."

"That's a good idea," she replied. She faced the glass and stared at him. He offered a lecherous smile in return. Then her middle finger went up and she waved it to make a point. He glared back and when he saw I was laughing, he muttered something and stalked away.

"What did he just call you?" she asked.

"I think he called me the c-word," I said. "But I don't care. He's a dumb f-word."

She burst out laughing and said, "I'm here to give you a ride."

"You are? I thought my P.O. was coming."

"Nope. I asked Charity and she said it would be fine. Is that okay with you?"

"Sure," I said. "Thank you, Jill. That's really nice."

"My pleasure. And my real name is Charlotte, but everybody calls me Char. You knew Jill wasn't my real name, didn't you?"

I knew she wanted me to tell the truth. "Yeah, I thought it was something else. Charlotte fits you."

Before we walked out, she looked toward the visitors' room and said, "I'm sure I can get your copy of *Macbeth* back for you. I'm a good friend of Ms. Sutton's."

"That would be great. I don't want her to think I didn't want her gift."

"No, she won't think that. I'll make sure she knows why you couldn't get it."

We headed to her convertible BMW and she put the box in her trunk. I turned my face up to the sun and closed my eyes.

"Does it feel good?" she asked.

"Yeah. Even though we went outside a few times a week for rec, this sunshine feels different. Does that make sense?"

"It does."

I slid into the smooth leather seats and inhaled a fresh scent that weirdly matched the look of the car. The dash was pristine, no fingerprints or dust. There wasn't a speck of dirt on the carpeted floormats and I wondered if I should hold my feet up since I was still wearing my jail shoes.

And what a ride it was. Char started the car with a touch of her finger and the motor quietly came to life. I'd always thought it was silly that writers described an engine as purring, but it really did! We drove with the top down, my hair whipping around my face. It felt wonderful.

On the way back to the city Char asked me about school and life and what it was like to be in jail.

"I went to jail on purpose," I announced.

I could tell she was shocked. "Why would you do that?"

I told her the story about Cluckie knowing Tyrese. I expected her to stop the car and ask me to get out but she just kept her eyes on the road. Eventually she smiled and said, "Story, you don't know how flattered I am but that was the dumbest thing you ever could've done."

"I had to," I said. "I didn't see another way."

She glanced at me and her gaze returned to the road before she said, "No, I guess you didn't."

We got off the highway and suddenly the sun disappeared behind the clump of tall buildings that huddled together as Lakeview's downtown. They were the center and then the buildings got shorter and shorter, kind of like those stick-figure families on the back of a van that stand in a row. In Lakeview those two- and three-story buildings on the edge of downtown were dilapidated apartments, or in my case, Trailer Town.

Lakeview was an old, little city and only a few office buildings were necessary to do its limited business. Most of the people, including my relatives, had worked for the handful of manufacturing plants near the water. The plants closed in the eighties and the buildings had sat empty for years—until Charlotte Barnaby arrived. Now they were being converted to upscale lofts.

We turned on Division Street and crossed the train tracks, the dividing line between the downtown and the poorest community in Lakeview, the Cheshire District. Char pulled up to the first stoplight and I automatically glanced around us but Char didn't seem to care. Carjackings happened daily to people in nice cars or rides with rental stickers since tourists routinely got off the interstate one exit too soon.

"You can just drop me off anywhere. I can take the bus from here."

She made a face. "Absolutely not. There's no way I'm leaving you on a corner in jail clothes. Tell me where you live."

I really didn't want her to see our shitty trailer. Then I remembered it was the second of the month. Even though I'd begged Mom to pay the bills and follow my system, I knew she hadn't done it. She'd said she'd deposited the money into the savings account because that was on her way home from the coffee shop where she usually met her term paper clients. The dashboard clock said two thirty. I could quickly check the accounts on my phone to find out how much we owed and then hit the bank. "Actually, if you could drop me off at First Bank of Lakeview, I'll be able to pick up some cashiers' checks and pay the bills."

She frowned and I thought she might be mad. But while I looked up the electric and water bills, she navigated the streets to the bank and finally pulled up to the front doors. "I'll wait here. You go in and get your checks. If the traffic gets bad, I'll circle the building, but I *am* coming back," she said emphatically.

I nodded and ran inside. I was embarrassed she was chauffeuring me around. It was great to have a ride and I loved her Beemer, but it felt like a guest looking in the medicine cabinet when they asked to use your bathroom. Mom would be furious if she found out a stranger knew our business. Still, if Char didn't help me, I'd never get all of this done. It was too late in the afternoon to work my system on foot.

Sure enough, Char was waiting in a loading zone when I exited the bank with the cashiers' checks. "So, Lakeview Electric isn't far," she said. "Is that where we go next?"

I nodded with my head down. It was humiliating.

"Story, just so you know, I used to go to the welfare office with my mom."

I stared at her. "You did?"

"Uh-huh. Until I was old enough to go to Head Start. My mom couldn't hold a job. She had terrible OCD, but we didn't call it that back then. People just thought she was crazy." She glanced at me to see my reaction.

"I'm sorry," I said. "That sounds hard."

"It was. And I don't tell a lot of people that story but I thought you'd appreciate it. I know this must be difficult for you, having me drive you around. I just want you to know I get it."

"So your family was poor, too?"

"We were. I'm the fifth and last child. My father left after my mom got pregnant with me and then she struggled to cope. My oldest brother was the one in charge."

Her voice cracked and I could tell she was getting emotional.

"Thanks for sharing that. It makes me feel better."

I explained my system and stopped worrying about why we were driving around. Instead I leaned back and enjoyed my first ride in a Beemer. It was four thirty by the time we finished and Char insisted we stop for ice cream at Mr. Fizz's Candy and Ice Cream Palace to celebrate my release from jail.

When she turned on to Cameo Avenue the scenery completely changed from drab and depressing to bright lights and bold colors with metal and chrome. This was the heart of the *new* downtown, the part that Char had completely redone with some of her billion dollars. At night the street was bathed in light from giant billboards and electronic signs that lined the freshly poured sidewalks, leading visitors to the new sports arena on the next block, which was sandwiched between a three-story shopping center and a collection of restaurants. It was like these few blocks belonged somewhere else, somewhere really exciting.

One vacant lot stood out. A chain link fence wrapped the perimeter, protecting the construction equipment inside. An architect's rendering hung on the fence and announced the new Lakeview Library would open in nine months.

"Can I ask you a question about Lakeview?"

"Sure."

"Um, why didn't you renovate the other streets, like the ones in the Chesh?"

"Well, my goal wasn't to push out the people who lived there by gentrifying the area and making it impossible for the residents to stay. And if I tore down all the older apartments and buildings, the people who live there now couldn't afford the new rents. So my idea was to bring opportunity and services into the area so people could rise up on their own. I know the apartments don't look great, but every building has been brought up to code, new flooring installed, walls painted, and every apartment has Internet."

"Really?"

"Yes. My company, Second Beginnings, believes access to the web in the digital age is no longer a luxury—it's a right— like running water or electricity. Eventually, I'd like to see every household in Lakeview have Internet."

"That would be fantastic! I know I'd love to have it in the trailer."

She nodded. "You will. We're piloting it right now. And we've opened a free medical clinic, a three-acre community garden is thriving, and Second Beginnings has sponsored a few hundred microgrants for the citizens of Lakeview."

"What's a microgrant?"

"Well, my definition of a microgrant is an amount of money Second Beginnings gives to entrepreneurs who want to start a company or business that helps the entire community. Just yesterday we gave a microgrant to a woman whose store will sell goods that help save the planet."

"That's cool. So when she makes a profit, she pays you back?"

"Hmm, not with money. She pays back the community by being a part of the economy—with a good cause."

I smiled. "I like it. That's really generous of you."

She laughed. "Thanks, but even after taxes I ended up with over a billion dollars. I can afford it."

She didn't sound snotty about it at all. She sounded like it was her duty to help people.

We pulled up to a parking meter in front of the most colorful store on the street—lime green paint, blinking neon lights that spelled out *Mr. Fizz's Palace* and an enormous, spinning ice cream cone that rose from the roof. Anyone strolling down Cameo Avenue during the day could see that cone, but at night it blended in with all the other blinking lights. Nighttime reminded me of what I thought Las Vegas or Times Square would look like.

"You've been here before, haven't you?" Char asked as she opened the door, our senses suddenly filling with every type of sweetness imaginable.

"Oh, yes. My mom and I come here about once a month."

"Glad to hear it. My uncle opened this store in the fifties."

"Oh, wow," I said, studying the list of forty ice cream flavors. "I knew your family was from Lakeview but I didn't know they owned the candy store."

"Yes, indeed. This was the very first place we renovated." She looked around and made a face. "At the time I liked the idea of making it more modern but now I'd like to make it retro. Take it back to what it looked like when my uncle opened it. What do you think?"

"I think that would be cool. My mom has lots of stories about this place. I know she'd love that too. Retro has memories."

"That's the way we approached the remodel of the Cameo."

The Cameo was Lakeview's first and only theater for a long time. It was a historic building that was almost torn down—until Char stepped in and saved it. I hadn't been inside since the renovation but I was really curious to see it.

"What are you going to get?" Char asked, pointing to the list of ice cream flavors on the wall.

"Chocolate-peanut butter."

"Me too!"

We laughed and chatted as the long line snaked around the shelves of candy and treats. Char may have had a billion dollars but I guessed there was at least a billion calories in this store! Periodically people would wave or call out a hello to her and I realized I was hanging out with a celebrity. We returned to the

Beemer with our cones and I really hoped Mom hadn't made anything special for dinner. I rolled my eyes at the thought. *As if...*

The time went so fast. It felt like it was a different me riding around, not the neighborhood version of Story but somebody else. I sat taller and was extra careful not to get ice cream on the leather seats. But by the time we pulled up to the trailer park, my old self was back. I quickly gobbled the rest of the cone but I didn't know what to do with the wrapper.

"Just leave it with me," Char said, taking it and setting it in the cup holder. "It's our secret."

I sighed in relief. Mom would yell at me if she knew I'd been to Mr. Fizz's without her. Char popped the trunk and I grabbed my box. "Thanks again for the ride, the ice cream...just thanks."

"My pleasure. Don't forget about the ninth."

"I won't."

How could I forget about the presentation that might change my life forever?

CHAPTER EIGHT

After I put the rent check in Ms. Finnerly's drop box, I trudged toward our trailer with my stuff. The light by the front window was on so I snuck a peek through the window. Mom was stretched out on the sofa, smoking and reading a book about Gettysburg. She wore walking shorts and a button-down shirt which meant she was expecting a client. She'd told me many times, "Story, people equate normalcy and intelligence with appearance." I knew that if she wasn't expecting a client, she'd be wearing her crappy board shorts and an old concert T-shirt.

A stack of ten books sat next to her on the end table. A short stack of five books sat on the floor. She couldn't learn my bill-paying system, not even sober, but she had a system of her own when it came to reading. She'd get ten to fifteen books at the library, depending on how many she could carry and stuff in her backpack. When she got home, she'd set them on the end table. As she finished each book, she'd place it on the floor. When they were all on the floor, it was time to go back to the library.

She loved reading and history in that order. She claimed she was a victim of her time. "Story, if I'd been born fifty years sooner, I never would've become an addict. None of the drugs invented then were nearly as addicting as meth. Nothing."

I wasn't sure if that was true but I wouldn't disagree with her. Even when I was right, she assaulted me with ten arguments from a plethora of different sources and drowned me out. Her photographic memory was her greatest weapon and I'd learned that every issue or opinion had three sides—the right, the wrong, and Mom's.

I wasn't in the mood to face her yet. I pulled out my phone and perused the last three weeks of my life. I knew most of the emails would be crap so I checked my texts. A few from Ivy, hoping I was cool "serving my time." Two from Theresa and a bunch from Bertie. She'd sent me a long text every single day. They all started with, "I know you won't get this until you get your phone back…"

I quickly scrolled through all of them. Some were funny, others had pictures or GIFs—lots of puppies—and all ended with, "I love you."

I came to the last one, sent this morning.

Sorry can't pick u up. Stupid rule about being 18. But I've had to work all day. Just know ILYSM and I'll think of you each time someone bowls a strike.

She'd added a ton of emojis, including one of a bowling pin. For our first date we'd gone bowling and I managed to knock down four pins in the whole game. Bertie, the athlete, got a bunch of strikes. When I accused her of deliberately picking an activity that made me look bad, she said it gave her the chance to touch me while she showed me different stuff like how to hold the ball and how to release it. Yeah, she'd touched me a lot.

I'm home!! I'm free!! ILYSM.

I waited a minute to see if she would text back and when she didn't, I knew she was still working at the bowling alley.

I picked up the box, stared at our sad trailer and sighed. "Gotta deal with her sometime."

Mom looked up when I came through the door and said, "See? You don't know everything. I didn't get your system done and we still have lights." She picked up a mug from the coffee table. "And the water's still on for my tea. Didn't have anything to worry about," she muttered as she went back to her book.

I just nodded. I couldn't tell her why the utilities were still working. Defending my system would mean explaining how I got everything done while carting my box of belongings all over town.

Still holding my box, I cocked my head to the side and read the titles on the end table. All of them were nonfiction and there seemed to be a theme: the American Civil War.

"Anything good so far?" I asked.

She waved her hand sideways, meaning so-so. Our conversation over, I went to my room and fell onto the bed. It was a lumpy old mattress but it was better than the cot in jail. I looked around and smiled.

I thought about how different my life might be in a month. I wondered where Char would send me to school. I thought about Tyrese, Cluckie's friend, who went to college. I presumed Char's school would be better than stupid Franklin High. I pictured people having important discussions, using my own computer, reading the classics and meeting other girls who were super smart. And a girl who liked other girls…

I shook my head. I shouldn't be thinking about that since Bertie was still here. Sweet, wonderful Bertie.

Still… The possibilities were endless. Hope wrapped me in a tight hug. I'd accomplished what I'd set out to do by going to jail.

I changed my clothes and took a long shower, picturing the three weeks in jail swirling down the drain. Then I headed back to the living room and crouched in front of our one bookshelf. Mom owned few books but the ones she'd kept from her short time in college were classics. On the bottom shelf was *The Complete Works of Shakespeare*.

"What are you looking for?" she grunted.

I held it up. "I was reading *Macbeth* and I want to finish it."

"One of his best," she said. "I doubt it will surprise you to know the witches were my favorite characters. Fair is foul and foul is fair."

"Um, Mom, can I ask you a question about them?"

She held up a finger, which meant I needed to wait until she finished the page. She hated to have her reading interrupted for any reason, but she demanded the interruption occur at a logical place. I waited until she set the book across her chest.

"So, what was the role of the witches? What was their purpose?"

She thought about the question and then asked, "How far are you in the play?"

"Act Three."

She shook her head. "Can't tell you or I'll ruin it for you." Then she added, "But be thinking about when the witches appear and what action Macbeth takes as a result of interacting with them."

"Okay, I'll keep that in mind."

There was a knock on the front door. Mom rolled her eyes and got up. "'Bout time he showed up. This is the reason I didn't pick you up from jail." She grabbed a brown envelope from the coffee table and opened the door to a girl dressed in a fancy leather jacket.

"You're not Lloyd," Mom said.

"No, I'm his girlfriend. He had to work." She held out two Benjamins and they made the exchange.

"Um, do you write theology papers?" she asked timidly.

Mom laughed. "Honey, I write anything you need. Let me give you my card." She plucked one of her cards from the stack she kept on top of the TV. Printed on the face of the card was a Lakeview Community College email and nothing else. The LCC system thought Mom was a student named Edith Cross, thanks to one of her previous customers. Not only did she have an email account, but she also possessed a real student ID with her picture. She often laughed at the irony: she committed plagiarism for LCC students with an LCC email and she typed the papers on the library computer.

"Cool," the co-ed said. "I'll be in touch."

Mom waved goodbye and shut the door. "Another satisfied customer." She handed me the money and scratched her head. "Now, where was I? *Macbeth.* Finish it tonight and we'll talk about it."

I snorted. "I doubt that's gonna happen. It takes me forever to get through one scene."

She made a face. "Why?"

As a genius, she had very little understanding of people's educational struggles.

"It's the language. I have to translate everything from Old English to real world English."

"Real world English." She laughed. "That is the real world, Story, at a very different time."

"I get it," I said, too tired to argue with her. "I just won't be done with it tonight."

I headed back to my room but I heard her book smack shut. I closed my eyes and sighed. *Why did I say that?* If she stopped reading it could only mean one thing: field trip.

We roamed the third floor of the Lakeview Community College library, the home of the reference section. Mom stood on tiptoe to see the titles on the top shelf. I had no idea what she was looking for specifically, but the minute I'd proclaimed my ignorance about Old English, she was ready to educate me.

"Here it is," she said, handing me an oversize paperback.

"An Introduction to Old English." I flipped through several pages and saw it was a dictionary, one that provided synonyms for Old English words and phrases. "Cool," I said. "This will make it go a lot faster. Thanks."

"Meet you at checkout," she said. "I'm off to get a 'C' in World Ideologies." She headed to the computer lab and I went to the reading area, now armed with a way to untangle the language of Shakespeare. Two hours later I was falling asleep in my chair, completely tired from my long day—leaving jail, driving around with Char, and walking two miles to the library. I groaned at the thought of trekking home loaded down with books at midnight.

I awoke to my mother shaking my shoulder. "C'mon, we gotta go. The place closes in five minutes."

I followed her to the checkout line. On her trek from the computer center to the reading room, she'd grabbed five random titles she'd never read. She pulled out her bogus student ID, which gave her unlimited access to the reference section. The library served as the town's library and the students could check out reference books, something Mom wouldn't be able to do if she just had a public library card. That card meant the world to her. It was the only thing she cherished. If the trailer ever caught on fire, I knew she'd lay her hands on that card before she checked on me.

"How about a mocha latte before the walk home?"

My tired eyes narrowed. "Where is my mother and what have you done with her?"

"Ha!"

"Seriously, how are we going to pay for the drinks? You know those are five bucks apiece."

She winked and said, "I got it covered. Now tell me where you are in *Macbeth*."

"I got through all of Act Four tonight. I think the witches are either a statement about choices and free will or they're a reminder from Shakespeare that we can't control fate. Our destinies are sealed and the witches are professing what they know is coming."

"I think it's the second one," she said as we trudged over the hill toward the campus coffee shop that stayed open all night. "People want to believe they control their fate but that's all bullshit. We're just pinballs, Story, in some crazy pinball machine called life."

"But we have choices. We make decisions."

"Of course, but there's a set of natural reactions that occur, which puts us in those situations to make the choices. Look at you. You're a perfect example. We're gonna go see some presentation about your future. But if I hadn't landed square on that sofa when I flew over that cliff, you wouldn't be deciding about your future. *You* wouldn't have any future."

I couldn't think of a counter argument. "So you think the big stuff's already decided for us and we're just making decisions that are inconsequential?"

She shrugged. "That's close. It's nihilism."

"What's that?"

"Look it up." When I groaned she added, "It's got an 'h' in the middle."

It turned out the coffee shop's graveyard shift clerk was one of Mom's newest term paper customers who kept her loaded in caffeine. Armed with lattes to warm us, we continued the trek home. I was still thinking about the witches, free will, and nihilism. I'd looked it up on my phone and learned it meant a belief that life was meaningless.

"So if life is meaningless then why try at all?"

"Exactly my point. It's just gonna happen. Do what you can to make your existence comfortable and try to duck when it rains shit."

"I don't agree. Maybe that's true for some people," I added, trying very hard not to personalize the conversation, "but I think some lives have a lot of meaning."

"Like whose?"

I sighed. I thought about the first time I met Char when I thought she was Jill. "Thomas Jefferson."

"You know he was a slave owner, cheated on his wife with one of his slaves and had children with her?"

"Okay, but he wrote the *Declaration of Independence*. That was meaningful."

"For some people," she said with a snort. "Pursuit of happiness, my ass. If you're rich, white and male, then yes, it's meaningful. For everyone else, not so much."

"It's not a perfect world. I get it. But that doesn't automatically translate to meaninglessness. Shouldn't we try to find some meaning for ourselves? Didn't you used to feel that way, like when you were my age?"

The question seemed to jolt her and she slowed her pace. "Yeah, I thought differently when I was your age," she admitted. "In fact, I was voted Most Optimistic my freshman year of high school."

I stopped walking. "You're kidding, right?"

"Nope."

I hurried to catch up with her. Perhaps it was the caffeine but Mom rarely talked about the past. "So when did you become a nihilist?"

"When do you think?"

I took a deep breath. She'd opened the door to talk about her addiction and numerous failed recovery attempts, although she'd just passed two and a half years of sobriety in June. I thought about the timeline. "If you were an optimist during your freshman year of high school, and you became a nihilist during your freshman year in college, what happened during those years between?"

Her face changed and I could tell she regretted bringing it up. "Nothing. Let's just walk." That was code for, "Don't bother me, kid." She picked up the pace and I struggled to keep up with her. Mom was a great walker.

"How can it be nothing? It's probably really important. I—"

She stopped again and I almost ran into her. She faced me and shouted, "Drop it, Story! I never should've said anything."

I glanced at the dark houses along the block and worried someone would call the police. Fortunately, no one's lights came on. Mom charged ahead as if she could outrun the question. Now I was more curious than ever. I'd always assumed her meth addiction was a fluke because she'd met my dad. I thought it was unrelated to her life before college. Now I wasn't so sure.

We walked the rest of the way home silently. I didn't have Mom's photographic memory but Gran had always said I inherited her curiosity in full buckets. Something had happened to her when she was about my age. I couldn't stop wondering if I'd become her—and was there anything I could do to stop it from happening?

CHAPTER NINE

"So, what do you want to do for your sixteenth birthday?" Bertie asked.

"Be with you," I said, snuggling closer to her as we walked along the pier.

"Well, that's obvi, unless there's somebody else you'd rather hang with on your sweet sixteen."

I could see her bright smile in the pale moonlight and it made me smile. "Then you're all I need."

"Oh, so you're not expecting a present?"

"Uh, well…"

She laughed. "Don't worry. I've got it covered…assuming you'll still be here for your birthday."

"Why wouldn't I be here?"

"What if Char Barnaby whisks you away after the presentation next week?"

I snorted. "I doubt there'll be any whisking. My mother has to say yes to this and when it comes to agreeing about anything that's a change to *her* life, it takes a while."

Bertie glanced at me with a concerned look. "But she really wouldn't deny you the opportunity, would she?"

I knew Bertie wouldn't—couldn't—understand. These moments reminded me that we didn't know that much about each other, and while I'd never say it out loud, a part of me was grateful that she'd leave for North Carolina before she ever could learn those things about Mom and the way I dealt with Mom.

Bertie had met her twice when she'd come to pick me up—for a total of five minutes. And that's how I preferred it. I'd met Bertie's mom, dad, and two younger siblings a few times and I'd had dinner with them once. They were sweet and kind...and *normal*. Bertie swore she'd not told them anything significant about my life—especially that I'd been in jail. When they'd suggested Mom and I come for dinner, I nodded, knowing it would never happen even if I had to tell them an absolutely ridiculous lie like Mom had been abducted by a serial killer who only attacked people in trailers.

We'd come to the end of the pier, my favorite place to think, but I hadn't answered Bertie's question. Maybe that was my answer. Bertie was suddenly very quiet, staring out at the water.

"You know I'll help you however I can," she said softly.

"I know."

But what we both knew and didn't say was that I'd have to do this myself and I'd probably have to defy my mother.

* * *

It was the day of Char's presentation. I woke up early and made coffee for me and started the teakettle for Mom. She had used the last week to torture me. She would threaten not to attend and a few hours later she would say she wanted what was best for me—if I did whatever she said at that moment. So I'd gone to the library with her twice, made gallons of her tea and played chess with her three times a day. And I'd done it all with a smile on my face.

The presentation was at ten a.m. and she got up that morning in rare form. As she strolled into the kitchen, she had a perplexed look on her face. "Hmm. I know there was something I was supposed to do today." She tapped her chin. "What was that?" She looked at me, her brow furrowed. "Do you remember, Story?"

I just rolled my eyes and she laughed. While she ate the eggs and toast I made for her, I cleaned the kitchen and then took a shower. I wanted to dress nicely without looking like I was ready to go to the prom. I settled on chinos and a button-down shirt. Once I'd finally dressed and brushed my rather unruly hair, I emerged from my room—to find Mom asleep on the couch, a book over her chest.

Unbelievable! I bit down on my lip to prevent a scream from escaping.

"Mom, wake up," I said, glancing at our cheap wall clock in the kitchen. It was 9:05 a.m. The bus ride would take twenty-five minutes and it was a ten-minute walk to downtown. "You only have fifteen minutes to get ready."

She blinked. "Oh, I'll never make it. My makeup artist isn't coming until nine thirty. Then there's the matter of what to wear…" She shrugged and I realized she'd not been asleep at all. Yet again, she was being a manipulative jackass.

"Mom, this is important to me. I've done everything you asked this week and I'm just asking this one thing. This one time." I took a deep breath and added, "Please."

She smirked. "Oh, all right." She slowly nestled her bookmark between the pages, closed the book, and reverently set it on the end table. *If she treated our relationship with that much care…*

She disappeared into her room and shut the door. I sat on the sofa, my foot tapping like mad. I needed to do something so I grabbed my backpack and pulled out *Room*, a book Ms. Sutton had recommended. I figured if I could go to the special school, I'd probably start right away. Undoubtedly, there would be more homework so I might not be able to finish this. *Focus, Story. Read.*

It worked for a few minutes but eventually I was just pacing, looking at my phone every thirty seconds. At nine thirty-five I trudged back to Mom's door and knocked. "Mom, are you almost ready? We've got to get to the bus stop."

"Almost," she called.

I shook my head and pounded my fist against my open palm. She was doing this deliberately. Mom never took any time to get ready unless she was meeting a client. Most days she just changed out of her pajama bottoms and wore whatever top she'd worn to bed. I considered that a win. She'd say, "Story, it's winter. We're bundled up in our sweaters and coats. Nobody's gonna know if I'm wearing my old Guns 'n Roses T-shirt with the hole in the armpit."

I paled at the idea that she would be wearing that T-shirt…

The door swung open and I gasped. Mom looked nice. She wore black dress pants, a lavender blouse I'd never seen, and… her Chucks. Her hair was pulled back into a bun and I thought she might be wearing makeup. I could see the shadow of her old self, that pretty college student in the photo with my father.

She threw up her hands. "Well?"

"You look great," I said sincerely. I glanced at my watch. "It's nine-forty. We have to go."

"Let's go, then," she said, marching to the living room, grabbing her purse and darting out the front door.

By the time I got my purse, flipped off the lights and locked the front door, she was out of sight. I ran. When I turned the corner, I saw the bus coming toward the stop. Mom got there just in time to hold it for me. I ran and we made it but we were going to be late.

When we got off the bus at the mouth of Cameo Avenue, I power-walked like I was in a 5K.

Mom shouted, "Crap, Story! Slow down! If I have a heart attack, you won't be going to any fancy school. You'll be home-schooled by me so you can nurse me back to health!"

I slowed so she could catch up. My phone read 10:04 a.m. *We're already late. Either it matters or it doesn't.*

The Cameo Theater sat at the other end of the street. It wasn't as magnificent in the daytime, but at night a string of white lights outlined each letter of the word CAMEO, and floodlights bathed each of the medieval sculptures that wrapped around the entire building. Behind the Cameo sat a high-rise, a multiuse building with residences and several dozen shops. I'd been to many of them with Mom, and we especially liked the coffee shop.

Char Barnaby was rumored to live on the top floor. Her company, Second Beginnings, took up the entire eighth and ninth floors, at least that's what I'd read on the building directory.

We reached the last cross street and the front doors of the Cameo were in sight, when Mom suddenly grabbed my arm and turned left, pulling me toward the back of the Cameo. "What are you doing?" I cried. "We're late and now you're going in the wrong direction! We can't get in this way."

"I know," she said. "I've done a little investigation into Ms. Billionaire and I need to confirm some intel I've received."

I rolled my eyes. "Intel? What are you? An FBI agent?"

"No, but I'm easy to talk to. When I talked with CO Wood the other day about his daughter's paper, I mentioned this presentation and he told me something very interesting."

"What? What did he say?"

"Oh, no. A good spy doesn't reveal the intel." She turned right at the corner of the building and we were directly behind the Cameo near the loading dock. No one was around but three long buses sat in a row. "Okay, let's go," she said, making a one-eighty turn and pulling me back up the street toward the front door.

"What was that all about?"

"Nothing. Intel confirmed."

I shook my head. I just needed to let it go.

No one was outside but when we barreled into the lobby, there were at least two dozen people standing around. *Thank God they haven't started yet. Breathe!*

"Hi, Story," a voice called.

Margaret, the interviewer I'd met in detention, greeted us.

"Hi, sorry we're late."

"You're fine." She turned to Mom and extended her hand. "And you must be Ms. Black."

"Patty is fine."

"Patty, I'm Elle. I met Story at detention. You have an exceptional daughter."

I knew her name wasn't Margaret! Elle fit her.

"I hope so. This seems like a lot of fuss for a school admission."

We looked around. There were at least two dozen teenagers, each with an adult. I hoped this wasn't a competition like *The Hunger Games*. I'd lose for sure.

"Let me show you to your seats," Elle offered.

She escorted us through the lobby and my gaze went everywhere. All of the original columns were still in place…the detailed scrollwork…the ornate woodwork. I was impressed. We went through two large oak doors and into the main hall. While the art deco proscenium and balcony had been preserved, the theater seats were gone. Sofas, couches, and chairs were scattered throughout the audience. It looked like a huge living room. I choked up, remembering that the last time I'd been here was to see *Finding Nemo* with Gran.

Elle led us to a single couch in the middle of the room. I noticed that while some people sat alone like us, most parents/children sat next to another duo. I wished we had someone else to talk to, maybe someone who knew about the special school and could convince Mom.

I looked around to see if I knew anyone. I guessed there were about seventy-five people, mostly white with a few Asian-Americans. Some wore uniforms or work shirts, like they'd taken off a couple of hours from their jobs to come to this presentation. A lot of people were in jeans and I was glad Mom and I had dressed up.

My gaze drifted to the mural on the ceiling and then the balconies. Char was sitting alone in one of the balcony boxes. She wore a headset and seemed to be talking to someone. When she saw me, she smiled. I think she might've winked too, but she was too far away to know for sure.

Mom nudged me. "Look over at that woman on that awful blue couch, the one in the green scrubs."

I found the woman, who was texting on her phone. A lanky, tall boy with glasses sat next to her. He looked like a young John Lennon. "What about her?"

"Doesn't she look familiar?"

I squinted to get a better look. "I don't think so."

"Hmm. I know her," Mom mumbled.

My foot started tapping. While I was just gazing at the crowd, waiting for the show to start, Mom was scrutinizing every person and every action. Her photographic memory and her unbelievable attention to detail made me nervous. If she found just one reason to say no to this opportunity, she'd do it.

"Why're you so nervous, Story?" she asked, placing a hand on my bouncing knee.

"I'm not nervous."

"Like hell you're not," Mom huffed. She gave a long look to her left and then swung to the right, literally making her own panoramic picture. "We'll see how this goes." She looked back at the woman in scrubs and murmured, "Where do I know you?"

Fortunately, the lights dimmed and a serious cello piece began.

Mom leaned over and whispered, "Bach, from his cello suites."

Pictures of Lakeview splashed across the enormous screen— empty lots, shuttered buildings, a closed school with a sign taped to the front door that read, *Hope died here*. A deep voice cut off the music. "This is our home. This is Lakeview. Before the arrival of Second Beginnings, unemployment reached an all-time high, violent crime threatened our safety, and home values had plummeted." A picture of a smiling man with few teeth filled the screen. He stood on his porch holding a homemade cardboard sign that read, *I'll give you my house for a new iPhone*.

More photos appeared of parents with their children: in a homeless shelter, waiting outside the welfare office and sitting on the stoops of the Chesh. The last photo showed a guy standing in an alley, his arm around a kid with similar facial features. Both of them carried pistols, grinning.

The deep voice said, "Please welcome Dr. Isaiah Baxter."

"Who's he?" Mom asked as we politely applauded.

"I don't know."

A young, African-American man strolled to the edge of the stage. He sported a short afro and a goatee, wore a white dress shirt, a dark blue vest and matching jacket, and black jeans. What was most noticeable was his bright multicolored bowtie.

"Good morning, I'm Doctor Isaiah Baxter. I have the great honor of serving as the principal for the finest school in America." He smiled and gazed at the audience. "I know that sounds like I'm bragging, but really I'm just speaking the truth. We've invited all of you here today to share an opportunity." He folded his hands in front of him and crossed the stage. "What if you could give that special young person in your life the greatest gift of all?" He paused for effect and stared at the crowd. Many of the adults nodded. Mom just looked skeptical. "I'm not talking about a car, a vacation, or money. I'm talking about a future. A future that will guarantee the young person you love will never be this guy!" The picture of the toothless man holding the sign appeared again.

A murmur went through the crowd and most of the adults whispered to the student next to them—but not Mom. She ignored me and watched everyone else. Dr. Baxter came down the steps into the audience and a technician handed him a microphone. He strolled to a balding, short man in a mechanic's uniform. Next to him was a girl with blue hair. "Hello, sir. May I ask your names?"

"I'm Ron, and this is my daughter, Hazel."

"Welcome to you both. Ron, do you want a different life for Hazel?"

"I do."

"One without poverty or crime?"

"Absolutely."

"Do you want Hazel to fulfill her dreams?"

"Yes."

"Do you want Hazel to go to the very best school and onto college?"

"Yes!" He practically shouted and the crowd applauded.

"Then this is the school she should attend." Dr. Baxter pointed to the stage and the words *Tabula Rasa* appeared. "May I introduce you to the educational opportunity of a lifetime, Tabula Rasa."

"A clean slate," Mom whispered.

The lights dimmed again. Some upbeat piano music started… and then pictures: a group of students building a computer, two students solving a formula together on a whiteboard, a circle of students wearing Virtual Reality goggles, a fitness center, an amazing green space with a life-size chess board! But the best pictures were the last ones—two students building a bridge together. It was like they knew me and my dream of being an engineer!

I swallowed and felt the lump in my throat. My eyes were wet. I quickly wiped them before Mom could see but she was already staring at me.

The film ended and everyone applauded. Dr. Baxter approached a stocky white boy and asked him, "What are your career interests?"

"I want to design video games," he said into the microphone.

"Excellent." Isaiah turned to the audience and said, "All of our students learn coding and we have integrated technology with every discipline." He pointed at the boy and said, "You'll learn everything you could ever want to learn."

He stopped at a yellow couch in front of a girl with short red hair who sat next to a woman in a polyester fast-food uniform. They introduced themselves as Shelby and Dina.

"What are you interested in studying?" he asked Shelby.

"Quantum physics. I like to read about it."

"That's amazing," Dr. Baxter commented. "At Tabula Rasa—"

"Who made the first quantum hypothesis?" Mom shouted.

I gasped and grabbed her arm. "What are you doing?"

"Figuring something out," she growled.

Dr. Baxter paused and everyone looked at us. Mom stood, just as she might have if she'd been called upon to answer a question in a college lecture class.

"Well?" she asked sarcastically.

Shelby looked at her mother and then Dr. Baxter before speaking into the microphone. "Um, I didn't read about that. Sorry."

"Excuse me," Dr. Baxter said, stepping in front of the girl. "Perhaps you could enlighten us with the answer?"

"Max Planck," Mom said distractedly, her gaze scanning the crowd.

I tugged at her arm again. "Mom, sit down. You're embarrassing me."

I glanced up at Char, who was still in the balcony. She was speaking into her headset. I could imagine what she was saying. She'd never want me in her school now.

Mom stalked over to them and yanked the microphone from Shelby while Dina put a protective arm around her daughter. Two security guards appeared and flanked Dr. Baxter, waiting for a command.

"Okay, you don't know who Max Planck is," Mom continued, "but surely you can name one, just one, of the scientists credited with discovering quantum mechanics."

"Ma'am," Dr. Baxter said, again stepping between Mom and Shelby, "why don't you return to your seat? I think—"

"*I* think this is horseshit!" She pointed at Dina and said, "You're feeding her the answer!"

"Only because you're bullying her!" Dina barked.

Her pronouncement silenced the crowd. No one whispered to a companion or commented about the crazy woman as I would've expected. *This is weird.* I remembered my interview with "Margaret" and "Jill." They'd tried to trick me and make me believe Margaret was in charge…

All eyes were on Mom. She turned a full circle. "Who are you people? You," she said, pointing at Shelby, "have never read an article—and certainly not a book—on quantum physics if you can't name Albert Einstein!"

She strolled to the blue couch and pointed at the woman in the scrubs. "I've seen you before. You do those commercials for the Dodge dealership on the highway!"

The woman said nothing, too stunned to reply.

Mom stared at Dr. Baxter. "Who the hell are you?"

In an even tone, he said, "Ma'am, I'm exactly who I say I am. I am Doctor Isaiah Baxter, principal of Tabula Rasa."

"Well, you may be legit, but none of these folks are," she accused. She hurried across the room. "Is someone going to tell me what's going on?" She tapped the mic with her finger. "Hellooooo."

I looked up at Char, hoping to get some guidance. She saw me and tossed her chin toward my mother. She wanted me to take charge.

I jumped up and went to Mom. "Please come sit down," I said firmly. "Let them finish the presentation."

"Something's going on, Story. I—"

"I don't care!" My voice echoed in the room. I took a breath and said, "I'm begging you." I stared into her eyes, knowing I'd start sobbing in just a few more seconds. "This is important for both of us. I'll clean the trailer for a month. I'll play chess whenever you want and go to the park on Saturday. We'll go to the library and I promise I won't complain. Please."

Mom finally nodded and we started back toward our seats. She gave a hard stare to those she passed but she walked with me—until she didn't. She grabbed my arm and pulled me back. We were standing in front of a middle-aged Asian-American gentleman and his daughter.

"Wait a damn minute," Mom spat. She bent over in front of the girl and grabbed her necklace, seizing a gold medallion in her hand.

"Hey! Let go!" the man shouted.

"Mom! What are you doing?" I cried.

The security guards rushed over but backed off when she let go.

"Are you her father?" Mom said into the microphone as if she was a professional interviewer. When the man nodded, she said, "Really?"

Mom shoved the microphone in front of him and he said, "Yes."

"Being incredibly open-minded to any possibility, is she adopted?"

"What?" the guy asked, puzzled.

"Is she adopted?" Mom repeated.

He glanced at Dr. Baxter and said, "No."

Mom stood up straight and stared at Dr. Baxter, a smug look on her face.

Oh, God. I knew that look. Mom wore it every time she beat me at chess or proved me wrong.

She glanced at me before she announced, "If she's not adopted, then I'd like to know how a *Chinese* father wound up with a *Korean* daughter. Whoever hired you obviously thinks all Asians look alike."

A murmur surged through the crowd and the man and girl looked at each other, stunned.

"How do I know this?" Mom asked. "Because the young lady is wearing a medallion with the Korean symbol for peace, while the gentleman's jacket is emblazoned with a name of a company written in Mandarin." She leaned closer and added, "If I'm translating this correctly…Sung Ho's Trades and Exports."

I felt like throwing up. I dropped onto an empty couch, my head in my hands, while Mom paced. I didn't dare look up at Char right now.

"You ain't foolin' me now," Mom bellowed at Dr. Baxter. She jumped on the stage and said to the crowd, "Show of hands. Students, how many of you could write the quadratic formula right now?"

Most of the students raised their hands.

"How many of you know the capital of Sweden?"

Most of them raised their hands again.

Mom nodded. "Very interesting. How many of you can name the most significant battles of the Civil War?"

Nearly every hand flew into the air.

"I'm impressed." Mom paused and added, "And utterly confused." She searched the auditorium and her gaze landed on the box where Char still sat. "Maybe Ms. Billionaire can enlighten me?"

Mom and Char stared at each other while everyone else watched. I knew if Char didn't answer her, Mom would drag me out of the Cameo and I'd never see Char again.

Char stood. "Lights up and doors open."

The lights came up and four blue doors on the opposite side of the theater opened.

"Ushers, lead them out, please!" Char announced.

Ushers in red coats and white shirts directed the audience out, closing the doors behind them, leaving me, Mom, and Dr. Baxter—and Char, towering over us.

"Where are they going?" Mom asked.

"That's not your concern," Char snapped.

"They wouldn't by chance be getting back on those buses that are parked outside in your loading zone, going back to wherever they came from?"

Char looked surprised but she didn't answer Mom.

I couldn't believe it. "Mom, what are you talking about?" I was so angry with her. And confused. And frustrated. Mom was ruining my chance. "Why are you doing this?"

"This was a sham, Story. This whole thing was a setup. I don't know why, but I intend to find out."

My shoulders sagged. I looked up at Char. "The school isn't real?"

"Oh, no," Dr. Baxter interjected. "The school is quite real."

"Story," Char said, "all you need to know is that we want to offer you the opportunity of a lifetime. This," she said, gesturing to the auditorium, "was an attempt to persuade your mother to let us help you."

"Who were all those other people?" I asked.

"Actors?" Mom guessed. When Char said nothing, Mom added, "And I believe, Story, those teenagers you saw were actually students at Tabula Rasa."

"They were?"

"Yes," Char said hesitantly.

I still didn't get it. It didn't make sense. "Why go to all that trouble…" Char looked away and Dr. Baxter had dropped onto a sofa and was cleaning his glasses.

I could see the wheels turning in Mom's brain. She pointed and said, "Where do those doors lead?"

"It doesn't matter," Char said flatly.

"Oh, yes, it does," Mom disagreed. "Because that's where the sausage gets made, right? That's where all the particulars of this little arrangement are spelled out." She gazed around the room and added, "Judging the great effort you've gone to for Story, the gobs of money you've spent to make this little presentation happen, I'm guessing there are a few conditions that I won't like, right?"

Neither Dr. Baxter nor Char would answer her.

Suddenly a skinny teenage girl with longer wavy hair burst through one of the middle blue doors. When she realized she wasn't alone, she immediately halted in mid-step. It was almost comical and I nearly laughed. Her jaw hung open and her eyes were wide. She didn't know where to look first. She finally settled on Char. "I'm sorry. I…I left my jacket…"

"Who are you?" Mom asked, still talking through the microphone.

The girl immediately glanced at Char, who nodded. "I'm Jamison."

"And you go to Tabula Rasa?"

"Uh-huh."

"So would you recommend this school to my daughter?"

Jamison looked at me and smiled. She was super cute so I smiled back. "Yeah, it's a great school. You should come." She looked at Mom. "You should let her come. I mean, yeah, this was a really weird Convincing Hour—"

Mom held up a hand. "A what?"

Jamison shifted from one foot to the other. "Um, it's the Convincing Hour?"

"Thank you, Jamison," Char called. "Go ahead and get your jacket."

She went toward the back and picked up a windbreaker. She mouthed "Sorry" to Char, smiled at me once more and waved. When I looked back at Mom, she wore an enormous grin.

"Convincing Hour," Mom murmured. "Clever. Well, I'm not convinced." She held out the microphone and in dramatic fashion did a mic drop like a celebrity. Feedback from the clattering mic resounded through the theater. "Let's go, Story," she said as she headed toward the exit. When she realized I wasn't following, she whirled toward me. "Let's go!"

"I'm not going," I announced.

She marched back to me. "What did you say?"

I thought of the day in Marvin's store, the moment I hurled that brick through his window and his angry look. He was a nice man and I'd made him hate me. I thought of jail, the bad food, the boredom. And Ms. Sutton. I'd done things I'd never do just to get to this moment.

I wasn't sure what had happened or if Mom had been deceived…or if Char was a good or bad person, but I didn't think bad people took you out for ice cream and played chauffeur for an afternoon… I stared Mom down. "I'm not leaving, at least not like this. I want my chance."

"Your *chance*? What the hell does that mean?"

"I want to go to Tabula Rasa."

"Fine. Go. I don't care where you go to school."

"Really?"

"Really. But I don't think it's quite so simple, is it Ms. Million—excuse me—Ms. Billionaire? If it were so simple you wouldn't have needed all of this." She gestured to the seats. "If it were so simple, you wouldn't need a *convincing* hour."

Char put her hands in her pockets and studied Mom. "What do you want?"

Mom held up a hand. "I don't want anything. But my daughter wants her chance."

Char looked at me, not with anger or hatred but with a sad smile. When she turned to Mom her expression shifted to stone. "Fine. I'll explain everything to you but not today. We'll make a new appointment. We'll sit and talk."

"Just the two of us?"

"No," Char and I said at the same time. Char looked at me, surprised…and pleased.

"This is about Story and she needs to be there," Char insisted.

Mom offered a smug grin. "Fine. Nice meeting all of you." She flung her chin toward Char and said, "Have your people call my people."

CHAPTER TEN

The text arrived just as we stepped on the crowded bus to go home. I could feel the vibration in my pocket, but I'd silenced my phone for the presentation so Mom didn't hear it. Even her hypersensitive senses were dulled sometimes, like when we were in a crowd.

It was nearing lunchtime and the bus was crowded so we couldn't sit together. Mom always headed for the back and I took the very first open seat I found—two rows past the driver and next to someone in a ballcap. Their head was down, scrolling on a phone, and I wasn't sure if it was a boy or a girl, but I thought it was a girl. She—or they—didn't look up when I sat down. I quickly removed my phone from my pocket. It was Char texting me and I remembered I'd given her my number the day she picked me up from jail.

Don't give up hope. We're not mad at you. We want you to have your chance. Try not to irritate your mother. See you in a few days. Now delete this text.

I hated deleting her words. I couldn't believe they still wanted me after my mom had made a fool of herself in front of

Char, the principal of Tabula Rasa, and all the strangers. It had been weird to watch the entire audience walk out. Mom babbled on the way to the bus stop that the Billionaire Lady hired all of them just to convince her—of something.

"She wants you, Story, but it's not just to go to school," she said. "I don't know what their game is but we're gonna find out. I wouldn't get your hopes too high because I ain't feelin' too agreeable."

I immediately texted Bertie: *Hey, can u talk?*

For a sec. TELL ME! NEW SCHOOL 4 U?

Not quite. Weirdest thing ever. Really.

Suddenly my phone rang. Bertie couldn't wait. I hated talking on the bus and I knew Mom would drill me if she saw me talking to anyone. She'd probably think it was Char.

"Hey," I said.

"I really only have a couple minutes. What happened?"

I recounted what had happened and how Mom had discovered their whole scam and then Jamison appeared.

"And she called it the Convincing Hour?"

"Yeah. It was like a whole room full of fakers and their job was to convince Mom to let me go."

Bertie laughed. "I'll bet that just pissed Patty off royally. I'm surprised she agreed to meet Char."

"Well, I was insistent."

"You stood up for yourself? Great job, Story. I know how hard that must've been for you."

"It was. But I went through too much to get this, you know?"

"Yeah. I'm proud of you. I know that sounds lame, but—"

"It doesn't. I'm proud of me too. But Mom thinks they've got some diabolical deal going on. Maybe like they're going to kidnap me and harvest my organs or something."

Bertie laughed again. "I doubt it. But it is weird how much trouble they went to for you. It's also super flattering." She sighed and said, "I've gotta go, but I'll see you tonight, okay?"

"'Kay. See you then." I pocketed my phone and glanced at the person next to me. Although her head was cocked to the side, I could tell she was staring at me. It was Jamison.

"Oh, my God."

"Stay cool," she murmured. "Don't look at me and face forward. I'm sure your mom would recognize me since she's uber observant."

I studied the cowlick of the guy in front of me. "Yeah, she would. What are you doing here?"

"Just…checking in. What'd your mom say after you left?"

"She's sure there's something super shady going on. She said Char wants something from her." I took a breath and said, "Is that true? Is there something shady?"

"Not really," Jamison said hesitantly. "It's more about doing what's best for the student and not the parent. Char's asking you to go to Tabula Rasa, not your mom. Did she say anything else, make any guesses?"

"No, she's just thinking there's more to the offer than what she's being told. Mom hates not knowing something and she detests lying."

"I get it. Did you like the presentation?"

I turned and smiled at her. I couldn't help it. I looked right into her sparkling blue eyes. It was like looking at the sky.

"Story?"

"Oh, sorry." I turned away. "Yeah, I thought it was great. Tabula Rasa looks so cool."

"It is. You'll love it there." She paused and asked, "Is it true you went to jail on purpose?"

I felt my cheeks burn. I refocused on the guy's stubborn cowlick. "I did. Char said that wasn't very bright."

She chuckled. "I think it's totally badass."

"Thanks."

She held out her hand. "Give me your phone. I'll give you my number."

"Uh, really? You can have phones at Tabula Rasa?"

"Of course," Jamison laughed. "It's a school. Not a prison." She tapped in her number and called herself. "Now I have your number. Would it be cool if I called you sometime?"

"Um, sure," I said, already feeling the burn in my cheeks.

"Cool. And if you have other questions about Tabula Rasa, you could always ask me."

"Cool as well," I said.

She looked through the window and pulled the cord. "My stop. Stay strong, Story. Remember, this is about *your* future."

She hurried off, keeping her head down so Mom wouldn't recognize her.

I thought about how much trouble Char had gone to so far to get me to Tabula Rasa. She was in my corner. Ms. Sutton was in my corner. And Bertie. And now Jamison. The only one who seemed against it—against me—was Mom.

CHAPTER ELEVEN

The next day Mom said Char was coming to the trailer three days later, on Tuesday. I didn't understand why Mom had to be involved. She never cared about my schooling after I was old enough to make my own lunch and walk there alone. She never came to conferences or signed permission slips. Gran did all that even when Mom wasn't in rehab. I hoped Char wasn't expecting her to volunteer at the school, go to PTA meetings, or chaperone field trips. She probably wouldn't show up and if she did, she'd make a scene.

I felt stupid for not preparing Char. My mom had the keenest eyes and she knew a lot from her reading, like the difference between Korean and Chinese. She never forgot a face or anything she read.

Jamison surprised me with a text—and a picture of her room. Well, her half of the room. *So this is where I live, Ginsburg Hall. I share with a cool girl named Sage.* It seemed pretty standard, except for an electric and acoustic guitar hanging on the wall and two retro concert posters above her bed—one for Heart and the other for Joan Jett. We texted back and forth and Jamison promised me a private concert if I came to Tabula Rasa.

I didn't know how to reply. Was she flirting with me? Had Char encouraged her to contact me? Was this a big game or was Jamison maybe interested in me?

Stop overthinking and focus on Bertie.

I sent Jamison a dorky smiley face.

Char had said not to irritate Mom so when she suggested we go to the park Saturday morning and play chess with the regulars, I agreed.

Post Park was the nicest park in Lakeview, another place that Charlotte Barnaby's company, Second Beginnings, had renovated. Before it had been a haven for junkies and hookups in the bathrooms. The grass had turned to dirt and the few picnic tables were covered in gang graffiti. Now it was clean and beautiful. Sprawling grassy lawns were filled with families picnicking, a yoga class practicing its moves and the chess lovers huddling around a cement circle of chessboards.

Many of them were homeless people who hauled their belongings around in shopping carts. I couldn't help but stare at the loads, knowing we were just a few term papers away from pushing a cart ourselves.

"Story!"

Amblin' Amber threw an arm around me and I tried to hold my breath. She reeked of garbage and marijuana. "Hi, Amber. How's it going?"

"Going well. Getting ready for the cold. We're winterizing the underpass. You ought to come see the way we've insulated it."

"Great. That's a good idea."

Since the weather was good, she wore a flannel shirt over a T-shirt. Her round face was dark like shoe leather, a perpetual tan from living outdoors for the last decade. Her nose and cheeks were red and her clear, crystal blue eyes were windows to the past. At least that's what Mom said. Amber camped under the overpass on the far side of the Cheshire district, refusing to take a bed at the shelter.

While Mom rarely shared the stories of her homeless friends, she'd told me Amber's biography as a lesson. "Story, whenever you start feeling sorry for yourself and the fact that you're stuck with me, just think about Amber. We've got the best luck in the world compared to her."

Amber had been a lawyer for a small firm. She'd lost her job when the company declared bankruptcy. Then her husband abandoned her and their son, leaving her with a ton of debt. The week before the bank foreclosed on her house, she'd been rushing to get ready for a job interview and greeting the babysitter who'd arrived late. The sitter thought Amber's son was with her and Amber thought he was with the sitter. They didn't realize he'd learned to open doors and he'd toddled out front to make chalk drawings on the driveway. Amber backed out of the garage and didn't notice she'd hit him until she'd put the car in drive and glanced back at the driveway out of habit. Once the police cleared her of wrongdoing, she walked out of her house with the clothes on her back and never returned.

Mom said guilt ate her soul. "It's the most powerful negative emotion there is, Story. Don't ever feel guilty about anything. Own your choices even when they're bad, and when accidents happen, don't feel guilty. That's why they're called accidents. Amber couldn't see that."

While Mom chatted with the others, Amber whispered, "I heard you might be going to that secret school."

I couldn't hide my surprise. "You know about it?"

"I do."

"Do you know where it is?"

"Not around here," she snorted.

"How?"

"Heard people talkin' downtown. Thing about the homeless, Story, is that people think we're invisible and we're all wrong in the head. There's nothing wrong with my head or my hearing. Everybody just keeps talking while they're walking." She patted my shoulder. "Is your mom going to let you go?"

I shrugged. "I don't know."

She gazed at me thoughtfully. "Story, how old are you?"

"Almost sixteen. Why?"

She looked like she wanted to say something but she just asked, "Want to play a game?"

"I promised Mom I'd play with her first, but how about you play the winner?"

Amber nodded and followed me to the table where Mom waited. As always, I was white. She'd brought her old timer, the only memento she had from her "childhood as a richie," as she called it. Gran had married four times, but Mom's father, Husband Number Two, was the richest. He'd left when Mom was six and she had little recollection of him. I knew she liked him better than Gran's third husband, a man she wouldn't even discuss. Beyond that information I knew absolutely nothing else and I'd never seen a memento of any kind—except the timer.

Mom hit my clock and I opened with pawn to e-three and then I hit the lever to activate her clock. Mom moved her knight to c-six and we exchanged moves quickly.

"You're getting faster, Story. That's good."

Our hands and eyes followed the pieces around the board. A crowd formed as we traded moves swiftly. I liked the strategy of chess, although Mom always figured out mine long before I recognized hers. That was our life. She was always three moves ahead of me. Hopefully Char was a better strategist or I'd be graduating from Franklin High.

"Checkmate," she called.

I pushed my king over and slid off the cement bench so Amber could take my place.

"Do you see where you went wrong, Story?" Mom asked. "I forced you to walk the plank."

I nodded. I'd gone for a bold series of moves to isolate her queen and wound up with my king down at her end of the board. Mom always said the queen was the key. As hard as I tried, I couldn't capture her queen so in all the games we'd played, I'd never won.

While Mom played, I scoped out the park for anyone I knew. A man lounged on a park bench nearby. He didn't have much hair and dressed in sweatpants, a long-sleeve T-shirt and expensive sneakers. He looked familiar and I wondered if Char had people watching me.

A basketball bounced his way and a young black guy who'd been playing three-on-three came to retrieve it. He had a few words with the guy in sweatpants as he handed him the ball. Neither of them looked our way so I told myself I was being paranoid. But he looked really familiar too.

I turned back to the chess game. Mom stared at me while Amber planned her next move. She hated playing with anyone but me, but the rule of the park was winner takes on all willing opponents. Others wanted to challenge her even if she didn't want to play them. Games took three or four times longer when she played someone else, and by the end of the game she was terribly bored. She referred to these challengers as the Post Pawns.

Only one guy had ever beaten her. He was a professor from Western Michigan. He'd heard about Mom and driven twenty miles to challenge her. He lost the first game but won the second. He'd come down two or three more times and the result was always the same: each won and lost a game. The third visit he invited her out for coffee. She'd said, "Hell, no," even though she liked him. After she declined, we didn't go to the park for two months.

"Are you afraid of him?" I'd asked one Sunday morning when she refused to go to the park.

"Are you crazy?" she'd bellowed. "He's not any good." We both knew that wasn't true. He was better than me but she didn't know what to do with him. So she just made him go away. When she finally got the nerve to face him again and we showed up to play, she learned he wasn't coming down anymore. She went on a terrible bender and disappeared for two weeks.

I analyzed the board and saw Mom's next four moves and Amber's countermoves. She'd have Amber checkmated in five. But I missed a move and she did it in four.

Amber threw up her hands and laughed. "This time it took you twelve moves, Patty. I think you're losin' your edge."

Mom laughed good-naturedly. None of the other Post Pawns wanted to play, so I slid back onto the cement seat. We set up quickly and I opened with a pawn to a-two.

"Unusual choice," Mom murmured.

She countered and I tried a different strategy, knowing it probably wouldn't matter. I'd tried playing without a strategy, which was what most of her opponents chose to do, but when I did it, she got mad. "Damn it, Story, quit jacking around! You're better than the Post Pawn Pushers."

Although she looked down on her competition, she still came to the park regularly. It was important for her ego since it was the one thing she did well that people acknowledged.

I tried the French defense, which I'd heard about in chess club at school. Three moves into it, she paused before she took my bishop. I'd interrupted her flow and made her think for a few seconds. Of course, within the next four moves I was back on the defensive when she thwarted the strategy.

"Checkmate," she said.

I nudged my king over and said, "Good game."

"Let's go," she said. We relinquished the board and said goodbye to Amber and the other Post Pawns. The guy on the bench checked his phone as we passed. Mom stopped and faced him. He looked up casually and she said, "We're leaving now and if you keep following us, I'll probably do something like tear my clothes off and scream rape. You ought to just go back to the billionaire lady and tell her you lost us."

His face fell and he nodded.

"Good choice."

CHAPTER TWELVE

Mom agreed to meet Char at four p.m. Unfortunately that was the day I volunteered to help at the animal shelter until three thirty. I burst through the door at three-fifty, knowing I would find dishes in the sink, Mom's books scattered about and a thick crust of dust on every surface. Sure enough, when I opened the trailer door, she was on the couch in her Blondie concert T-shirt and skinny jeans. She had a bad case of bedhead and smelled of cigarettes. Nope, not even a shower.

"Could you have at least cleaned up your dishes?" I asked, scooping up her cereal bowl from breakfast, two cups of tea and a plate that smelled like tuna.

As I rushed past her she called, "We're not high society, Story. If Ms. Billionaire is expecting a butler to answer the door, she'll need to try a different trailer park."

I did what I could and hid the rest in the small bathroom. I was in my bedroom changing when there was a knock on the door. When they knocked again, I knew Mom wasn't moving.

"Can you get that, please?" I called sweetly.

She yelled, "I'm coming!" and I just shook my head.

I toed on my flip-flops and hurried out to the living room. Mom stood in the doorway, blocking Char from entering. Mom said, "I thought there'd be more of you. Maybe the guy from the park."

"No, I just brought my associate, Tyrese," Char replied from outside. "I didn't want to overwhelm you."

"How considerate."

"I don't need any backup," Char continued. "I'll present you with an idea and you'll either be amenable to it or not. Are you going to ask us inside or should we just talk here?"

I immediately pushed into the doorway. Char wore a lavender silk blouse, her jeans and those awesome boots. "Hi, Char," I said with a smile. "Mom, can you please allow our guests to come in?"

Mom turned away with a groan and I motioned for them to enter. Once inside Char said, "Story, this is Tyrese."

My eyes widened and I shook his hand vigorously. *He really exists!* He was tall and hunky with a great smile. He was better dressed than all of us in a navy blue, three-piece suit with a white dress shirt and a red tie. His hair was in cornrows and I immediately realized he was the basketball player who chatted with the guy Mom saw in the park.

"Oh, my gosh. I'm thrilled to meet you," I squeaked. "You're a legend! You're the reason I went to jail."

"Excuse me?" Mom snapped.

Oops. Mom doesn't know that part. "I meant that when I was in jail, I heard stories about Tyrese going to this uber-fabulous school. That's how I knew I wanted to go there."

"Um, well…"

"Sorry for embarrassing you."

"It's okay," he laughed.

I hadn't planned on two people coming. I offered Char the wooden chair I'd pulled out from the corner. I looked around for another seat but Tyrese said, "I'm good to stand."

"Can I get you anything to drink?" I asked.

They both said no, but Mom said, "You ought to take her up on her offer. She never waits on me like this."

"Mom," I scolded.

She shrugged and leaned back on the sofa. "Well, it's true."

"You two play chess," Char commented, pointing to the chess set on the coffee table.

"We do," I said pleasantly.

I hoped she didn't look too closely at the dust bunnies floating across the board.

"Are you surprised?" Mom asked sarcastically.

"No," Char said. "Anyone who can tell the difference between Korean and Chinese probably knows how to play chess."

"Well, I'd gladly play you, but Story and I are in the middle of a game. Chess is our thing that we do together, but you know that since you had us followed."

"Mom, stop."

"I don't know what you're talking about," Char said mildly. "I—"

"Lady, let's get one thing straight. Don't mess with me, not if you want Story attending your school. Understood?"

She cleared her throat. "Understood."

"Okay, we've had enough pleasantries. This is your show. Make me an offer I can't refuse." Mom gave a wide smile, revealing her awful teeth.

"Oh, you can refuse it," Char said, "and many parents do."

Mom's smile disintegrated with Char's matter-of-fact approach. "So is this like a charter school?"

"No, this is a private school. Charters siphon funds from public schools. I have no intention of doing such a thing."

"How noble." Mom pulled a cigarette from a pack on the end table and held it out. "Want one?"

"No, thank you."

"So you don't take money from public schools but I'll bet you recruit their teachers."

Char stiffened at the comment. "I have employed teachers who were ready to quit and were giving up on the system. They wanted a change and I saved them from leaving the profession they love. And in answer to your first question, Tabula Rasa is a boarding school."

"Huh," Mom said. She took a drag on her cigarette and exhaled. "I went to boarding school."

I couldn't believe it. "When? I've never heard that."

"There's a lot you haven't heard," Mom said. "I went there until my junior year. Place in Arizona called the Willoughby School." I shook my head and Mom tossed her cell phone to me. "Look it up."

"I believe you. I'm just surprised. Why did you leave?"

"Not important," she retorted. "But the teachers were actually sorry to see me go. Said I had a gift for writing and science." Mom sat up straight and added, "I was a regular Renaissance woman."

"What's a Renaissance woman?"

"You tell her, Mr. Detective," Mom said to Tyrese as she sprang from the couch and went down the hallway. *Where is she going?*

"The term is really Renaissance man," he said, "a person with brilliance in all areas. During the Renaissance period knowledge was greatly respected and people like Da Vinci were revered."

"Actually," Char interjected, "While it's true Da Vinci was seen as a Renaissance man, the term was coined by someone else."

"Leon Battista Alberti," Mom said as she returned. "He was an architect, painter, scientist and poet." She held up a plaque so we all could see it. The inscribed letters were horribly worn and the metal plate had suffered many scratches and dents. It read:

> Patience Mary Black
> Renaissance Woman of the Year
> Willoughby School
> 2000

Mom handed it to me. "Wow, Mom, this is great. Why haven't you shown this to me?"

"That's ancient history," she said, plopping back on the couch. "And I was pretty damn good at that, too," she laughed. "Just know your mother wasn't an idiot."

"I've never thought that."

"Well, I'm not a bragger," Mom said, shifting her gaze to Char. "I don't have to tout my accomplishments all the time. I have humility."

"And you're saying I don't," Char answered.

"Lady, you control Lakeview. You've got this town in your hip pocket. Might as well call it Charlotte Barnaby City."

Char smiled. "That actually has a nice ring."

When their eyes met again, Mom was frowning. Her attempts to goad Char weren't working.

Char glanced at her watch. "I have to be somewhere soon so I'd like to tell you about the school."

Mom stretched out on the couch again and laced her fingers behind her head. "Go right ahead. I'm all ears."

"Tabula Rasa offers the best high school experience possible, one that will truly prepare Story for the rigors of college. She'll also learn a vocation and she can dabble in a foreign language, although we know most won't be able to master it in such a short time. And after she graduates, we'll pay all costs for her to attend any college that accepts her."

"Stay away from those frat parties!" Mom laughed heartily.

I held up a hand. "Just listen and please stop being rude."

"Fine." Mom sat up and leaned forward. "Let me summarize. You have an amazing school, according to you, one that will, according to you, prepare Story for college. You'll help Story get into whatever school she wants." Her gaze never left Char's face. After a long pause she asked, "So what's the catch?"

Char shifted on the chair and looked at me. "This is a different kind of boarding school."

"How *different*?" Mom asked sharply.

This was the moment. It felt as if Mom was pushing Char against a dark wall in an alley and I was powerless to help her. I glanced at Tyrese. He seemed tense. I guessed he might be feeling the same way.

Char gazed at me. "At Tabula Rasa, students build a community that nurtures them all the time, including weekends and holidays."

"I don't get it. How is that any different from any other boarding school?"

Instead of answering my question, Char looked away and I turned to Mom. She was shaking her head. In the silence, the whirr of the air conditioner harmonized with the high-pitched wheeze of the running toilet at the end of the trailer.

"It means, Story, that you'd never come home."

I winced. "Really? Never?"

"Yes," Char conceded.

"You want to take Story away from me."

"Mainly we're taking her away from this neighborhood," Char said. "There are too many distractions and temptations." She looked at me. "And think about your school. Your classes are boring and the teachers spend most of their time dealing with the troublemakers. They can't teach the way they should."

Mom pointed the burning ember of her cigarette at Char. "We agree on that point. That school is awful."

"Exactly. Ironically, in detention Story proved what she's capable of doing. She's brilliant and she could be successful under the right conditions." Char smiled at me and I felt my cheeks burn.

"So if it's all about the school, why not just move us to some swanky neighborhood? I'd go," Mom said.

Char paused before she said, "I think you know the answer."

I was confused. There was stuff I was missing. "What answer?" I asked Mom.

Mom pointed at Char. "Oh, no, Story. Ms. Billionaire needs to share this part with you. I want you to hear it from her. You see, this is about *me* and *my* bad influence on you."

I looked from Mom to Char. A part of me wanted to agree immediately. Gran had spent most of her old age being a mom because Mom couldn't. I'd figured that out when I was nine. But Mom tried…sometimes.

Mom pointed at Char. "I want your *perspective* about my life. What do you think you know about me, Ms. Barnaby?"

Char took a deep breath, like she was preparing to give a speech. "I know…I know that where you are now isn't where you thought you'd be twenty years ago."

Suddenly Mom let out a huge laugh and Char flinched. She kept going, stamping her feet and clapping her hands. It was completely over the top. I rolled my eyes and shrugged at Tyrese. He hadn't moved or said a word. He was like stone.

Finally Mom stopped and wiped tears from her eyes. "That's the biggest understatement I've ever heard! Thank you so much for summing up my life so diplomatically. If I ever had a shred of respect for you, which I don't, it would've picked itself up by its dirty britches and hauled ass out of this godforsaken hell hole." She rose from the couch and planted her feet shoulder-length apart. "Who the hell are you to come into my house and decide that my little girl doesn't belong with me? What gives you the right to say I'm ruining her life?"

"I'm not—"

"Yes. You. Are. That's one hell of a God complex you've got."

Mom towered over Char, who remained in her chair. I was glad the coffee table was between them.

We listened to the whirr of the window air conditioner until Char said, "What I started to say was that I'm not here to save you. It's too late." She looked at me with a gentle smile. "I'm sorry, Story, but it's the truth."

"Are you kidding! That's not true at all!" Mom shouted. "How dare you come into my house and call me an unfit parent! You are a complete stuck-up bitch and I want you the hell out. Now!"

Mom came around the coffee table and Tyrese sprang into action, stepping between Mom and Char. Mom continued to rant while Char headed out the door. I followed after her.

"I'm sorry, Char. Please don't leave."

Char turned and said, "I have to for now. We'll talk soon."

Mom came barreling out the door with Tyrese behind her. "You're a bitch!"

Char glanced at me and said to Mom, "I'm not sure you'll want Story to hear this."

Mom crossed her arms. "We have no secrets. And as you say, she's brilliant."

"Fine," Char conceded. "Then let me make this clear. The opportunity for you to turn your life around passed about three rehab trips ago. You're a failed sociological statistic. A smart high school sophomore could predict what remains of your life. Story certainly knows the score. You're done but she's not." The bravado and cockiness evaporated. Mom couldn't find a place to land her gaze so she stared at the dirt. "What is it you want, Ms. Black? What can I offer you to consider this opportunity for your only daughter?"

Mom looked up and sneered, "I want to know your secrets. I want to know how your little show runs."

"Why would you want to know that?"

Mom sighed. "Come now, Ms. Barnaby. You're a former principal, which means at some point you were a teacher, right? Surely you recognize an inquisitive student. I was a scientist. I had dreams of working on the Human Genome Project, or didn't your extensive background check reveal that?"

Char couldn't hide her surprise. "Of course not. We have no way to know your dreams."

"There is if you ask me," Mom fired back. "When I got to college, I told everyone my dreams."

Char shuffled her feet. "What were you like?"

"I was curious. A dreamer. And sheltered. Far too sheltered." Her smile faltered and she opened her eyes. "Rupert, Story's father, saw my vulnerability. I so wanted to be like the other girls. To be accepted. To be…cosmopolitan." She turned her nose up and tossed her hair back for effect.

"And what happened?"

"You know what happened." Mom's toe made circles in the dirt. "You're right. It was as cliché as a greeting card. But to be clear, my thirst for knowledge has never extinguished. Did your background check tell you how often I go to the college library? Or the number of times Story and I go to the park to play chess?"

Char nodded but didn't say anything.

"In case you were wondering, Ms. Barnaby, my thirst for knowledge is as much a habit for me as meth. But to be clear, I've been clean and sober for over two years. Story plays a key role in feeding my thirst for knowledge. If she goes away, it will be much harder to satisfy my cravings for intellectual conversation and stimulating discussions."

"So, it's all about you. Your needs. Your desires. When does Story get something for herself?"

"She can have whatever she wants."

"Really?" Char gestured and said, "Look around. This place is nirvana." She leaned in and whispered, "You're doing a hell of a job."

Mom stiffened at the caustic remarks. "So you want to save her."

"I won't save Story. Story will save herself. I just want to give her that chance."

If I could've opened Mom's brain, I was certain I'd be watching all the little synapses firing. Eventually she stared at Char.

"No," she said simply. "No."

"What?" I cried. "Seriously?"

"Why?" Char asked. "Why would you deprive her of this chance?"

"Yeah, why?" I repeated.

Mom shook her head. "This just isn't right," she said sincerely. "What you're doing…it's against all ethics. Removing children from their families? That goes against everything in sociology. Children need their parents."

For the first time since they'd arrived she sounded normal. Practical. For a few seconds I believed her.

"That might've been true thirty or forty years ago," Char disagreed, "when parents did their job, when so many kids didn't live in terrible poverty. When parents had the means to help their children. It was different then."

"I don't disagree, but Story will make it without your help. I believe in her."

"You can believe in her and that's very important, but the odds are definitely against her."

"They're against a lot of kids but some do fine."

"A few," Char said softly. "But only a few."

"So, you think Story'll turn out to be some hooker?"

She paused before she answered. "No, worse. She won't fulfill her potential."

Mom snorted. "Potential. Who the hell can judge that?" She shifted her weight and crossed her arms. "And what will happen to her in twenty years? Are you still going to invite her to the school for Christmas dinner? People need their kin."

"She'll be a different person by then. In twenty years you can see her whenever you want. She'll be a strong, brilliant woman with a wonderful career. None of this existence will matter."

Mom took a step closer. "This *existence* may not be the ideal life, but don't you think for a moment that you know what I want for my daughter. Just because you send some guy to follow me doesn't mean you know my life."

Char stepped away and turned to me with a sad smile. "I have to go, Story." She steeled her expression and said to Mom, "I hope you'll reconsider your position. You've said you have no interest in this opportunity, but we do offer help and support to parents. If you really want to kick your habit for good, I can send you to the most successful treatment facility in the nation. We could help you find a job, a better place to live. If you finally wanted the opportunity to go back to college—"

"So you're offering me a bribe," Mom summarized.

"Not at all. We aren't going to *give* you a dime."

Mom scratched her chin. "Let's say I agreed to this little arrangement, and then a few months from now I change my mind. I tell you to send her back. What happens then?"

"That won't happen," Char said.

"It sure as hell might."

"It won't happen because you won't have any authority to make such a request. For Story to be admitted to Tabula Rasa you will rescind your parental rights and agree to her request for emancipation."

Mom scowled. "Emancipation? Why in the hell would she want to do that?"

Char looked at me and said, "Because she can—in a month. With or without your consent."

Mom's jaw dropped. She clearly hadn't thought about that. Very rarely was she surprised. Very rarely was anyone else one move ahead of her. I didn't even really know what emancipation was.

Mom looked at Char as if she had three heads. "Who *are* you people? Who made you God?"

"The California Lottery Commission," Char growled. "I'm someone who can guarantee your daughter will have a better life than you will ever be able to provide for her."

"This just isn't right," Mom murmured. "It just isn't." She took a deep breath and asked, "Why us? Why not someone else?"

"Because Story is special and you know it."

"What I know," she snarled, "is that Story is mine."

CHAPTER THIRTEEN

The pier was my thinking place where I watched the boats on the lake. The ones in the distance looked as if they were leaving Lakeview for good but really they weren't going anywhere. They'd circle the lake and return to the harbor. They could enjoy the water and the sky, but they were landlocked and their adventure was limited. I imagined their disappointment when they steered back to the pier at the end of the trip.

If Ms. Sutton were here, she'd ask me to explain the symbolism of the boats to my life. No brainer. I didn't want to spend my life circling Lakeview. Tabula Rasa looked incredible. What would it be like to walk home, pack my suitcase, take the bus to Second Beginnings and show up at Char's door?

What would it be like to leave for good—or at least leave until after college? *Buh-bye, Lakeview! See ya!*

Could I do it? *Absolutely.*

Would I miss Mom? *A little.*

Would I worry about her? *No.*

"That's not true," I whispered. "Her sobriety would tank."

Do I care, knowing no one can remain sober for anyone else? *No. LIAR!!* I made a fist. I did care even if I didn't want to.

Gran taught me about sobriety on my ninth birthday. Mom was about to finish rehab for the fourth time. Gran had built up her homecoming as my big ninth birthday present. Mom said she was going to stay sober as *her* present to me. We were having a party with us, my friend Theresa, and a kid from around the corner. There were decorations and Gran even got a store-bought cake.

Then Mom showed up high just as we were finishing a game. Apparently the cab that Gran had paid for made a stop along the way—at Mom's dealer.

There was my answer. Staying or going had nothing to do with her sobriety. So if I managed to get out, would I ever come back? Even to visit Mom?

Gran used to play a game with me when I was younger. We'd go online and look up different colleges. We'd stare at the images and she'd point at a picture of smiling students and say, "Look how happy they are to go to college! That will be you, Story. You'll love every minute of it."

I never mentioned they could be smiling because someone paid them to smile for the picture. I just nodded, wanting to believe. Getting out of Lakeview had always been our dream. Going to Tabula Rasa was the key to reaching that dream. I'd pictured life without Mom many times. But what kind of daughter abandons her mother? What did that say about me?

"What kind of mother continually abandons her daughter?" I mumbled to the wind.

What if she OD'd when I left? I pictured Ms. Finnerly, the trailer park manager, pounding on the front door. When nobody answered, she'd use her key and find Mom dead on the couch, probably with a book lying across her chest.

I'd seen her death in my dreams many times but Gran was always there to comfort me. Now I was on my own. Would I really care if Mom were gone? When I was in jail, I didn't miss her. It had been like a vacation.

The wind picked up and my teeth started to chatter. My phone buzzed. It would be Mom, wondering where I was. When she was sober she texted a lot. It was the only bad thing about her sobriety.

I read the text and sighed. Char.

Your mom wasn't ready to hear what I had to say. I'd like to meet and talk and I'll bring your copy of Macbeth, too. Coffee shop inside the MR building?

I texted back. *Sure. Just let me know when.*

Probably next weekend. It will give me time to think about everything.

Ok.

I reread her text. She was rethinking her decision. The closer I got to home, the angrier I was at Mom. She'd ruined my chance. *No, wait.* I stopped walking and said into my phone, "Emancipation laws for Michigan."

I scrolled through a few pages of entries. One thing was clear: I could legally separate myself from Mom in just a few weeks, if the Michigan courts agreed. I was pretty sure I could convince them that I could live on my own, especially at Tabula Rasa.

My phone buzzed again. It was Bertie. I'd told her about the big meeting and she'd offered to take off work and be there but I couldn't let her do that. She was just a few weeks away from moving to North Carolina and she needed every dollar she could earn.

How did it go?

HORRIBLE. Predictable. I think I lost my chance.

No. Char wouldn't do that to you, would she?

IDK. T2UL.

She sent me a heart emoji. We'd said we'd make a clean break when she went to North Carolina and we'd just be friends, but there was always this hope—at least in my mind—that all of those winter and summer breaks would be reminders, like little links in a chain. Maybe we'd be together after college? But if I went to Tabula Rasa and never came home… It wasn't just Mom I'd be losing for good.

Next to my family, Bertie's family looked rich, but really they were just middle-class people. They joked that every one of their kids needed a scholarship to go to college. Just from being in their home and sitting at their dinner table I knew their kids would get those scholarships. They would make it happen.

When I reached the trailer park, I saw smoke billowing through our kitchen window. I flung open the trailer door and gasped for air. Whatever she was doing would've set off the smoke alarms, if we had any. She was leaning against the sink. She held her lighter in one hand and something white in the other. She brought it to the orange flame repeatedly.

"What are you doing?"

The tiny bit that remained unburned looked oddly familiar. I whirled toward the coffee table. The chess set was gone. She waited until I turned back before dropping the blob of plastic into the sink with what appeared to be the remains of the entire white team, as well as several black pawns.

"Mom, stop it!"

I reached for the lighter but she turned away. I pushed past her, hoping to rescue the rest of the set, but when I saw there were only ten pieces left intact, I gave up. I turned on the water to drown the smoldering plastic mess just as Ms. Finnerly appeared at the window. She was an older woman with stringy hair that never looked clean. She wore a prominent mustache that Mom had ridiculed many times.

"What's on fire?"

"Just some cooking problems," I said casually.

Her eyes narrowed as she peered through the screen. "Not the illegal kind, right?"

"No, ma'am, not at all. I've got it under control."

Our eyes locked and she nodded. "Fortunately, you do," she said, before she left.

"What the hell does that mean?" Mom shouted from the couch.

I whipped around and hissed, "Be quiet. She can throw us out whenever she wants."

Mom snorted and lit a cigarette. "Yeah, who else would pay for this charming chateau? Whoever waxes her upper lip? Oh, that would be no one!"

I slammed the kitchen window shut. Inhaling the smoke would be better than Ms. Finnerly hearing Mom's wisecracks and kicking us out. I gazed at the melted chess pieces and tried not to cry. Gran had given me the set after Mom came back from her second rehab trip. She'd promised me a present if I gave Mom another chance. I was only six but I'd learned how it went. Gran didn't know how to play chess so it became a bridge between Mom and me. Most of our good times occurred around the chessboard. And now it was gone. Why had she done this?

Chess glued us together. It was always a conversation starter even when we weren't playing. While we ate cereal at the sink or walked home from the library, Mom would share a strategy she knew from her days on the high school chess team. Sometimes she got so excited she'd grab my arm and we'd go next door and beg Mr. Hallman to use his Internet so Mom could show me some moves on YouTube.

I found an old coffee can and cleaned up the mess while she watched. As I dropped each piece into the can, my anger intensified. It wasn't just about ruining the chess set. She'd destroyed a piece of Gran. That was unforgiveable. I debated whether to go to my room, stuff my little suitcase with everything I valued and leave.

I marched to the coffee table and smacked the can down loudly. "Why did you do this?"

She shrugged. "Felt like it. Seems you and Ms. Billionaire have everything planned out. You don't need me. Who else will I play with once you're gone?"

"This wasn't yours to destroy. It was mine."

"No, it wasn't. I hope that bitch gets murdered for her money! And who does she think she is?" She jolted upright and pointed her cigarette at me. "Story, do you know what she's doing? Do you really understand?"

"She's trying to help me! Help other kids have a better opportunity. Help—"

"That's only part of it! I've heard the talk on the streets. Any parent or guardian that won't fade away, that won't nod their head and say, 'Sure, Ms. Money, my kid can go to your school,' gets the treatment."

I made a face. "The treatment?"

"Her organization digs up whatever dirt they can find, and of course, there's always dirt, usually illegal, and she threatens them. 'Give up your kid, or else!' That's the treatment."

I was still processing. "Or else what?"

She started ticking off answers on her fingers. "Or else I'll call the police and have you arrested. Or else I'll call Social Services and have your kid removed anyway. Or else...*I'll ruin you.*" She paused, her gaze fiery, and added, "That's the treatment. What do you think of that?"

I swallowed hard, not wanting to believe Char could be so ruthless. *Her motives are good. She wants to help me.* I thought about what she could do to Mom. She could tell the university about Mom's business. They'd ban her from the library forever. Not only would that ruin her business—the business that made sure we had a roof over our heads (a pathetic roof, but still...). But more than the business, losing the library to Mom would be losing...*her mind.*

She must've seen the look on my face because she smiled. "You get it now, don't you?"

I shook my head. "It still doesn't mean that the end doesn't justify the means. I've *known* some of the kids who've disappeared. Their lives were shitty."

Her gaze narrowed. "Are you saying your life is shitty?" I looked away and she stood. "Story, she has no right to break up families and decide who has a shitty life and who doesn't. She has no right to take you away from the woman who gave you life. The woman who raised you—"

I whipped my head up. "Raised me?" I couldn't believe it. "You think that's you? No, Gran raised me. Gran was the one who read to me, who taught me right from wrong, came to school and took me home when I got sick in class. That was Gran. You showed up when it was convenient. When you weren't high. When you weren't in rehab. When you *felt* like it. If you don't want to do something, you just don't do it. I'm the one who does it now, and before me it was Gran."

She curled her upper lip and exposed her gritted, rotting teeth. "I am so sick of hearing about Gran the Saint! Newsflash, Story. She wasn't as perfect as you think."

"I never said she was perfect. She was here for me."

"Well, that makes one of us."

I threw up my hands. "You always say that. What the hell do you mean?"

She looked away and took a long drag from her cigarette. When she blew out the smoke she seemed to blow out her anger as well.

"Story, you need to understand what we're dealing with here," she said, returning the conversation to Char.

It was like that. Whenever the topic of Gran came up, she'd get angry and change the subject.

"The *type* of woman we're dealing with. She has no regard for us. She's trying to make herself look good. She has her own motivations. This isn't about you and your chance. This is about her. That's why she has that huge show! So she can tout her accomplishments." She stretched out on the couch and picked up a book, ending the conversation as far as she was concerned.

"Are you keeping me from fulfilling my potential?"

"Yup."

"So when should we invite her back?"

She dropped her book and glared at me. "No, Story. It's the end. She's not coming back. I'm not changing my mind. And you're going to figure out how to make it work at that awful Franklin High. I'm sorry about that part but if you keep your grades up, you'll be eligible for a scholarship." She snorted and added, "And I doubt you'll fuck it up the way I did."

She resumed reading and I stormed back to my room. The residual smoke and the smell of burnt plastic had given me a headache. I opened my window and fell across my bed. I couldn't believe I'd lost my chance. Then again, I'd never really had one. If Char had listed her conditions when she interviewed me at the jail, I would've excused myself and gone back to the unit. She didn't know Mom the way I did.

My phone chimed. A text from Jamison. Suddenly I realized my heart was pounding.

Want to show you something super cool. This is the largest tree in MI.

It was indeed enormous and so big it didn't fit into the picture.

You probs can't see me, but I'm hanging from the low branch on the right.

I enlarged the photo and saw a figure hanging from the branch—upside down. *Talented!* I wrote. Before I sent it, I added, *Can I ask you a question?*

Sure.

Have you heard of "the treatment?"

The text dots bubbled and bubbled but there wasn't a response. I shouldn't have asked. Now Jamison probably hated me. I watched and waited—and paced. The bubbles disappeared and then the phone rang with a video chat. *Jamison.*

I quickly looked in the little mirror on the wall, making sure I didn't look too bad before I pressed the accept button. "Hey," I said, hoping I sounded casual.

"Hey. Yeah, I couldn't answer your question in a text."

She was outside, sitting against that tree. She gave me a smile and her bright blue eyes just pulled me in.

"Oh, that's cool," I said. "I mean, you don't have to answer the question at all—"

Her smile vanished. "No, I want to explain, at least I can tell you a little about what I know and that's not a lot. I just know my own experience."

"Okay..."

"I went to detention two years ago for selling drugs at my high school. Wasn't my first offense so they gave me six months. I'm not proud of it but that's how I survived living with my stepfather. And he was a bad dude." She sighed, looked away and whispered, "A bad dude in a lot of ways. That's all I'll say on that."

"I get it. Um, can I ask where your mom was?"

"She OD'd a year before."

"I'm sorry."

"It's okay. So while I was in detention, I took the SPOT, had my interview and when I got out, Char had a Convincing Hour for my stepfather. She didn't do the big show like she did for you. I'd told her I'd do anything to get out of his house, so she just laid it on him. Told him that I was going to her school, he was going to let it happen, and six months later, when I turned sixteen, he'd be supplied with emancipation papers that he would sign…or else."

"What was the 'or else'?"

"She'd expose his drug business and have him arrested."

"She can do that?"

Jamison laughed and her blue eyes looked happy again. I decided I liked seeing them that way. "Story, she has a billion dollars."

I rolled my eyes. "Of course."

"So that's the treatment," she said with air quotation marks. She stared at me intently and I saw those blue eyes blur with tears. "She saved my life, Story."

"That totally makes sense. Who knows what would've happened after you got out of detention?"

"I think it would've been a pretty predictable ending. I really hated myself. If Char hadn't come along…" She looked away and wiped the corner of an eye. When she composed herself again she said, "And that's what happened, well, except for one little detail."

"What was that?"

"About a year later, after I was completely immersed in Tabula Rasa, had totally forgotten about my stepdad's disgusting ass, Dr. Baxter asks to see me. Do you remember him, the principal?"

I nodded. "Yeah, I loved his bowtie."

She laughed. "We tease him about his bowties. Anyway, he tells me that he just wanted me to know that my stepfather was killed during a raid by the feds."

"Oh, wow."

"He asked if I was okay, which I was, and that was the end of it. All I see now is what's in front of me, my future." She brought the phone closer until her face filled the space and I could see a little dimple on her left cheek. "Your future's in front of you, Story. What's gonna be your story…Story?"

We both laughed and she said, "Sorry, lame. But I had to."

"Just one more question. What's the deal with that big show? Why go to all that trouble?"

She nodded. "Every new student asks that question. Thing is…You know about lemmings? The little creatures that'll go over a cliff because the ones in front of them are doing it?"

"Yeah, I've heard of them."

"A lot of people are lemmings. If they see a crowd at an event, they're more than likely going to want to go. If someone famous tells them to buy something, they'll be more inclined to try it. It's advertising. Marketing. Only with the Convincing Hour, we're marketing the school. More times than not, it works and Char doesn't have to use the—as you called it—the treatment." She looked up and nodded at someone I couldn't see. "I gotta go. My partner's bugging me."

"Oh, sorry to take you away from your girlfriend, I—"

"No, no. She's not my girlfriend. She's my chemistry lab partner." The blue eyes seemed to turn a shade darker. "I don't have a girlfriend—now."

* * *

The trailer was quiet for the next few days. I came and went while Mom parked on the couch. She moved very little and didn't bother to change her clothes for days. I noticed, though, her stack of books changed, which meant she'd gone to the library at least once.

I'd been to the library a few times myself, learning about emancipation. I studied the qualifications and the process. It wasn't easy but I thought it could be a way through the problem. Mom was all about going through problems—except ones that involved her.

I told Bertie everything I'd learned about emancipation during our freebie date, a date we took turns planning. It could be anywhere but it had to be free. Tonight she'd chosen the Boardwalk, a mile of shops and condos adjacent to the marina. According to Mom, this area had been rundown and disgusting before Char Barnaby renovated it with ritzy high-rise condos and upscale restaurants.

"But could you really do that to your mom?" Bertie asked after I'd told her more about emancipation. "Could you spend all that effort basically saying your mom sucks—to a judge?"

My gaze shot to her. "Do you think it's a bad idea?"

She grimaced and shook her head. "I don't think it's about good or bad. It's about what you can live with. And I'll tell you that I'm really super pissed at your mom."

"What? Why are you mad at her? I mean, I know why I'm pissed at her. She destroyed my chess set, the most important thing Gran ever gave to me."

Bertie took my hand and squeezed it. "I'm pissed at her because she's the most selfish person I've ever met. I'm sorry if I sound really mean. And how childish is it to burn up a chess set?"

A couple of passersby looked at us oddly since Bertie was practically shouting. She blushed and raked her curls away from her face. She looked out toward the darkness that was the lake. It was her "thinking look." If she wanted to say more, she would. I leaned against her, looped my arm through hers and thought about my life without her.

CHAPTER FOURTEEN

On Saturday I decided to stay in my room for the day and read in bed. Mom and I hadn't spoken for nearly a week and I thought it would be better to hide out. I'd just started *The Color Purple* when Mom barged in and threw off the covers.

"Let's go," she said.

"Where are we going?"

"To the park to play chess."

"Mom, I don't want to go. Play with Amber."

She made a face. "Amber doesn't play chess, Story. You know that. Amber moves pieces around the board. It's like playing with a black hole. Nothing there." She turned to go and said, "You've got five minutes. Get ready."

I didn't move and kept reading. If I ignored her long enough, she'd go away. Five minutes later when she came back and saw me still in bed, she put her hands on her hips and said, "Story, moping around isn't going to get you anywhere. Okay, you're not getting your *chance*. Sorry I ruined it for you but I won't disown you because an egomaniac wants me to. You know she's cracked, right? You know she's not right in the head, don't you?"

I'd spent the week thinking about "the treatment." It didn't matter which way I thought about it, the scales tipped in Char's favor. "She seems fine to me." I stared at Mom and said, "Why don't you want me to succeed?"

She sighed dramatically and turned away. "I refuse to answer that question."

"Why?" I cried. "Every time something good is about to happen you mess it up for me." I gestured toward the kitchen. "Look what you did to my chess set—"

"*Your* chess set? That was my chess set!"

"No, Gran gave it to me right before you got out of rehab for the second time. I didn't want to go back to you but she said she'd give me something if I did. So I came back and got the chess set."

She pursed her lips. I could see she was fuming. Gran apparently never told her that story. "So your grandmother and Ms. Billionaire have something in common. They both bribe people to get what they want."

"It worked, didn't it? And you ruined it. Just like you ruin everything!"

She waved me off. "Stop being so damn melodramatic and cliché. 'Just like you ruin everything.' You are not an average teenager. Stop talking like one. Now, either get dressed or I'm going to spend the next hour ruining that book for you because it was one of my favorites and I remember every single plot point. Then I'll postulate on string theory for the rest of the day."

I moaned and pulled myself out of bed. All parents had ways of annoying their children. Mine became Wikipedia. It wouldn't be so bad. We'd go play chess and then Mom would take me to Subway for a hoagie. The weekend manager was another term paper client. Then Mom would come back to the trailer, take a nap and lose herself in a book. That was how she fought her addiction. She read.

"Story, every addiction has triggers," she'd explained. "I get cravings in the late afternoon. The only way to get rid of them is to yield to my subconscious so I read and I nap."

When we got to the park, the regulars were huddled around the chess area. In addition to Amber there were the two old dudes, Stanley and Mort, who lived in the apartments across from the park, a young, nerdy guy named Kwan, who Mom sometimes agreed to play, JoJo, a vet of the Gulf War, and Xavier, another vet who suffered from serious PTSD. Mom told them Ms. Billionaire wanted to kidnap me and take me away. I shook my head in protest but everyone watched her as she recounted Char's visit.

"She thought she was so damn high and mighty," Mom said. "I handed her ass to her. Billions or not, she's not taking Story. She's not better than me."

They nodded and shouted encouragements—everyone but Amber. She'd turned away and seemed to be staring at a tree. I moved behind her and realized she was staring at the M-R building in the distance. A single tear streaked her cheek. She quickly wiped it away and stuck her hands in her pockets.

"Why are you crying?" I asked gently.

She couldn't look at me. She stared at the dirty yellow mittens covering her hands. "I was thinking of Billy, wondering what I would've said if Charlotte Barnaby had asked me to give him up."

"And?"

"If he'd wound up in jail like you did, I would've thought it was my fault."

"You can't think that way," I disagreed. "I made those choices. Mom doesn't have anything to do with it."

She narrowed her eyes. "Doesn't she? Are you really being honest with yourself, Story?"

I glanced at the group surrounding my mother. I could only see the top of her head. She loved being the center of attention and she'd say just about anything to draw a crowd.

"I convinced Ivy to rob the store with me," I admitted quietly. "It was my fault she got arrested."

"I wondered about that," she said. "Ivy's half in love with you. You know that, right?"

"No, I didn't."

We stared at each other and I realized how clear her green eyes were. She lived on the streets but she'd never taken any drug stronger than pot to dull her pain, almost as if she wanted to feel horrible, like she deserved it. I suppose if I'd run over my own son, I'd feel pretty guilty.

Amber threw her chin in the direction of the M-R building. "Have you told her how much you want to go to her school? Does she know what you did to meet her?"

"Yeah, but it doesn't matter. Mom's never going to agree. I'm supposed to meet with her tomorrow and I'm sure she's going to drop me."

"So, it's just her decision? You don't have a say?"

I was confused. "Who do you mean when you say *her*? My mom or Char?"

"Both, actually."

Amber bit her lip, exposing her black and yellow teeth. I pictured what she'd looked like in her other life. I probably never would've noticed her walking down the sidewalk in a stylish winter coat, talking on her cell phone. Char never would've shown up on her doorstep in her old life. She had it covered. Billy would've been fine. Then everything changed in a second.

"Story, do you know what emancipation is?"

I nodded.

"And do you understand that in the state of Michigan, anyone who is sixteen or older can petition the court to become emancipated?"

"I knew that. I've been studying it. As a lawyer, did you ever help anyone get emancipated?"

"Once."

I glanced toward Mom, just to make sure she wasn't paying attention to us before I asked, "Would you help me?"

The corners of her mouth lifted. "Of course." She leaned closer and whispered, "You need to take control, Story. If Char Barnaby's thinking about dropping you, then you need to tell her how far you're willing to go to get what you want." Amber glanced at the crowd and said, "Go. She actually lives in that building. She's probably there since it's still early. Go now."

My gaze flitted from the M-R building to the crowd. My feet started to move toward the park exit. I'd need to leave before Mom saw me or she'd run after me. Amber joined the group, blocking my mother's view of the exit.

I had no idea what I'd say to Char. I could tell her about Amber helping me to become emancipated or maybe I could get her to change the admission requirement. Mom was certainly unlike most people. She should have her own set of rules. Perhaps I could visit her once in a while or maybe we could Skype. If Mom knew she hadn't truly lost me and I could still remind her to pay the bills, she'd sign anything. I just needed to negotiate.

CHAPTER FIFTEEN

As I raced down the sidewalk away from the park and Mom, I thought about what I would say to Char. I looked over my shoulder six times certain Mom was charging toward me until I stepped into a wedge of the entrance's revolving door. A half turn later it spat me out into a grand foyer bustling with people shopping at all the stores that took up the first three floors.

All the businesses were locally owned and there wasn't a chain store anywhere. Char had helped all of the business owners. It was one of the reasons so many people remained silent when old-timers talked about the "old Lakeview" back when nearly everyone worked at one of the factories, long before the "billionaire lady" appeared on the scene. Char had positively touched so many people's lives that few could talk against her.

I stopped at the Guest Services desk and a pleasant African-American man with graying hair and a goatee asked, "May I help you?"

I told him who I was and why I was there, and then he went to work on his comm unit, pressing buttons I couldn't see and touching his earpiece. It reminded me of the bridge in *Star Trek*. If he asked Scotty to beam me up on a transporter, I wouldn't have been surprised.

"You can wait in the vestibule behind me. Please wear this lanyard while you're here."

"Sure. Thank you."

Attached to the lanyard was a bright red visitor's badge and a tracking device. These people were serious about security. The vestibule was shaped like a pod with soft lighting that would've seemed eerie except for the relaxing, whispered classical music that filled the chamber. The pod had to be soundproof because I could barely hear the chatter and noise from the busy stores that surrounded it.

Three couches formed a semicircle and a coffee cart with beverages and snacks was positioned behind them. Toward the end of the pod was a single elevator with a pale blue door, which I guessed was only used by important people. I thought about sitting down but I was drawn to an architect's model of M-R, the centerpiece of the room. I peered through the Plexiglas at the detailed exterior walls and the tiny windows. It was beautiful.

I heard the elevator doors open and I took a deep breath. *Don't take no for an answer.* I'd practiced my speech on the walk over here. Before Char could offer a greeting, it all tumbled out. "I'm really sorry to barge in on you. I'll say what I need to say and then I'll go. I know you're super busy. I really want to go to Tabula Rasa. I'm sorry about my mom's behavior but it's her strange way of caring. What upset her was the idea of not seeing me. If there's any way you could put that requirement aside and let her see me a few times a year, I think she'd let me go to your school. And I'm talking to an attorney about emancipating myself when I turn sixteen. And that's really soon," I added.

Char looked stunned. I'd obviously caught her in weekend wear—faded Levi's, a blue work shirt and sneakers. She smiled easily and after a long pause she said, "How would you like to go get a latte? I could really use a caffeine jolt."

"Oh, okay, sure."

We took the special elevator to the third floor and walked to Uncommon Grounds. I'd been there before with my mom—

several times. Mom was a coffee connoisseur and she claimed UG, as we called it, brewed the best cup.

I knew the dark-skinned man behind the counter, Zane. He wore a dashiki, and he grinned when he saw us approach. "Greetings, Char. And hello, Story."

"Oh, you two know each other?" Char asked.

"We do," Zane said. "Where's Patty?"

"She's not here," I said. "And when we come in next time, please don't let her know I came here without her." Zane pressed his index finger to his lips. "Thanks," I said, relieved. Mom could be petty over the smallest things.

"I know Story will have a mocha latte," Zane said, "but what would you like, Char?"

"That sounds great. I'll have the same."

We waited off to the side and I pulled out my phone. "I should text my mom and tell her where I am."

Char nodded. "I'm sure she'll be thrilled."

Met a friend at the park. Gone for coffee. See you at home.

Mom immediately replied. *What friend? I didn't see any of your friends at the park!*

I guess you didn't. I switched the phone to vibrate and stuck it in my back pocket.

Char eyed me suspiciously. "Is this okay? I don't want you to be in trouble."

"It's fine," I said. Eager to change the subject, I gazed at the stores across from the coffee bar—a woodworking shop called Turning, a bakery named Daily Bread, and an interesting shop called Mosaic. I pointed and asked, "What's the history on that place?"

"That's a newer addition run by several international relief organizations. They sell trinkets and goods made by people in third world countries. All the profits go back to the local communities."

"That's very cool," I said.

Zane brought over our drinks and said to Char, "Sorry to interrupt when you have a guest but I wanted you to know that Konoki had her baby."

Char's face lit up. "That's wonderful! I'll stop by her place tomorrow. Thanks for telling me."

Zane nodded and said, "Good to see you, Story."

"You too," I said. After Zane retreated behind the coffee bar, I asked, "Who's Konoki?"

"One of Zane's employees. She lives on the fourth floor with her husband and two—now three—children."

"Wow. Is her husband like a CEO or something?"

Char cocked her head to the side. "Why would you ask that?"

I felt my cheeks burn. "I know what people make who work in a coffee bar, and I'd always thought the apartments in here were super expensive."

Char shrugged. "It varies. And to answer to your question, her husband Efraim is an accountant with my company so he's not rich. But he is an excellent accountant so he does well. He's a very honest but shrewd man."

"Oh, yeah, I'd imagine you need a great accountant. There's a lot to count."

Char laughed. "I need a great team and I have one." She narrowed her gaze and asked, "How would you like to take a drive?"

By the time we'd piled into Char's Beemer my phone had vibrated four more times. I knew it was Mom but I wasn't letting her ruin this afternoon like she'd ruined my chess set. Even looking at her texts would wreck my mood. Then Char would take me back. I couldn't help reacting to my mom. It was completely reflexive.

We headed toward Sellis Avenue and Char pointed at the stereo. "What kind of music do you like?"

"All kinds, really."

"Well, go ahead and surf the controls. This thing has everything but I've never bothered to program it."

"I bet I could figure it out. What kind of music do you listen to the most?"

"Pop, jazz, a little hip-hop."

"Well, what's your favorite and I'll program that first." Char just shook her head. "What's wrong? Do you like something totally weird like funeral marches?"

She laughed. "Thanks. Now I don't feel so weird about it. What I like the most is music from the seventies. You know, disco, club music. All that stuff." I bit my lip and stifled a giggle. "See?" Char teased. "You're making fun of me."

"No," I argued. "In many ways the seventies were completely misunderstood. A lot of great music came out of that time. Some of Elton John's best stuff, Loggins and Messina—"

"You know Loggins and Messina? Do you like their music?"

"I do." I messed with the console and a few seconds later the opening riff of "Your Mama Don't Dance" began. We sang it twice and serenaded several people at red lights.

Char pulled onto the highway and headed north. We talked more about music and books and stupid stuff. We were both giddy and I couldn't remember the last time I'd laughed so hard.

We sipped our lattes and let a comfortable silence settle between us while I thought of my next strategy. This was like a chess game and I needed to win to get what I wanted. Char hadn't said anything about the speech I'd vomited up when I arrived at M-R.

"Can I ask you a question?"

"Sure. I may not answer if it's really personal."

"No, it's not personal to you. It's personal to me. I want to know if you think my relationship with my mom is typical. I don't have anything to compare her to. I get that most people don't have a mother with a meth addiction but lots of kids have parents who are addicted to alcohol or painkillers. And some kids have parents who beat them constantly. I've never had that happen. I figure you've seen a lot of parents so I'd love to know what you think."

Char glanced over at me. Her fingers tightly gripped the steering wheel and I could tell she was choosing her words carefully. "I think," she said slowly, "that your mother has an amazing intellect—"

"Yeah, I know. Amazing intellect that faced unfortunate circumstances. I don't mean to be rude by interrupting you, but I've heard all that from several school counselors. I want to know if you think she's horrible and unredeemable."

"No," Char said adamantly. "She's primarily hurt herself. She's not engaging in criminal behavior that hurts others." She shrugged. "Well, it's *unethical* behavior that violates several parts of the university code, but I doubt she'd be arrested. Has she ever paid her taxes?"

I shrugged and shook my head.

"Yeah, I think we both know the answer to that one."

"If she's not unredeemable then why does she have to give me up?"

Char chuckled. "I walked right into that one, didn't I?"

My heart beat faster. I was on a roll. "I understand I'm affected by her choices but she isn't like most bad parents. She just can't function well. If I go away, she'll never remember to pay the bills."

Char raised a hand. "Hold on. I can't have this conversation while I'm driving." She turned off at the next rest area, pulled into a secluded spot and killed the engine. "Story, I understand what you're saying and you're right to some extent. I'm not sure I've ever encountered a parent—maybe another human being—with an I.Q. comparable to your mom's. She's unique in that way but she's incredibly predictable too."

"How? I'd never call her predictable."

She touched her temple and closed her eyes. When they flew open again she said, "Story, *you're* the mom, not her. You take care of her and not the other way around. Think about the day you got out of jail. A lot of kids would be running to find their friends or go to the movies. They'd do something fun that made them feel free. What did you do? Paid the water bill, the electric bill and the rent. You've had to be hyper-responsible to survive." She paused and said, "I know from experience."

"What happened to you?"

Char looked away. "I told you my mom struggled to work. Your mom has an addiction and mine had a disease, OCD. When

I was ten, my oldest brother Damon packed my suitcase and sent me to live with my aunt here in Lakeview. Damon knew he wasn't going to leave the streets. None of my older brothers did, but he took me out of east LA to escape that life."

"That's why you have that admission requirement," I murmured.

"Yes."

"What did your mom say about you leaving?"

"When we told her, she got really upset and started yelling. Then she looked over my head at the wall where we kept family portraits. And she just stopped talking. She got up and adjusted some of the pictures, trying to make them perfectly straight even though there wasn't anything wrong with them. She forgot our conversation entirely."

"Did you ever see her again?"

Char nodded. "She visited me a few times, but by my junior year she was incapable of caring for herself and my brothers put her in a facility."

"Wasn't that expensive?"

"Yeah, but my brothers had money. They hadn't earned it legally but the care home didn't ask where they got it." She took a breath. "I saw her once more before she died. By then I was at Berkeley and she was starving herself to death. Eating had become incredibly difficult. She didn't want to put food in her mouth. She thought it was dirty."

My eyes filled with tears. "That's so sad but I'm glad you told me. Thank you."

She squeezed my shoulder. "I know this is hard but you have to fight for your future. Until your mom learns how to take care of herself you shouldn't be around her. She needs some tough love right now and it will probably get worse before it gets better. You've never let her hit rock bottom. That will probably happen before she can pull herself up." She paused before she added, "So, no, I can't change the admission requirement for your mom. She actually needs it more than most parents. Do you see that? And I'm sorry for sounding so harsh."

"No, it's okay," I said. "I guess we should probably go back." Now I looked away. I didn't want her to see me cry.

"I know that tone, Story. You're giving up, aren't you?"

I shrugged. "There's nothing else to do. It's the laws of physics. You're immovable and *I know* my mom is immovable."

"So you'll survive at Franklin High and on the streets? This entire opportunity will become an amusing anecdote your mom shares whenever she wants to boast? How she bested Ms. Billionaire. Am I right?"

Tears streamed down my face. I couldn't speak so I just nodded.

"What about the idea of emancipation?"

I stared at the stand of oak trees in front of us—strong, unmoving, unwavering. *Could I be that strong?* I wiped my eyes and shook my head. "I don't know if I could do it."

She started the car and pulled out of the rest area, but instead of turning left and heading back toward Lakeview, she turned right.

"Where are we going?"

"You need to see what you're giving up."

It only took a moment for the statement to make sense. "We're going to Tabula Rasa?"

"Yes," Char said. "If my team knew I was taking you there, they'd be pissed."

"Well then—"

"Don't argue," she ordered, pointing at me. "I'm the boss. It's my choice."

I raised my hands in surrender. "Yes, ma'am." I cleared my throat and whispered, "Can I ask why? If this is something you never do and it's going to get you in trouble, why? Why me?"

She didn't answer and I thought maybe she hadn't heard the question, but after we'd traveled a mile or so she said, "You have to fight for your future, Story. Sometimes you have to fight people who think they're doing the right thing for you. I gave up on my future a lot of times until Damon took me to Aunt Olivia's house. I want you to see where else you can be, somewhere that isn't an aisle at Walmart. Isn't a stoop in Cheshire. It's easy to slide back into the comfort of the street.

People do it every day. I probably would've done it, if it hadn't been for Damon."

We drove for another fifty minutes, deeper into the woods of Western Michigan. Char wouldn't have to worry about me telling anyone the location of Tabula Rasa. I had no idea where we were.

What was obvious was the shift in her body language. She sat straight in the seat, both hands on the wheel, staring through the windshield. Maybe she was just being super attentive in case a deer or a raccoon ran across the road but I knew something was bothering her.

"So, you've never brought any kids up here for a tour?"

She pursed her lips and set her jaw. She started to speak but stopped herself and exhaled. Eventually she said, "Only once."

"What happened?"

"What happened was…"

She glanced at me like she was wondering if I could handle hearing the story, which was obviously bad.

She stared at the road for another minute before she said, "We guessed wrong. We thought Jack, that was his name, would be more motivated to do well in detention and not get as many strikes if he saw what awaited him."

"Tabula Rasa."

"And he loved it. And he did better while he was in detention."

"But?"

Char exhaled. "While he was finishing his sentence we did more checking into his life. He had an alleged abusive foster parent but he also had two younger siblings who depended on him. If we took him away from them, he'd have a great life but they'd lose their protector."

"I'm guessing he didn't take it very well."

"Not at all. When he realized that his abusive foster father was the barrier—for his life and his siblings—he flew into a fit of rage. The father came home one night, plopped down into his favorite chair and demanded a beer. Instead of bringing a beer, Jack grabbed a kitchen knife, came up behind him and slit his throat."

I gasped. "Oh, my God."

"He showed absolutely no remorse for what he'd done. Since he was nearly sixteen, they tried him as an adult and a year later he was killed in a prison knife fight that he started."

"That's horrible."

Char nodded and wiped a tear off her cheek.

I wanted to tell Char it wasn't her fault. The foster father was the abuser but I understood her guilt.

Suddenly the radio was interrupted by an incoming call from Dr. Isaiah Baxter, the principal of Tabula Rasa. Char offered a pained look and tapped her steering wheel control. "Hi, Isaiah."

"Please take me off speaker phone," he said curtly.

"I can't. I'm driving."

"Uh-huh. I see. Are you with Story Black?"

Char smiled at me. "As a matter of fact, I am."

"Hello, Story."

"Hi, Dr. Baxter," I said, wincing. If somehow I did go to Tabula Rasa, I didn't want the principal to hate me.

"I told her about Jack. She gets it."

"I see."

"Is there anything else?" Char asked, leaning toward the speaker.

"We'll see you when you get here."

When he disconnected, I said, "If this is a bad idea, we don't have to go."

"No, I think it will help if you see it," she said, but I heard uncertainty in her voice that wasn't there before.

We drove another mile before we turned right onto an unmarked road that was well hidden by the trees. The trees suddenly disappeared and the road cut through a grassy meadow. Up ahead a cute little cottage sat next to the road. Scattered across the meadow were yellow metal boxes, each with a long rod sticking up in the air, holding a flat black panel angled toward the sun.

"You have solar," I said.

"We do. We use as much alternative energy as we can. We recycle as much as possible, collect rainwater, and compost."

Beyond the cottage was a hill that was as wide as the meadow. The road continued—into a tunnel. There were words above the tunnel, but we were still too far away to read them. I imagined Tabula Rasa was on the other side of that hill. I felt my heart beat faster. I was super excited.

Char stopped at the cottage and three men came out—Dr. Baxter, Tyrese, and a Hispanic man, who was dressed in black pants and a tight polo shirt that barely fit over his muscular chest and arms. I guessed he was the security for Tabula Rasa.

"Our welcoming committee," Char joked. "Wait here."

As she joined the trio on the porch, the Hispanic man gave her a big hug, as if he hadn't seen her in a long time. I guessed she didn't get out to the school very often. She stood with her back to me as the men made a semicircle in front of her.

I leaned closer to the windshield and tried to make out the signs above the tunnel. *Learn. Live. Renew.* The enormous hill masked everything beyond it, although I could see the canopy of an incredibly tall tree. To the left of the tree was a constant glint, the sun reflecting off something I couldn't see, something else that was tall.

I pulled out my phone, which had been vibrating like crazy in my back pocket. Fourteen texts, all from Mom.

Where r u?

By the fourth text she was demanding I call her, and by the tenth, I was a selfish bitch. I needed to make the most out of this afternoon because when I got home…

Dr. Baxter pointed at Tyrese, who pulled out his phone and showed something to Char. When his finger swiped the screen, I imagined they were looking at screen shots and possibly photos. He spoke while he showed her stuff on the phone until eventually he nodded and tapped on it. When I heard a ping inside Char's Beemer, I knew he'd sent her a text or email. I saw the glow of her phone screen from inside her purse, which sat between us in the front seat. I casually reached for the phone while I stared out the windshield. I glanced at the text on her home screen. *Patty Black and Hayden Runyon.*

I'd never heard Mom mention a Hayden Runyon. Of course, she barely talked about her life when she was my age. Maybe Hayden Runyon was a good friend. Maybe he was a boy she liked before dad. I thought about asking her, but I didn't think she'd tell me and she'd probably fly into a rage.

Tyrese also sent an attachment but I didn't know Char's password, and I felt extremely guilty for even a little snooping. I let the phone drop back in her purse and watched them. Dr. Baxter was talking again, gesturing, pointing in the direction of the school. Char crossed her arms, looked at the ground and nodded. I got the feeling the afternoon was about to change. I wasn't going to get to see Tabula Rasa and it was all Hayden Runyon's fault.

CHAPTER SIXTEEN

"I'm sorry, Story," Char said as she turned the car around and started back toward the road. The three men stayed on the porch and watched us leave. "I have a great team of people and sometimes they have to protect me from myself. As much as I wanted you to see the school, I have to think of the big picture."

"It's okay. I completely understand." I really wanted to ask about Hayden Runyon but then Char would know I violated her trust. My phone vibrated in my pocket again, reminding me of what waited for me back at the trailer park.

"It's only four. Can we do something else?"

Char smiled. "Sure. How would you like to have dinner with me and my girlfriend?"

"I'd love it! Do you think she'll like me?"

Char chuckled. "I'm sure she will, but you need to text your mom and make sure it's okay."

I pulled out my phone. There was no way I was asking permission to eat with Char. I wasn't *asking* for anything.

I'm out with a friend. Home later.

I expected the replies to start immediately and when they didn't, I frowned. "That's weird. She sent me several text messages and now that I'm replying she's not answering me."

"Are you worried? Should I take you home?"

"No, I'm sure she's just pouting. She does that whenever I'm not following her schedule or paying enough attention to her. It's really annoying but I've learned not to feed it."

Char shook her head. "Story, you are truly older than your chronological age."

"You think?"

"I do."

"Thanks." I shifted in my seat and asked, "So did you come back to Lakeview because your family was here?"

"Partly." She smiled. "I had good memories of going to the candy store when we visited."

"I'm pretty sure Gran used to take Mom there. My family has been here for generations and my great uncles worked in the shoe plant."

Char chuckled. "Small world. It's very possible some members of our respective families knew each other."

"Wow, that would be weird."

Char nodded. "I wanted to help a place I knew could succeed. I'm not trying to make Lakeview like it was in the past. Those times are over."

"Like Thomas Wolfe's saying, 'You can't go home again'?"

"Exactly. But I knew Lakeview could have a future. People just needed opportunities. You know, one and a half billion seems like a lot, and it is, but I'm helping an entire city so if I just handed it out, the money would be gone quickly. I'm just giving people a lift so they can help themselves. Trying to make up for the bad luck, even some of the bad decisions they may have made. Just balancing the scales. The rest is up to them."

I thought about how much I wanted this opportunity and what I'd done to get it.

"After I won the lottery I knew almost immediately that I wanted to do good with the money. I really wanted to make a difference with kids. During all the years I'd been a principal,

I'd heard so many heartbreaking stories…So many brilliant kids trapped in situations they never should've faced and not enough caring adults. There was one girl the last year I was a principal…Breanna Waits. She had a horrible life with a mother far worse than yours. I wanted to help her. I should've helped her. But at the time I didn't know how. She was the inspiration for Tabula Rasa."

She paused and took a deep breath. I could tell it was hard for her to talk about this student.

"But I know that education is tied to community," she continued. "If kids aren't thriving, it usually means the economy in that area isn't thriving either."

"Like all of us who live east of the railroad tracks don't have a great school and it's falling apart—or it was until you came along."

"Yes, we're making strides, but it takes a while for some people to appreciate change. And there are a lot of cities in the United States that need desperate help. My team looked at several different cities and a whole lot of data. Then we picked Lakeview. Not everyone was thrilled to see us at first, but now that we've been here four years, they see that we're not about just helping Democrats or Republicans, or Blacks and not Whites. Most everyone recognizes that we want everyone to be successful, and things are starting to change."

"I'm not trying to argue," I said slowly, "but if things are changing, why do the kids at Tabula Rasa have to leave their families?"

A little smile crept across Char's face. "I think you know the answer to that."

I thought about how bad things still were in the Cheshire District and how many kids at Franklin High bought and sold drugs. "Because change takes time," I said softly. "And we—I—don't have that much time."

As we pulled into the M-R parking garage, Char asked, "How are you with cooking?"

"Haven't had much practice. We just eat whatever's in the fridge or something that can be heated in the microwave."

"Sometimes we do that too but not tonight. You're a guest so we'll do something special. But I'll need your help."

"Okay. I'd love a cooking lesson."

I'd wanted to learn to cook but Mom certainly wasn't going to teach me. "Story," she'd said, "cooking is horribly overblown. You're an animal. All you need is simple care."

We rode the elevator to the market on the second floor. We wandered past the stalls and booths, gathering produce for a salad, stopping by the fish market for fresh bass and heading to the baker for a loaf of French bread.

Our arms full, we went up to Char's loft. Glass windows filled the exterior walls, offering a view of the harbor. The kitchen, dining area, and living room all shared one enormous space. High ceilings and skylights added to the dramatic effect.

"Wow. This has a lot of the same features as my dream house. It's like you read my imagination."

Char winked. "Great minds think alike."

After a quick tour I got a lesson on chopping vegetables. Mom believed there was little nutritional difference between a bag of frozen peas and fresh snap peas, so I'd never had a salad at home in my entire life.

I said as much to Char who agreed. "I totally get it. I'd been the same way until I went to Aunt Olivia's and we created a garden. There's something truly rewarding about growing your own food."

"Is there a garden at Tabula Rasa?"

She looked at me with a mysterious smile. "There is."

We set Pandora to a '70s station and rocked out to Earth, Wind and Fire's "September" while we prepared dinner.

"Crap!" I suddenly cried. I'd sliced my finger with the knife.

Char rushed over. "Let's get it under water to see how bad it is."

Please don't let me need stitches. If Char took me to the ER, Mom would make a huge scene.

"I'm so sorry."

"Hey, it happens to all of us. Keep it under the faucet for a minute. I'll go get some disinfectant and a few bandages."

My heart stopped pounding once Char had wrapped my finger and I realized we wouldn't be going to the hospital. Still, it was a deep cut and the blood seeped quickly through the bandage.

"I'm fine," I said casually. "It'll be good in a few minutes. I always bleed a lot."

"I think your chopping time is over," Char joked. "Why don't I get you something to drink and you can keep me company while I finish this?"

"Yeah, okay. Sorry I'm such a klutz."

"You're not. These knives are very sharp and I should've warned you. How does some mango iced tea sound?"

"Great."

We talked for another half hour. I tried not to think about my phone and the fact that Mom had never texted me back. I quickly forgot about her, though, when the front door opened just after Char popped the fish into the oven.

I couldn't believe it. "Ms. Sutton!"

I flew off the stool and into her arms.

"Hey, what a greeting!" She hugged me tightly, then stepped away.

Tears streamed down my face. "Sorry, I'm such a baby. I've missed you so much."

She handed me a tissue and stroked my shoulder. "It's okay. I've missed you, too."

I looked at Char. "How could you not tell me Ms. Sutton was your girlfriend?"

"And miss seeing the look on your face? No way." Char slid her arm around Ms. Sutton's waist and kissed her. "Hi, baby."

"Hey. What smells so good?"

"Story and I made dinner."

"No, that's not quite true," I disagreed, holding up my finger. "You made dinner and I just made a mess."

"Ouch!" Ms. Sutton exclaimed. "Are you okay?"

I studied my finger. "Yeah, I'll live but I think I need a new bandage."

"Char can finish and we'll go see if we can dress this wound a little better."

We went back to the bathroom and Ms. Sutton pulled out the official first aid kit. I was beyond embarrassed. I'd been so nervous cutting the vegetables that my hand shook as I tried to slice the cucumber. Who knew they were so slippery?

"I'm really sorry for making a mess."

Ms. Sutton flashed a warm smile. "It's not a big deal. I've cut my fingers on those knives more than once. Char takes them to be sharpened every other month because she can't stand using a dull knife in the kitchen." She held up my newly bandaged finger. "This is often the result. We're going to check it again before you leave, and if it hasn't stopped bleeding, we'll have to go to the ER."

I nodded, praying that didn't happen. It would just give Mom one more reason to hate Char.

"Hey," Ms. Sutton said. "Don't be sad. I know what you're thinking but it's going to be fine. Don't spend the rest of the night worrying about it. Okay? Does your mom know you're here?"

"I left messages so she should. I think she's pouting."

"Why? Because Char kidnapped you and took you to Tabula Rasa?"

I laughed and said, "She didn't kidnap me. I wanted to go. And we didn't get to go inside."

"Yeah, I heard. Maybe soon?"

"I hope so, Ms. Sutton."

She patted my arm. "You can call me J.B. I'm not your teacher now."

I knew my cheeks were turning red. I giggled, "Okay, J.B."

We went out to the dining room table. Char had poured wine for herself and J.B. and she'd set the table with expensive dishes that had little flowers around the edges. There were cloth napkins and the room smelled of baked bread. J.B. motioned to the head of the table but I shook my head.

"Oh, no, I shouldn't sit there."

She disagreed by pulling the chair out for me. "You're our guest of honor."

I felt weird sitting in front of them but it also felt special. I'd never been a guest of honor. Char presented the bass on a serving dish and my mouth watered. I was unusually hungry and I had to remind myself not to eat too quickly and use the manners Gran had taught me. "Story," she'd said, "there's eating at home manners and eating out manners. Learn the difference or you won't go out much."

I must've had an odd expression on my face because Char said, "Story, are you all right?"

I nodded. "Yeah. It's just been a long time since I've sat at a table for a meal. Mom and I usually grab things out of the refrigerator and stand over the sink when we actually bother to eat."

They nodded but the look in their eyes told me they felt sorry for me. Usually that look made me mad but this time it didn't. I felt sorry for me, too.

"Story, what have you been up to? Read any good books?"

"I finished *The Color Purple* and I've been reading *Room*."

J.B. nodded. "Both are great."

"I still wish you were my teacher."

She smiled and squeezed my shoulder. "Thanks. I wish I were your teacher, too. You were one of my best students."

I looked at Char. "Could I ask you a couple questions about how kids get into the school?"

"Sure. I just can't talk about anyone specifically."

"I understand," I said. "Are all the kids from Lakeview or are some from other places?"

"No, they're all from Lakeview, just different high schools."

"And they all gave up their families?"

Char's eyes narrowed before she said, "The families realized they were standing in the way of the student's potential." She pointed her fork at me. "Think back to when you told me about the mother in Walmart, the one pushing the shopping cart, standing between her own mother and her daughter. Remember what you said?"

"Um, sorta. I was pretty stressed out when I met you." I looked at J.B. and added, "I was really nervous."

She reached over and patted my arm. "You were obviously great or Char wouldn't be inviting you to the school."

I looked back at Char. "I think I said something about her knowing she was stuck."

"Exactly. You told me she knew she was stuck and she'd made sure her daughter was stuck, too. You said she probably felt guilty. That's what most of the parents of our students realize. We have something to give their children and they shouldn't stand in the way. That's what I'm trying to get your mom to see."

"I'm not sure she'll ever understand. I think she wishes she were me."

"What do you mean?" J.B. asked.

"I think she's asking herself, 'Where the heck were you when I needed someone? Send *me* to Tabula Rasa.'"

"You think she's jealous," Char summarized.

I nodded and we suddenly stopped talking, like they were thinking about what I'd just said. I stared at my plate. It was so pretty with the little flowers around the rim. I'd never had a dinner like this.

"Are you enjoying the bass?" J.B. asked.

"I am. I don't think I've ever eaten anything this good. Thank you for inviting me to dinner."

"You're welcome," Char said, offering me another helping of salad.

I looked at my plate and realized I'd gobbled all the food up quickly. I'd completely forgotten my manners. I pictured Gran staring down from heaven, shaking her head at me. I tried very hard to eat my salad in slow motion.

"Story," J.B. said, "if you could travel anywhere in the world, where would you go?"

"England," I said automatically.

"Why there?" Char asked.

"Because that's where all my favorite writers are from. Chaucer, Jane Austen, George Eliot, Shakespeare, all of them. I heard that a lot of the famous people are actually buried in the churches."

"That's true," Char said.

I looked at J.B. "I'm a huge fan of Shakespeare now, thanks to you."

"Glad to hear it. I think you would love going to England and seeing Shakespearean theater. They rebuilt the Globe theatre in London and you can stand on the floor like the groundlings."

J.B. had told us the groundlings brought sacks of rotten fruit and vegetables to throw at the actors if the play was bad. I pictured myself standing in the crowd with my bag of rotten tomatoes.

"Of course, when Char and I went," J.B. continued, "we sat in the gallery on cushions."

"I wasn't standing for a three-hour play," Char agreed.

"How long have the two of you been together?"

"Nearly two years," Char said.

J.B. reached for Char's hand and I saw love between them. I guessed Bertie and I looked like that to other people. Then I thought about saying goodbye to her. Forever.

Char touched my arm. "Story, are you okay."

I blinked away tears. "Yeah. Watching the two of you…I was thinking about my girlfriend. She's moving away to college."

J.B. squeezed my shoulder. "That's hard. Is she your first love?"

I nodded. "She's super cool. She's taught me a lot but I've learned a lot about myself too. Kinda strange, huh?"

"Not really," Char said. "The greatest interactions are those that leave both people a little better than they were before."

"I like that."

"I imagine it will be hard for you and your girlfriend to leave each other," J.B. added, "but there will be others."

I thought about Jamison immediately. *I don't have a girlfriend—now.*

Char dabbed her lips with her napkin. "It's just my opinion but you don't want to get too involved with anyone at your age."

I knew what she meant. I'd seen all the pregnant girls sitting on the stoops. Their boyfriends had said they loved them just to get them into bed. Once there was a baby, the guys were usually gone or onto the next girl.

"My mom says the same thing," I told them. "I think you're both right."

"Your mother and I agree on something?"

We all laughed at that.

"Char says you like to play chess," J.B. offered.

"I do."

Then I remembered my mom bragging to the Post Pawns about how she'd thrown Char out of the trailer. Mom didn't care that I wanted to go to Tabula Rasa. She'd fight to keep me and my only hope was emancipation. And if I did that, I realized I'd probably never see her again.

"Story, are you crying?" Char asked.

I nodded but couldn't look up so I was really surprised when J.B. wrapped her arms around me and pulled me into a hug. That just made me cry harder. Nobody but Gran ever hugged me and I didn't cry in front of Mom. "Story, cryin' is for babies," she'd said. "You're not a baby. Pick yourself up and make yourself happy again. That's all you can do. I will not indulge your sorrow."

I buried my face in J.B.'s shoulder and she whispered, "It's going to be okay. It really is. Just let it out."

"She'll never let me go," I whispered.

I kept crying and I couldn't turn it off. I'd kept the tears in a vault since Gran died, and Ms. Sutton—J.B.—came along with the secret code to unlock it. Then they were suddenly freed. Char handed me a tissue and I dried my eyes. I felt embarrassed all over again and wished I hadn't cried in front of them.

"I'm sorry I ruined dinner," I blubbered.

"You didn't ruin anything," Char insisted. She got up and disappeared into another part of the loft.

"Sometimes we just need a good cry," J.B. agreed. "Think about it, Story. Most of the great female characters in literature allow themselves one good cry per book."

"That's true," I agreed. "But not British characters as much."

We laughed and she added, "Yes, they're so proper. Score one for the Americans."

She'd made me laugh and suddenly I wasn't sad or embarrassed anymore. Char returned with a box, its outside a checkerboard pattern—a chess set.

"How about we play one game before I take you home?"

"Sure."

"You two play," J.B. said, "and I'll clean up the dishes."

"Oh, I'll help," I said, rising from the chair.

J.B. put her hand out. "You *are* helping me, Story. I'm no match for Char. She thrives on healthy competition so you take her on and I'll take on these dirty dishes."

Char had already opened the box and was placing the carved figures on the table. It was the nicest chess set I'd ever seen. "Do you want to be white or black?"

"Black."

I suddenly realized the irony: Story Black playing black, practically for the first time ever. When I played with the Post Pawns I was sometimes black, but since I played Mom most of the time, I was white and got to go first. She likened it to a hunter giving its prey a head start. I'd run ahead a few hundred feet and then, bang! She'd shoot me dead.

I marveled at the intricate horsehead carving on the knight. "This is a beautiful set."

"I got it several years ago on a trip to India. I've always felt bad when I think about how the ivory was acquired but I still appreciate the gorgeous craftsmanship." She commenced her opening move, pawn to e-four.

I countered with pawn to e-five, and when she brought out her knight to f-three, I surmised she was using the Ruy Lopez opening. I answered with the expected Berlin defense and we exchanged the standard moves for five turns. Suddenly she changed strategies. I found myself staring at the board.

"You weren't expecting that, were you?" she asked.

"No. Huh," was all I could say. My mother was in my head.

After so many years of watching her patterns and standard moves, I was completely thrown when a competent player deviated from Mom's norm. I pushed Mom out of my head so I could study the board. I saw the next four moves anywhere I laid my eyes. I felt Char watching me while I decided.

I brought out my king's bishop to g-four. She looked up with a little smirk. Like Mom, she didn't want to lose. We continued back and forth and I guessed she was refining her strategy with each move. We advanced to the endgame. I saw daylight and sacrificed my bishop. When she took it, I slid my queen to e-two.

"Checkmate."

She chuckled and gently knocked her king on his side. "Well played."

"Wow, Story," J.B. said.

I'd been so engrossed in the game that I didn't realize she'd finished with the dishes.

"Thanks," I said. I glanced at my watch. It was nearly ten. "As much as I'd like to stay longer, I should probably get home."

We carefully put away the chessboard, placing each piece in its foam cocoon. J.B. walked me to the door and gave me a big hug. "We'll have you over again sometime," she whispered.

"I'd like that. Thank you."

"Let me see that finger."

I held it up. The blood had finally clotted and only a little red spot had seeped through.

"Excellent. Oh, wait." She had a surprised look on her face and ran to the bookshelf. She returned with her copy of *Macbeth*. "I know you finished reading it but I wanted you to have this copy since I inscribed it for you."

She held it out and I could feel the tears welling in my eyes. How could that be happening? I was all cried out. I nodded and took the book. I hugged her again and quickly went out the door.

Char caught up to me and put her arm around my shoulder. "You okay?"

"I don't want you to think I didn't have a great time because I cried so much tonight. I don't understand it, either. I'm usually not a crier."

We waited for the elevator and she pulled me into a hug. "Story, there's nothing wrong with crying. We're all criers.

We're all laughers, sourpusses, and sometimes meanies. We're everything and that's okay." She held my chin and said, "I know how much you want to go to Tabula Rasa and I'll do everything I can to make it happen."

I nodded and my tears instantly dried up. Her words fortified my resolve. I'd get there. I would go to Tabula Rasa, somehow.

As Char drove me home, I fought to stay awake. I was emotionally drained. It had been the best Saturday ever. I'd need to thank Amber when I saw her again, since running to the M-R building had been her idea. I couldn't believe how much had happened in a day—hanging out with Char, seeing Tabula Rasa (at least the outside), having dinner with Char and J.B., playing chess and getting back my copy of *Macbeth*.

"Thank you for giving me such a perfect day," I said quietly.

"You're welcome," Char replied.

I pictured hope as an extended hand, waving in the air, trying to get my attention. It was like someone in class ready to answer a question or someone standing on a corner trying to hail a taxi. But as we got closer to the trailer park, the hand of hope disappeared. Char had a billion dollars but I doubted it could buy my mother. I was stuck in a corner and the only way out was through the courts.

We didn't talk the rest of the way home and I was relieved. It would've been agony. I was determined to throw off my seat belt and offer a quick thank-you as I barreled out of the car and hurried inside.

But as she pulled up to the trailer park my mom stepped in front of the car, shielding her eyes from the high-powered beams. And from the way she staggered and swayed I could tell she was high.

Char slammed on the brakes as Mom drifted in front of the headlights. The nose stopped inches from her legs and I gasped. Char turned off the headlights but left the motor running. The running lights cast a soft glow and Mom lowered her hands from her face. She took a few steps toward the passenger's side of the car and stumbled.

"Oh, God," I mumbled, getting out and running to her. "Mom, what happened?"

"Just having a party with me, myself and I." Her eyes were glassy and her breath stank of cigarettes. I tried to take her arm but she yanked it away and almost toppled over. "Leave me alone!" Her gaze leveled through the windshield and she saw Char. "You bitch!" she shouted and pounded the Beemer's hood with her fist.

I motioned for Char to go but instead she got out of the car, holding my copy of *Macbeth*. She strode behind the car so I was between her and Mom.

"She has no right to take you, Story. None at all! Don't you believe her stories, Story. Ha ha. That's quite the pun."

"Mom, stop yelling," I pleaded.

"I will not!" She lunged for Char and when I pushed her back, she toppled onto the sidewalk. "Aaggh!"

"Mom, are you okay?" I asked, rushing to her side. "I'm so sorry. I'm sorry, Mom. Are you hurt? I'm sorry I hurt you. I never should've left this morning. I'm sorry. You've got to quit yelling. We'll get thrown out. Please stop. I'm so sorry."

I glanced up at Char. She just stood there with her arms folded, wearing a stony expression. She had no sympathy for Mom, who was struggling to right herself, her face full of pain. "C'mon, Mom. Let's go inside. Tomorrow I'll go look for a chessboard. Everything will be okay." I looked up. "Char, please go."

Yet she remained where she was. Mom glanced up at her and barked, "Why the hell are you still here? Get out of our lives!"

"Char, please just go," I begged.

"What the hell is going on out here?"

Ms. Finnerly and a man in sweatpants holding a bat joined us.

"It's nothing, Ms. Finnerly. My mother isn't feeling well."

"Ha!" Mom shouted. "I'll feel just fine once Ms. Billionaire leaves in her fancy car."

The guy with the bat whispered in Ms. Finnerly's ear and the two of them offered Char an unbelieving stare. I turned toward Mom, just in time to hear her say to Char, "*Zugzwang*."

"Mom, what did you just say?"

Zugzwang was a chess term that meant any move was a bad one. Mom frequently said it to me with that same grin on her face right before I made my last move in our chess games, when she knew I had nowhere to go and no way to win. Amid her meth-induced fog she knew what she was doing. It was an act!

She thought this was a life checkmate. She was being awful in front of two important people: someone I desperately wanted to impress and someone who could make us homeless whenever she wished.

"Story, can you get your mother back to the trailer without her making a scene?" Ms. Finnerly asked sharply.

Mom's eyes widened and she touched her hand to her heart. "A scene? *I'm* making a scene? Lady, that hairy lip of yours is the biggest scene of all." She laughed and spun around, almost falling on her face.

"That's it! I'm done with you, Patty Black!" Ms. Finnerly stalked away as the guy with the bat followed.

"Please," I shouted at Ms. Finnerly. "Please give us another chance."

"What the hell is that?" Mom asked. "A gift?"

I whirled around. Char had placed the copy of *Macbeth* on top of the mailboxes and Mom saw it. She staggered over and gripped the paperback as if she intended to crush it. She slowly turned to Char. "Look like the innocent flower, but be the serpent under it," she said, quoting Shakespeare. She held up the play and threw it on the ground.

"I guess you aren't a fan," Char said.

I reached for her. "Mom, c'mon. Just come with me."

Char snatched the play and handed it to me. The look on her face said only one thing—rage. She leaned closer to Mom, who seemed to shrink. "You are the most pathetic excuse of a human being I have ever met," she said quietly. "Not only did you deprive the world of your gifts, you have made it your life's work to squash your daughter's equally amazing potential. People like you are the reason I'll spend a billion dollars cleaning up the mess you made. You, Patty. You!"

Mom exhaled and Char made a face and backed away. Her hands were fists and I wondered if she might hit Mom. It was as if all her anger had traveled to her hands.

"Char, please go."

I was crying and didn't realize it. Char looked at me tenderly, squeezed my shoulder and nodded. Her phone rang and her Apple Watch sounded. Somebody really wanted to get hold of her.

"Yeah, you get on out of here!" Mom gloated, grinning from ear to ear.

Suddenly Char was in her face and hissed, "Hayden Runyon."

Mom's face fell and she stumbled toward the trailer as Char hurried to the Beemer, leaving me standing there by myself.

CHAPTER SEVENTEEN

I spent the entire night and most of Sunday hovering over Mom. She'd sob in my arms, saying she was sorry for getting high, calling herself a horrible mother. The first time she said it, I disagreed and told her she wasn't all that bad. That just made her cry harder. We both knew it was true so there wasn't any point denying it. I asked her about Hayden Runyon and that made her wail. I didn't mention the name again.

Once she was cried out she'd lie on the couch nearly catatonic, staring at the opposite wall, curled up in a ball. Talking to her when she was like this didn't help so I went to my room and reread *Macbeth*. Mom had mangled and dirtied the copy J.B. had given me, but I straightened the pages as best I could and reread her inscription over and over.

Dear Story,

May your first exposure to Shakespeare lead you to enjoy all his plays and poetry. You are an incredibly gifted young woman, and I feel fortunate to have met you.

All the best,

Ms. Sutton

I appreciated the sentiment but I wasn't feeling worthy of her kindness. It was my fault Mom had blown her sobriety. She'd been doing so well, over two years. I knew she probably would've matched her record of three years and two days had I not disappeared with Char. I felt incredibly guilty. Mom had been using all of her techniques to avoid meeting her dealer, but when I wouldn't answer her texts she'd gone to find him.

When I was growing up, whenever Mom needed a fix she'd leave me with Gran. I think Gran knew what was happening, and as much as she hated the idea of Mom using drugs, my safety was more important than preaching about sobriety. Mom would make up a ridiculous story about a friend calling or a job interview but Gran always cut her off once I'd crossed the threshold of Gran's house. We'd wave goodbye and make cookies after Mom left.

Usually she didn't come back for days, sometimes weeks, but Gran was always there—until she found out she had cancer. For a long time I didn't know she was sick. Then Mom changed and tried to be better. She couldn't remember much about how to live but she stayed sober because Gran was permanently leaving us at some point. I realized it was a choice: stay sober or deal with life. She couldn't do both. That was the part Char didn't understand. Mom's sobriety consumed her.

In the end it was all about choices. I always thought the scariest part of parenting was dumb luck. Gran could've been the best parent in the world and my father still could've convinced Mom to take that first hit. And what if Mom had never gone to that frat party? My father would've hooked a different pretty girl on meth and I wouldn't exist. Mom reminded me of that fact constantly.

I knew what she'd say when she finally came around. "Story, all I can do is try. It's back to square one. Just like Sisyphus. I roll the boulder up the hill and it rolls back down. All I can do is roll it up again. I'll go back to the meetings and I'll do the steps. Blah, blah, blah."

I went in search of something to eat and found some peanut butter and crackers. It had been twenty-four hours since I'd sat at Char and J.B.'s table eating the wonderful dinner. I'd had so much fun. It was *normal.*

My phone chimed. A text from Bertie. *RUOK?*

My mood instantly improved. *Yeah,* I replied, not sure that was the truth. *I thought you had to work tonight???*

Nope. It's a special day... Put on something decent and meet me outside the trailer park.

I threw on some clothes, grabbed my bag and tiptoed out the front door. Mom was snoring so I knew she'd be out for hours. Bertie's old Honda was parked in the spot where Char's Beemer had parked the night before. A Happy Birthday balloon was tied to the passenger door handle.

I'd completely forgotten that today was my birthday.

Bertie was dressed in her usual jeans, retro loafers, and untucked white button-down shirt. She opened her arms and I walked into a hug I didn't realize I needed. She held me tightly and we stood there together for a long time, not caring who saw us. I inhaled the lavender-scented soap she liked so much. She gave me a sweet kiss and looked puzzled. "Peanut butter?"

"You caught me having a snack."

She whispered, "I have an idea for a better snack."

Her breath tickled my ear and sent a shiver down my back. I'd read romances about women feeling a sensation to their core and now I knew what they meant. I groaned and said, "What's the plan?"

"Well, our first stop is dinner."

I raised an eyebrow. "First stop? There's more than one stop?"

She furrowed her brow and pursed her lips. She'd said more than she wanted.

I giggled and said, "Where're we going?"

"Nope," she replied, opening the passenger door. "Not telling. I've already given away too much. I'm taking the Fifth."

"Are you requesting an attorney be present?"

She tapped her chin with her index finger. "Perhaps."

I slid in and she handed me the balloon. When she climbed into the driver's seat, I immediately pulled our faces together for what I hoped was a great kiss.

Her eyes were wide when we parted. "Have you been practicing?"

I laughed and she joined me. "No, you're the only one I kiss."

At least for now.

She grinned and we drove toward the interstate. When we took the exit for Kalamazoo, I said, "Wow, we're going out of town."

"A sweet sixteen birthday needs to be done right. If you want, we can stop at the Motor Vehicle Department and you can take your driver's test."

She tried to keep a straight face but she couldn't. The inside joke was that I'd been driving since I was eleven. When Gran got sick and there was no one to take her to the doctor since Mom wasn't around, one of Gran's neighbors, a long-distance trucker, taught me to drive. I was worried that when I actually took the test, I'd look too experienced and they'd know at the DMV that I'd been driving illegally and refuse to give me a real license.

Even Mom was impressed by my driving ability. The last time we'd borrowed someone's car and I'd parallel parked in about five seconds with one hand on the steering wheel, she'd said, "Don't do that during the test. Nobody but New Yorkers can parallel park. Work for one level above incompetent."

"I want to make a pact," Bertie said. "Forbidden topics tonight."

I'd introduced this game to Bertie on our second date. Gran played it with me throughout my childhood whenever I was a whiny pain in the ass—her words, not mine.

"We don't talk about leaving Lakeview, your mom, emancipation, lottery winners, or glam rock."

"Glam rock? Why would we ever talk about that?"

"We probably wouldn't but it's not a topic I enjoy so I wanted to include it."

I laughed again.

I laugh a lot with Bertie. I'm happy with Bertie. I was this happy last night with Char and J.B. Bookends to a crappy twenty-four hours in between.

I put my hand out the window, touching the warm summer air. I leaned back and closed my eyes.

"We're here," Bertie whispered.

I blinked and sat up. "What?"

"We've arrived at our first destination. You took a little nap."

"Oh, my God," I cried. "I can't believe I fell asleep. How long was I out?"

"Only about fifteen minutes."

"I am so sorry."

She took my hand and whispered, "Actually, I'm sorry."

"What? Why?"

"I should've asked you if you were up for a birthday date after what you dealt with last night. Not just the scene your mother made but then the aftereffects of her high."

I shook my head. "You have nothing to be sorry about. *Nothing*. But you did mention a forbidden topic and brought up Mom so I think I should get ten minutes of Twisted Sister."

"Who?"

"Mom's fave glam rock band."

Bertie rolled her eyes. "C'mon, let's eat."

In front of us was a bizarre, multicolored old house. The main space, which I assumed was the original structure, was painted banana yellow. It was three stories high and several balconies wrapped around the second and third floors. All were filled with diners being attended to by waitstaff dressed in black. To the left and right of the yellow structure stood tall brick towers that looked as if they belonged in a fairy tale. I pictured Rapunzel opening the highest window and draping her hair to the ground. In front of the house was a squat, single-story, emerald-green building with a massive front door made of wood and iron. Hung in the center was a metal sign: The Towers.

My eyes couldn't focus on anything particular. It was too much.

"Isn't it cool?" Bertie asked.

"Yeah, um, I didn't know architecture could be so... interesting."

"Wait'll you see our table." She giggled like a little kid and there was a crazy glint in her eye. I had to laugh, it was so cute!

We walked into a room made completely of stone. "Please tell me we're not eating in a dungeon."

"No, I promise."

"Welcome!" a voice boomed and echoed, bouncing off the stones.

A knight dressed in chainmail, minus his visor, bowed in greeting. He looked like he belonged in *Game of Thrones*, complete with bushy beard, square jaw, and an eye patch.

Bertie gave the knight her name. He bowed again in reply and pulled a scroll from the wall. He scanned the scroll and suddenly said, "Aagh! You're the fair maiden, Story." He dipped to one knee. "Your highness."

My cheeks were burning. I shrugged at Bertie, who only laughed. I gestured and said, "Um, get up…um…rise, Sir Whoever-You-Are."

The knight jumped up and said, "Happy Birthday!" Then three doors flew open and the room flooded with damsels and knights and even a three-person band. Some held streamers and waved them in the air. An incredibly beautiful princess put a crown on my head, dressed me in a Happy Birthday sash, handed me a scepter, and bowed. They all sang what I guessed was a medieval version of a happy birthday song, shouted, "Hurrah!" and then disappeared as quickly as they'd entered, leaving us with Sir Whoever-You-Are.

Bertie's gaze shifted between the crown and scepter. She was biting down on her lower lip to keep from laughing. I was too stunned to say anything but when my crown started to fall off because it was far too large, I had the sense to grab it and resituate it on my head.

"Glad you caught it," Bertie said. "I paid extra for that."

"Let me show you to your table. It's right this way," Sir Whoever-You-Are proclaimed.

He took us into a little alcove where a very modern elevator awaited. As we boarded he said, "We're a very progressive medieval castle," and pressed the third-floor button. He offered a bow as the doors closed, leaving him behind.

I burst out laughing. "How did you know about this place?"

"My parents brought me here for my twelfth birthday."

"Are you trying to tell me I behave like a twelve year old?"

She shook her head. "I just think you deserve some fun."

My eyes watered and I knew if I thought about any of this too much, I'd cry. Instead I played the character. I tapped the scepter on Bertie's shoulder. "If I'm happy by the end of the night, maybe I'll make you a knight...or whatever."

The doors opened and a kitchen maid brandishing a rolling pin greeted us. "Welcome to The Queen's Tower. I'm Mildred, your servant for this evening. Please follow me."

The dining room wasn't very large and it was round. Tables lined the edge, each one beside a window. The humming chatter of the diners was interrupted by the bellowing servers. The whole room wanted to watch the show since each server had a different and outrageous personality. Mildred seated us at the only empty table, and I immediately looked out the window, disappointed to see the ugly rooftop of the building across the street.

"Don't worry," Mildred said, as if she could read my mind. "In about ten minutes you'll have a lovely view of the park."

I must've looked perplexed because Bertie added, "The room moves like a really slow carousel. It makes a full circle each hour."

My jaw dropped. I'd heard about these buildings, but I'd certainly never been in a rotating restaurant!

Mildred presented us with menus and Bertie and I laughed and joked. I took a deep breath and inhaled sweet and spicy, making my mouth water. We shared a turkey dinner and a big piece of chocolate cake for dessert—with a candle. Before I realized it, an hour had passed.

When it was time to go, I returned the crown and scepter, but I got to keep the sash. Sir Whoever-You-Are held the door open for us and bade us a fond farewell.

We waved goodbye and when the door closed, I declared, "I'm drunk."

Bertie looked at me sideways. "Say what? Did you get something extra in your iced tea?"

I took her arm and snuggled against her on the way to the car. "No, I'm happy drunk."

"Oh, okay. I think I get it. Like so happy you can't describe it?"

"Yeah."

"Feeling like there's nothing else surrounding you except happiness?"

"Yeah!"

"Like you're the filling inside a custard donut?"

"As long as it's vanilla." I grabbed her hands and twirled her in a circle. A few people in the parking lot looked at us weirdly but I didn't care.

Instead of getting on the interstate we took the side streets toward Kalamazoo's downtown. Along the route, colorful banners hung from the antique streetlights, announcing the Kalamazoo Playhouse's latest production: *A Midsummer Night's Dream*.

I turned to Bertie. "Are we going to the play?"

"Maybe. Maybe not. We could be going to a Growlers' game," she said, mentioning Kalamazoo's minor league baseball team.

"You wouldn't do that to me, would you? On my birthday?"

I knew that Bertie and her dad had season tickets to the Growlers and Bertie knew I disliked most sports. I had, however, made an exception and gone to two of her softball games in the spring. At least with softball there were girls to watch.

When Bertie turned in to the parking structure across from the Kalamazoo Playhouse, I had my answer. I squealed and clapped my hands. "You are the greatest girlfriend."

I took her arm and we followed the clusters of people heading toward the entrance. Other than a handful of college students, Bertie and I were definitely the youngest people there.

"A lot of gray hairs," Bertie whispered. "I don't see anyone we know."

"Did you think we'd recognize anyone?"

"No, but it makes this next move easier."

"What are you…"

Bertie climbed onto the cement foundation of the nearest light pole. With one hand around the pole and the other reaching out in a grandiose gesture, she shouted, "Ladies and gentlemen, if I may have your attention!"

I heard someone mutter, "She's gotta be drunk."

"My wonderful girlfriend Story is celebrating her sixteenth birthday. If you would please join me in a rousing chorus of 'Happy Birthday,' I would be most grateful." She started to sing and by the last line everyone had joined her.

After a great round of applause she jumped off the light pole and resumed her place next to me. Several people congratulated me and an older lady hugged me and told me I reminded her of her granddaughter. While I acknowledged everyone who spoke to me, my brain focused on the light touch of Bertie's hand at the small of my back, guiding us forward as the doors opened. I said thank you at least a dozen times. I'd never felt so honored in my whole life. I couldn't stop smiling. Those strangers had no idea how much I appreciated that they took the time to say anything to me. Except for Gran—and Bertie—nobody had ever cared that I'd been born.

"These are great seats," I said once we were situated in the center of the third row. "If I were a groundling, I'd have my bag of tomatoes ready."

"You'd throw tomatoes at Shakespeare?"

"Well, I might not know it was Shakespeare's play if I was watching it back then." I squeezed her hand. "Thank you for an awesome birthday present."

Bertie's cheeks turned red when she said, "You're welcome."

She laced our fingers together and gave me a kiss just as the curtain rose. I couldn't tell which made me happier, the play we watched on the stage or the show we made together in the third row.

CHAPTER EIGHTEEN

Bertie pulled up to the same spot where she'd picked me up five hours before, only her car was turned in the opposite direction—toward home and away from the fun we'd had.

"I wish our date didn't have to end," I whined. "Thank you for making it so special."

She nodded. "Sixteen's a big one."

I snorted. "You sound like it was twenty years ago when you turned sixteen."

She fiddled with the steering wheel. Her hair had fallen in front of her face and she made no effort to rake it back as she usually did. "No, I just remember a cool party. Thought I should do the same for someone else."

"I see. This was like charity."

Behind the hair I saw the corners of her mouth turn up. I leaned over and kissed her. She pulled us together and deepened the kiss. I stroked her strong arms, felt our breasts collide and wished we had some privacy.

When I couldn't stand it anymore, I pulled away. I guessed our expressions could be mirrors—turned on, frustrated, and sad. We both knew this was the top, the apex. There wasn't another date that would be this special. Not only had Bertie spent at least a week's salary on my birthday—a one-time deal for sure—we were almost out of time. But it was worth it. It was a memory I'd cherish forever.

I got out of the car and stuck my head through the window, clutching my bag, my balloon and my sash. "I love you."

Bertie slowly turned and looked at me. "I love you, too."

There were tears in her eyes and it was as if she was begging me not to say anymore. The date would speak for itself.

I turned away from Bertie's car—from Bertie—and toward my life. The Honda's motor came to life and she drove away. I halted for a moment. Even though I knew we still had two weeks before she left, even though I knew we'd probably see each other tomorrow—maybe even FaceTime later tonight—this goodbye felt permanent.

As I approached the trailer, I heard Mom and Char arguing. In between there was J.B. and a man's voice. *At least Char and Mom have some referees.*

I hesitated and looked back over my shoulder. Maybe I should text Bertie to turn around. *I might like North Carolina.*

"But I'm home," I muttered and pulled open the door.

Everyone looked at me—Mom, Char, J.B. and Tyrese. Mom stepped in front of me, hands on her hips and growled, "Where have you been?"

"Out," I said quickly and then I gave the three others a hug. When they looked as worried as Mom, I added, "Bertie took me out for my birthday." I glanced at J.B., and said, "*A Midsummer Night's Dream.*"

"Why didn't you leave a note?" Mom demanded.

I rolled my eyes. "Really? We never do anything for birthdays. I didn't think you'd care. You never have before."

Mom waved at a cake sitting on the coffee table where the chess set used to be. "Well, it just shows you don't know everything. I'm full of surprises. A girl's sixteenth birthday is special so I made a cake. My sponsor got me the box mix and a can of frosting."

I bit my lip, trying not to laugh or cry at the lopsided cake with patchy frosting and a candle tilting to the right.

"What do you think? Aren't you impressed?"

I nodded but I couldn't decide what was the right thing to say. She'd never done anything like this before…a magnanimous gesture. It would be wrong to ignore it, but if I thanked her for doing something out of the ordinary, she'd get defensive.

So I didn't say anything and she shook her head and her shoulders slumped. "Great. I try to do something nice and this is the thanks I get." She stubbed out her cigarette and grabbed the cake off the table. "Fine, you don't want it—"

"Mom, stop," I said, following her to the trash. "Don't throw it away. I'd like a piece."

"No, it's clear you aren't grateful for my efforts." She pulled out the trashcan from the cabinet below the sink, releasing a foul odor.

I sighed. "Don't throw away the cake, Mom." My voice was monotone. This was an old argument. Mom felt rejected and I had to reassure her. It was like dealing with a child. "I'd like to have a piece," I repeated.

But I could feel my anger building. I reached for those recent memories…just a few hours ago. Bertie and I bantering…the funny knight…the crowd at the play cheering for me. I'd felt so…special.

"Nope," Mom said. She picked up the cake and held it over the trashcan dramatically.

"Go ahead and throw it out," Char said, "or set it down and light the candle. Do one or the other but quit playing games."

Mom's gaze narrowed in disdain. Char had called her bluff and wouldn't play.

"Ms. Black, I'd like to have a piece of cake."

We all turned to J.B. While Char seemed more than happy to watch Mom squirm, J.B. wouldn't abide it. "May I have a piece of your cake, Story?"

I nodded and Mom looked unsure of what to do. After a long pause, she set it back on the counter. She found a knife that looked relatively clean and cut a slice for each of us. She'd acquired a motley stack of cheap paper plates that read *Happy Birthday*, *Congratulations* and *Happy Hanukah*. No doubt they were leftovers her sponsor had thrown into a cupboard after different celebrations.

Char and J.B. drifted back into the living room area and stood near the door with their cake while Mom and Tyrese leaned against the kitchen counter. I wasn't sure where to be so I went and sat on the couch, thinking it was like a neutral zone.

"Story, how was the play?" J.B. asked, smiling.

"It was wonderful. I didn't realize how funny Shakespeare is."

"Yeah, his comedies are great." She came and sat beside me. "What was your favorite part?"

I told her about the dream scene and she offered up a few quotations. We were laughing and I was finally enjoying this weird birthday party until Mom jumped in.

"What fools these mortals be!" she emoted, gesturing to J.B. and Char.

J.B. ignored her and squeezed my shoulder. "Though she be but little, she is fierce."

I laughed and said, "Well, thank you."

Mom's expression darkened. She could be so childish. "One sees more devils than vast hell can hold."

J.B. wasn't laughing now.

I tossed my cake plate onto the coffee table. "Jesus, Mom."

"Don't be mad at me! These people barge in—"

"You called us," J.B. said firmly. "Remember? When you couldn't find Story, you asked for our help."

"What I remember is that I spent an entire afternoon making a fucking birthday cake and you all came over and ruined the party!"

I couldn't take it anymore. I stood and got in her face "*They're* ruining the party? Seriously? That's what you think? These people have done more for me in the last few months than you ever have."

Mom swallowed hard and her bluster deflated. "I was just tryin' to get it right for you."

The look on Mom's face was pure and penitent. For a moment I wanted to forgive her as I'd done a hundred times before. But there had been many "cakes" in my life, even if they hadn't been made of flour and frosting.

I snatched my cake plate from the coffee table, breezed past her and tossed it into the trashcan. "Madmen have such seething brains," I said slowly. Then I picked up the cake and held it over the trashcan in a dramatic pause. I stared at Mom, pulled my hands away and let it plunge into the trash.

Mom flinched as if I'd hit her. A small part of me wanted to comfort her as I always did. But only a small part. I was much more concerned about the other people in the room, the people who actually cared about me and my success.

"I'm sorry," I said, making eye contact with Char and J.B. before I stormed off to my room. I slammed the pocket door shut and leaned against the wall. I closed my eyes and pictured the one normal birthday I'd had—my tenth. Mom was away and Gran invited my few close friends. Nothing ridiculous happened. There wasn't any screaming. It was just fun. It was just like tonight…until I came home.

Since my bedroom was right off the kitchen, it wasn't difficult to hear the rest of them talking. Mom shuffled into the kitchen and said, "Oh, well. Tasted like crap anyway."

"You know," J.B. said, "this isn't a competition."

"Of course it is," Mom replied. "You made it that way with your stupid rule about never seeing the family. You force kids to pick."

"And you really think that's a bad idea?" J.B. countered. "Ms. Black, I've met thousands of kids during my time as a detention teacher. Nearly every kid's biography is the same, although sometimes there are unique twists that make a kid's story exceedingly repulsive or ugly. But there's one thing they all have in common. Every kid has been poisoned by the adults in their lives. Our rule removes them from that poison."

Mom snorted. "Thanks. Appreciate you calling me a poison. And that rule is unethical and enforced illegally. You're separating families. Don't you even care that you're a homewrecker?"

"We do," Char said. "And that's why we pass on more kids than we pursue. Only in situations where we know the family will be okay without the student, do we make an offer."

"Oh, I feel so much better now, knowing you spare a few families. I've got your number, Ms. Billionaire. You guilt people into giving you their kid and have them sign a phony document that's not legal. Parents can't just sign a paper and give you their kid, but they're either too ignorant, too stoned—or both—to know the difference. And when they won't, when they stand their ground like me, you threaten them—with jail or ruin... or worse."

Mom's voice cracked, and even though I couldn't see her, I knew her eyes were brimming with tears. *I wonder if she's thinking about Hayden Runyon.*

"We do what we have to do to save these children," Char said. "Reaching their full potential can mean so much to their communities, to our country...to the world."

There was a long pause before Mom said, "What if I were to tell you I need Story to survive? What if I told you that I barely make it every day? Story..." Her voice broke and I could hear her sobs. She finally muttered, "Story's the only good thing in my life."

"Do you mean that or is this zugzwang?"

Everybody turned toward me and I realized I'd left my room without knowing it. I watched Mom, who was leaning against the counter as though it was helping her hang on. I'd never seen her this vulnerable. "Mom, do you really believe you can't live without me in your life?"

She wouldn't answer and I knew it was because everyone was watching her, doubting her. She deserved everything she got, too. She slipped past us all and disappeared into her room.

Char crossed her arms and faced me. "Does that change your mind? Do you want to give up your chance?"

Now I looked away. I couldn't say those words. I hugged myself tightly, picturing the three of them taking a vote about me—thumbs up or down, head nods or shakes. I couldn't tell if, for the first time in her life, Mom was being completely honest—or not.

I looked at each of them. I think my face said it all.

"Well, we're going to go," Char said, pulling me into a hug. I held her a long time, knowing the book on Story Black was closed.

When we parted I was crying, but I didn't want my last memory of Char and J.B. to be sad, so I laughed. "You know, it's ironic. I went to jail on purpose. Then I was so worried about losing my chance and now I'm giving up on it."

J.B. pulled me to her and cradled my face between her hands. "And still, meeting you has been wonderful. You're an extraordinary young lady."

Char reached into her bag and handed me a white envelope. "I have a birthday present for you."

"Oh, thank you," I said automatically, pulling out four sheets of paper. The top one was a form—Petition for Emancipation.

CHAPTER NINETEEN

"What the hell is that?"

From the repulsed look on Mom's face, I could tell she wasn't impressed with my new brown Drive-Thru Burger polyester uniform. "I'm finally old enough to get a job and we certainly need the money."

She watched me finish getting ready for my third day at work, which would be my first eight-hour shift. I hadn't told her I was getting a job but after a week of post-birthday moping, I knew it was time to move forward and get on with life. Well, I wasn't sure if I was moving forward but I was doing something productive.

"I'll be home around five," I said, heading for the door.

"What about the park?" she asked incredulously.

I shook my head. "Mom, I'm going to work. Saturdays at the park are over. It's time for me to start behaving like an adult." I headed out, hoping she didn't rant that I wasn't paying enough attention to her.

"You're not quitting school, are you?" she called.

"No, Mom," I yelled back without turning around.

Once I reached the bus stop, I pulled a library copy of Shakespeare's *Turn of the Screw* from my backpack. It reminded me of A *Midsummer Night's Dream* and the first half of my birthday evening. That part had been exceptional—dinner, the play, and the perfect evening with Bertie. The surreal second party, with Mom, Char, J.B., and Tyrese, had been a disaster. I still had no clue if Mom had manipulated me yet again, which was why the emancipation papers still sat in the center drawer of my crappy desk.

Right before I'd gone to bed that night I'd received two texts: one from Bertie wishing me sweet dreams on my sweet sixteen, and a second from Jamison.

It's up to you now. You're 16 and u don't need her bs. Fill out the form.

I knew she meant the emancipation form.

Thinking about it. Maybe.

She sent a few frustrated emojis and then, *coming 2 LV for a CH soon. Want to show you something. B ready.*

She was coming back for a Convincing Hour.

Ok.

It was nice having something to look forward to, although it wasn't the same as having hope. That was a much bigger word for important dreams. This was more like anticipation.

The bus pulled up and I scanned the seats. It was filled with tired people getting off the night shift and sweaty people coming back from their Saturday morning workout. Even though there was an empty row near the back, I took a seat near the front, next to a sleeping woman in a custodial uniform. Mom taught me the best way to stay out of trouble on the bus was to sit next to someone. "Story, you want to be in control on the bus. If you take an empty row, somebody is probably going to get on at the next stop and sit next to you. Might be some kid with lice, a handsy teenage boy or some gangbanger girl who wants to get in your face. Always take a seat next to people who are minding their own business. And when they get off, you move."

The bus lumbered to midtown and I stared out the window and yawned. We drove past the M-R building and I glanced at the front doors, remembering how I'd marched into the lobby and asked to see Char. Those doors had been the beginning of the greatest day of my life.

As far as I knew, Mom had gone back on the wagon. Her sponsor had called me the day after I turned sixteen and asked if I'd enjoyed the cake. I'd said yes, not telling her that I'd thrown most of it away. She went on about how hard Mom worked on it. Even though it was a little lopsided, the fact that she'd wanted to do something nice for me was monumental.

I closed my eyes, castigating myself again for being such a bitch and tossing it into the trash. I shouldn't have done it and if I could rewind like a DVR, I would've just stomped off to bed and left the poor, defenseless cake on the counter.

The bus stopped in front of the high school and a few adults and students got off, probably going to new student registration. School started soon and I wasn't excited at all. Everything I'd done this summer would be erased. At the welcoming assembly the principal would tell us about the "new" year, a "fresh" start and a "great" beginning. The cheerleaders would wave their pompoms and the band would play the fight song as we shuffled off to first period—like lemmings.

I got off the bus and walked the last three blocks to Drive-Thru Burger. There were a few good things about working there but the most important was the security. It was impossible to rob. Drive-Thru Burger only had one entrance—a solid, two-inch steel door for employees. The serving window was bulletproof glass. The manager told me whenever somebody stuck a gun up to the window and demanded money, the crew gathered together and made faces at him. One guy got so mad he shot the window a few times. Of course the cops showed up immediately and he went to jail. She'd pointed at the two pockmarks in the glass to verify her story.

The other great thing about Drive-Thru was that it didn't have a playground. I knew people at school who regularly crawled around in the McDonald's Playland, wiping down the plastic handles and cleaning up the messes in the tubes when kids barfed or peed everywhere. Drive-Thru Burger didn't even have a customer bathroom.

The only negative was the size of the building—tiny. I got a little claustrophobic sliding around the three other employees who worked with me. So far the worst thing that happened was a guy in a Benz yelled at me for giving him the wrong burger. When I tried to explain it was my first day, he yelled louder. I vowed when I had enough money to buy a Mercedes, I wouldn't treat people like crap, especially the people who'd never be able to afford a Benz.

By three thirty my legs and back ached from standing in such a confined space. My job was mainly to retrieve things from the compact freezer—the burgers, fries, and shake mix. My calves cried every time I bent over and I silently wished we didn't live in a trailer and I could take a bath instead of a shower when I got home. I missed Gran's tub.

By seven forty-five the dinner rush was over and cars dribbled in slowly. We were all ready to go home and we counted the minutes until the overnight shift arrived. The crew that worked swing shift with me was cool. Carlos and Malcolm were freshmen at the community college and Tiffany was a senior at Bellman High across town. She was the cute shift manager. Every time she moved around me she touched my shoulder or arm so I wouldn't back into her. At first I just thought she was being super considerate, but as we joked and laughed at the end of the shift, I caught her looking at me a few times.

The bell rang, announcing another car had pulled up to the speaker. Carlos took the order while Malcolm and Tiffany worked the grill and fryer. I stepped up to the window to act as cashier and was shocked when Ms. Sutton—J.B.—pulled up to the window.

"Hi, Story," she said.

Her smile sent a rush through me and I grinned. "What are you doing here?"

"I heard you got a job so I wanted to see for myself."

I rolled my eyes like it wasn't a big deal. "Yeah, it's a start."

She got a pretend-serious look on her face and pointed at me. "You're not dropping out, are you?"

"No, I've got a system."

She smiled. "Of course you do." She paid for her food and asked, "Do you have two minutes to talk if I pull around the other side?"

"Uh, let me check."

Tiffany said I could clock out a little early so I grabbed my purse and met Ms. Sutton outside. When she saw I was ready to leave she said, "Get in and I'll give you a ride."

"No, that's okay," I said automatically.

"Get in, Story."

I nodded and climbed into the passenger seat of her Subaru.

"I know this isn't as nice as Char's Beemer, but I like it."

"I think it's great. It suits you."

She chuckled as she pulled out. "How's everything going?"

"Fine."

She looked at me thoughtfully. "And?"

"And what?" I shrugged.

"You look a little…sad."

"Well, my girlfriend's leaving in a couple days and you know, we decided to break things off when she went to college…"

"I see." She squeezed my shoulder. "That's hard. Same thing happened to me when I was your age."

"It did?"

"Yeah. She was my first love."

I knew I was about to cry so I bit my lip and just nodded. She dropped the subject and I was grateful. We rode in silence and when we passed the high school, she asked, "Are you excited to go back to school?"

"I think you know the answer to that." When she didn't say anything, I asked, "Aren't you going to make a pitch for emancipation?"

She chuckled and shook her head. "That's completely your decision."

We pulled up to the trailer park and I said, "Sorry. Gran would say I've been a terrible conversationalist."

J.B. turned in the seat and smiled. "I just wanted to see how you were doing. I wanted you to know I'm always available if you need to talk." She held out a card with her name and phone number scribbled on the front. "You keep this, and if you need something or if you need advice or just want to talk, you call me."

"I will," I said, knowing she meant it.

She gave me a hug and I climbed out. She waved through the open window as she drove away. I watched her until she turned the corner. I stared at the card. How many times in the last few months had I wished I could've called her? Another irony.

I trudged slowly to the trailer, my calves screaming for a rest. As I came upon one of the community trashcans I stopped and dropped her card into the barrel, convincing myself that I wouldn't need it. I took three more steps—and went back. I fished the card out and put it in my wallet. How many people could say they were connected to a billionaire?

CHAPTER TWENTY

It was the fourth Sunday of the month, which meant it was my weekend day after I worked graveyard. While it messed with my internal clock, it was nice to have Sunday all to myself. School had started and after a single day of teachers handing out the rules, claiming they were in charge and then watching a handful of kids in each class defy their authority, I knew it would be a long year.

I slept in that Sunday and made omelets and bacon for breakfast—enough for both Mom and me. She actually thanked me and asked how I planned to spend the rest of my day.

"Bertie leaves today for college. I'm stopping by her house before she gets on the plane."

Mom set her fork down and her lips became a straight line. "Hmm."

"Hmm, what?"

She threw her chin toward the coffee table. "I found that on the doorstep last night. You must not've seen it when you came in."

My fork clattered to the plate as I rushed to the table. Sitting on the corner was a white envelope with my name on it—in Bertie's handwriting. My hands started shaking. I knew what she'd done before I read the words.

Dearest Story,

There's no way I can say goodbye to you. It would be so maudlin… so weird. I don't ever want to think of crying and think of you. Time to 'fess up as my grandma says. You're always mentioning your Gran, so I thought I'd mention mine.

I delivered this on my way to the airport. By the time you read it, I'll be in North Carolina. Moving on with my life. Without you. Sorry to be cold. But you need to move on with yours. You know what you need to do.

You always sounded cool with breaking up when I went to college but I could tell you hoped that I'd come back for holidays and see you and we'd hook up… No. Not gonna happen. My parents are taking us to the Bahamas for Xmas. And if I can help it, I'm never coming back to LV, at least not soon.

But maybe in the coming decades we'll be middle-aged Tik Tok friends, or whatever old-people social media looks like. We'll reconnect and remember your awesome 16th birthday.

Go, Story. Live.

B.

"She left, huh?" Mom asked. "Without a goodbye."

I closed my eyes, letting a black veil drop between my world with Bertie and…everything else.

I took a deep breath and said, "Yup," before heading back to my room and reading the letter again and again. *You know what you need to do.*

"Hey," Mom said from the doorway. "Come to the park and play chess."

"No, not today," I said, rereading the letter for the sixth time.

"Come on, it'll get your mind off her."

"No. No thanks."

"Story, c'mon. You know how I hate playing with Post Pawn Pushers."

I whirled to face her. "Yeah, I do know. And right now, I don't care. I'm not going to the park! It doesn't matter how much you whine. I'm not going."

I stared at her but my gaze drifted to the center drawer of my desk—and her gaze followed.

She nodded. "Okay, fine. Suit yourself."

She left with a slam of my door and a minute later the front door slammed. I dropped onto my bed, still holding the letter and staring at the desk.

My phone was chirping—repeatedly. I'd fallen asleep on my bed holding Bertie's note. I found my phone under a blanket and saw a text from Jamison.

Where r u? Third text!!! Cameo loading dock. 3PM. B there and b stealthy. ☺

"Be stealthy? What the hell does that mean?"

It was two thirty. If I hurried, I could make it. I texted her back, changed my clothes and slowly opened my door. Mom wasn't home. I practically ran to the bus stop just as it was pulling up. I hopped on and zipped into the first seat. I must've looked like a crazy person because the older woman in the adjoining seat moved closer to the window.

My heart was pounding. Probably from the running but maybe from…hope! Jamison had a plan. Maybe she'd figured out how to get me to Tabula Rasa! My foot was tapping like crazy. It reminded of that interview in detention. Back at the beginning. It seemed so long ago.

I darted off the bus and hustled the three blocks, veering around the Sunday shoppers who constantly stopped to peer in windows or chat with friends. I dodged left and right until I came to the street that led to the loading dock. If Mom hadn't dragged me down this road before my own Convincing Hour, I never would've known it existed. More irony, for sure.

I hurried down the empty street and casually looked around the corner. There were three buses like last time and the drivers were standing on the loading dock talking and drinking coffee. I checked behind me, just to make sure no one was lurking about because that's what happens in movies and this was feeling uber-covert like a movie.

It was three o'clock but nothing happened. My foot started tapping madly. 3:01. 3:02. At 3:03, my phone chimed in my hand and I nearly dropped it.

Coming out now. Blend in the crowd. Look for me.

I heard the people and I quickly came around the corner, moving toward them. No one seemed to care. I suddenly felt a hand on my right arm. Jamison grinned and pulled me through the horde of people to the first bus. It was clear now that the adults got on the last two buses and the kids got on the first one—to go back to Tabula Rasa.

Nobody seemed to care that Jamison was bringing a stranger onto the bus. The noise was intense as everyone tried to talk over everyone else. Most of them were dressed conservatively, probably because of the Convincing Hour, but their rainbow of hair color, piercings, and even a few tattoos, announced their individuality. Some gestured dramatically, others laughed and whispered. It was like the ride back to school after a field trip. Everyone was reserved and following the rules on the trip, but once it was time to head back, their individual personalities burst out.

She pushed me into the backseat and sat next to me, grinning. "Ready to break in?"

"What? We're going to Tabula Rasa?"

A tall, Hispanic boy with a goatee looked over the seat. "Who are you?"

Jamison said, "Hector, this is Story. Story, this is Hector."

Hector laughed. "Are you a stowaway?"

"I guess."

"Emancipation candidate," Jamison added.

Hector rolled his eyes and nodded. "Good luck."

He sat down as the driver got on and shouted, "Head count!"

I grabbed Jamison's arm. "What are we gonna do? They'll find out."

She laughed and winked. It was kind of sexy. "Don't worry. I got your back."

The driver slid into his seat and a blue-haired girl wearing a sundress slowly moved down the aisle, pointing her finger as she counted heads. *I know you.* She was the girl Mom had grilled about quantum physics at my Convincing Hour.

My foot tapped frantically. Jamison reached over and put her hand on my knee.

"Chill," she said. "That's Caitlin. She's the mayor."

When Caitlin finally saw me, she looked confused until Jamison nodded. Then she skipped me and kept counting. Then she pranced back up the aisle and shouted, "All here, Paul!" before she sat down.

The doors closed and the bus groaned as it pulled away from the Cameo. It wasn't until we were a few streets away from the M-R building when I finally exhaled.

"I don't believe I'm doing this," I laughed.

Jamison hugged me and kissed my cheek. "Story, it's gonna be supreme."

"And Caitlin's the mayor?"

"Sorta. It's her thing and we all go along with it."

We giggled and talked about normal stuff until someone wiggled down the aisle and pushed onto our seat. Jamison laughed and said, "Story, this is Wen. Pronouns are they and them."

"Hi, I'm Story, pronouns she and her."

Wen's kinky hair was tri-colored and their tinted, chunky, black glasses hid most of their eyes. They wore a fringed leather jacket with a dark black shirt and black pants. They almost looked like a cowboy, only funkier.

I pointed and said, "Kudos on the jacket."

"Well, thank you. Sorry to crash, but I really wanted to meet you, and Paul, the driver, has a major fest if we're not in a seat." Wen was extra emphatic as they said each word.

Jamison grinned and said, "I don't mind sitting closer to Story." She glanced at me. "Are we good?"

"We are…" She was pressed against my right shoulder and I'm sure she heard my heart pounding, but she didn't seem to care. I wanted to tell her that while I loved her flirting, I'd just lost my girlfriend.

"Okay," Wen began. "Your mother. I was there for your Convincing Hour. I want to know everything."

"Are you sure?"

"Yes."

And they looked like they really did.

Hector from the seat in front of us turned around. "Wait, that was your mother? Holy fuck." He wrapped his arms around the back of the seat. Others wanted to know what the big deal was. Soon I was telling my story to the last two rows of the bus.

CHAPTER TWENTY-ONE

When the bus turned onto the gravel road to Tabula Rasa, I looked out the window and saw the familiar cottage, the place where I'd learned about the mysterious Hayden Runyon. The place where Char had decided to turn the Beemer around. This time the bus zoomed past the cottage and went through the tunnel. *Learn. Live. Renew.*

I couldn't believe I'd shared my story with complete strangers. Some had chimed in, knowing exactly what it was like to have a drug-addicted, narcissistic parent, and they offered support. I'd never told anyone, not even Bertie, some of the stuff I told them. Once I'd said everything I wanted to and answered a bunch of questions, everybody settled back into their seats and fell asleep. Typical kids on a car ride. Doesn't matter if you're brilliant or not, a baby or a teenager, the repetitive motion of wheels on a highway affected us all the same.

Jamison shifted against my shoulder. She'd fallen asleep against me and Wen had fallen asleep against her. Most of the other kids were sacked out and a few were playing on their phone. She sat up, yawned and looked out the window. "We're almost there."

I looked around. "Um, I just realized, how am I going to get back?"

She barked a laugh. "Oops. I didn't think of that."

My mouth dropped open in shock. I knew I should be worried or upset but I wasn't. I just shrugged.

Jamison shrugged back. "Maybe you'll just have to stay."

You know what you need to do.

The bus headed into a circular driveway next to an amphitheater. Once it came to a stop, most of the kids popped up to leave, even the ones in the back. I worried that the driver would notice me, but once he opened the door, he was the first one down the steps.

"We're going to give you a private tour," Jamison said as we headed out.

Wen clapped their hands and passed the word to Hector and Caitlin. "Yay, tour!"

I asked them, "Have other students stowed away on the bus like this?"

"No," they said. "That's why this is so cool."

When I got off, I was prepared for Dr. Baxter, the principal, to be waiting for me with a stern expression on his face. And if not him, then Char. But there was no one around.

Jamison said, "Story, this is Caitlin."

Caitlin had a firm handshake. "Story, it's nice to officially meet you. Far nicer than meeting your mother."

I winced and she shook her head. "Don't worry about it. Jamison let me in on this little plan because eventually I'll have to explain what happened to Dr. Baxter."

I went wide-eyed. "Oh, I'm sorry."

She waved me off. "It's okay. He's used to us."

They all laughed, and in that moment, I really wanted to be inside that joke.

Caitlin led us around the amphitheater, a half shell with tiered seating. The audience area closest to the stage was cement but the rest was grass. I guessed that the season dictated where the school sat and watched. I thought it would be cool to lay on the grass, snuggling with Jamison, while we listened to some funky jazz.

"This is a great place for all the school bands to jam," Jamison added.

"There's a lot of musical groups?" I asked.

Caitlin snorted. "Too many to count. And I'm not saying they're all good."

"Ours is," Wen added.

"Agreed," Hector said.

A sidewalk cut across the back of the amphitheater. On the other side were five identical buildings. It was obvious these were the residence halls. Rows of balconies displayed flags, stored bicycles, and served as a closet.

"As you can guess, these are the residences," Caitlin said with a sigh, as if she was embarrassed that such a mess was in view. She pointed to the one farthest away. "That's Ginsburg Hall, where I live."

"And I live next door in Obama Hall," Wen added.

"Me too," Hector said.

I looked at Jamison. "Where do you live?"

She hooked her arm through mine and pointed to the last building. "Right there in Gish Hall. Actually, that's a nickname. It's real name is Kechewaishke. He was chief of the Ojibwe, now known as the Chippewa. This was their land once upon a time."

"Who picked the names?"

"The first class," Wen answered.

"Cool," I said, nodding.

We went through a breezeway between Obama and Baldwin Hall toward a garden where two boys were planting small starter plants. The taller one was lanky like a basketball player and the shorter one was chubby with a round face. When they saw Caitlin, they waved.

"Hey," the tall one said. "Is this the stowaway?"

"Yeah," Jamison replied.

"Good morning," the shorter one offered to the whole group.

Caitlin pointed at me. "Keshaun and Dante, this is Story."

Keshaun, the tall one, said, "Are you staying?"

"I…I don't know."

"You should stay," Dante said, crossing his arms. He looked at Caitlin and said, "She should stay."

"Thanks for your input, Dante. Why don't you tell Story about the garden?"

Dante waved at Keshaun. "He's the promoter."

Keshaun smiled and said, "Our vegetable garden makes us somewhat self-sustainable. We grow stuff here in the summer and in the greenhouses in the winter. All the students participate. Knowing how to properly use the earth, tend the earth and preserve the earth are life skills."

"Well said," Caitlin offered. "Gotta keep moving. Have a good day, guys."

They waved and returned to their work.

When they were out of earshot, I said to Jamison, "They seemed really nice."

"You wouldn't have said that a year ago," she said. "Dante stole a car and drove it through a market."

"I heard about that. It was part of his gang initiation."

Jamison nodded. "Exactly. He had to prove how tough he was, and back then he was tough—and dangerous."

"What about Keshaun?"

"He was abandoned by his birth mother when he was four and left in the foster system. Wound up in jail for dealing. He was also using drugs to forget about the foster family."

"Oh, that's awful," I said sadly. "And do they share their stories with everybody?"

She nodded. "We have to. I'm not telling you anything they haven't told others, but what I've told you isn't the most horrible parts of their respective stories. We don't focus on that here."

"Tabula Rasa," Wen said. "A clean slate."

"Exactly," Jamison agreed.

The garden was immense and just beyond it was an enormous green space that looked like a park. Benches, swings, Adirondack chairs, and lounges covered the grass that looked too green to be real. A huge tree stood in the center, the one I'd seen from Char's Beemer. And I recognized it as the tree in Jamison's selfie. Teenagers were sprawled on the furniture and the grass. Some were reading and others were chatting in groups. Two kids were playing chess on a life-size board and I automatically walked toward it.

When the students realized we were there, they ran to greet us. Soon we were surrounded.

A girl with pink hair and several piercings eyed me carefully. *I know you.*

"Colfax?" I asked.

She nodded. "Hey, Story. A long way from Ms. Sutton's class, huh?"

"Yeah. You look great. And happy."

"I am."

Jamison said, "When Lynette heard you were coming by, she wanted to make sure she was here to greet you."

"Thanks. That's nice."

"Okay, everybody back to what you were doing," Caitlin said, motioning for them to go. "Get on with your Sunday plans."

They offered goodbyes and returned to their spots on the lawn.

"Let's check out one or two of the classes," Caitlin said as we strolled across the lawn.

"People are in school now? On Sunday?" I asked.

"Of course. Classes occur Monday through Sunday, although you won't sit in a classroom all day, every day. We operate like a college. Classes have certain times they meet and you have additional responsibilities to the school. A counselor works with you to appropriately manage your time. You're expected to juggle academics, a vocation, community work that includes gardening, and a hobby. In your case, from the way you were looking at the chess board, I'm thinking that might be your hobby?"

"Yeah, it's my thing."

"I play chess," Hector said, pointing at me like it was game on.

I pointed back and he nodded.

We crossed the park toward a tall glass building and passed a long greenhouse. Caitlin pointed at the students caring for the plants. "They have an interest in horticulture and agriculture."

"They're super serious," Wen added. "Way over my head."

"Mine too," Jamison said with admiration.

"Wow, it's weird to hear super smart people be respected," I said.

"It's expected," Caitlin said. "Nobody here judges anybody, Story. Well, at least not after you have time to get over your shit."

"Yeah," Hector agreed. "Getting over your shit, you get a lotta room."

"Oh, that's good." I imagined myself wading through my shit. There was a lot.

Caitlin placed her palm over a pad next to the front doors. They whooshed open and she said, "There's no keys or badges here. Everything is coded for biometric authentication, mainly your palm print. However, there are some places that require a retina scan."

"Wow," I said.

She gestured at the grand lobby. "This is the main learning and studying building."

"Its nickname is the brain," Hector added.

The first floor had several workspaces with different colored furniture. There were the standard couches and stuffed chairs, but also some oddly-shaped pieces that I wouldn't know what to do with.

"This is the common area," Caitlin said. "We have several clubs that meet here. Each color represents a pod. At Tabula Rasa students are assigned to several dynamic teams but only one pod. There are interactive boards and tablets available as well as the standard whiteboard so when a pod meets, they can take notes."

"And then it's all downloaded to your tablet," Hector added.

"So is everything done with technology?" I asked.

"Yeah," Jamison said. "No paper anywhere."

Wen raised a fist. "Way of the future."

We followed Caitlin down a hallway to what looked like a traditional classroom.

"Come check this out," she said. We peered through the glass at seven students watching another class on the screen. "These students are taking a philosophy class with Japanese students."

I looked closer and noticed the split view of the screen between the two groups. They were having a discussion thousands of miles apart. "This is awesome," I said.

"I'm guessing your mom would know what they were saying," Hector joked.

We all laughed and I nodded. *I'm sure she would.*

We followed the hallway past several empty classrooms until we arrived at the end of the corridor. To my left was a glass elevator and to my right were two black doors labeled AR-VR.

I gasped. "Is this what I think it is?"

Jamison grinned. "It is."

Caitlin activated the retina scan, which brought up a holographic keypad. I was shocked. It was like being in a *Star Trek* episode. She quickly entered a super long passcode and the left door opened.

"That's a lot of security," I said.

"It is," Wen explained, "but we're probably the only school in the US with this much advanced technology. Char spent a huge amount of money on this."

The room was semi-dark and filled with couches, overstuffed chairs, chaise lounges, and even a barbershop chair. Along both walls were cubbies; each one contained goggles.

"A student is assigned their own goggle unit," Jamison explained, removing hers and showing it to me. "Right now, my engineering class—"

"You're in engineering?" I asked. "Sorry to interrupt, but that's what I want to study."

Jamison got a dreamy look on her face. "That's great."

Wen coughed several times and Jamison laughed. "I got it, Wen. Anyway, my class is studying the Roman period and we're looking at the bridges they built. When you put these on, you'll be in Turkey at the Caravan Bridge."

"Wow. I've seen that before on a PBS special."

"This is way better than two-dimensional television."

Jamison fidgeted with the controls and helped me put on the goggles. Suddenly I was standing in front of one of the oldest bridges in the world. I walked under the bridge and it was like I was floating on the water.

"Unbelievable," I murmured.

"Okay, show-and-tell is over," Caitlin said.

Jamison helped me remove the goggles and we both started laughing. "I could've spent all day there," I said.

Hector crossed his arms and leaned toward me. "If you want to do that, you gotta come to this school."

"Noted," I said with a nod.

We left the AR-VR room and Caitlin called the elevator. We rode up to the second floor, and when the doors opened, we were standing in a laboratory. Pairs of students huddled together and various computer parts were spread over the tables.

"Are they building computers?"

"Yes," Caitlin replied. "Each student has different needs. Depending on your chosen vocation and academic track, you're expected to design your own machine and keep it updated."

"I wouldn't know how to do that," I said quickly.

"That's okay," Jamison said gently. "Nobody is expected to know that when they arrive. Everyone gets a student mentor and eventually each student becomes a mentor."

"Oh, that's great."

"We believe *life* is your education," Wen said seriously. Then they looked at us and said, "Do I sound like Dr. Baxter?"

"You so need the bowtie," Jamison laughed.

Wen shook a finger at her and dug inside their backpack. "Wait…" They pulled out a bowtie and tied it around their neck. "You need to know many things, but you need to *do* even more. Every student leaves Tabula Rasa with basic skills, including auto maintenance, home repair, and like I said before, a vocation, like these students. They're studying to be computer techs, but others are learning welding, auto body, and cosmetology."

We crossed the lab and Caitlin palmed us through a different exit that led outside. We were on a bridge that overlooked a lush, green sports field. A soccer ball and four kids rushed under us. Caitlin stopped and pointed down at the goal. "Of course, we believe exercising the body is just as important as exercising the mind."

As someone who hated rec in jail, I withheld comment and nodded.

"I see that look, Story," Wen said. "I'm the founder of the walking club. While Caitlin and Jamison go out and whack each other with…sticks…or whatever you use for rugby, my group walks."

"Oh," I said, relieved. "Good to know."

Crossing the bridge led us inside another building. We made a series of lefts and rights, deeper into the building. Every windowless wall was covered with whiteboard paint or inspirational messages, math problems, or questions. It looked like people did their homework while they walked to class. Couches and beanbag chairs allowed students to congregate anywhere. I slowed as I read the messages and quotations. One whiteboard was a series of algebraic equations. The student had stopped halfway through and written in red marker, *Help me. I'm stuck. Thanks in advance, Byron.* I stopped in front of the problem and studied his calculation. He'd made a mistake near the beginning. I saw a cup of whiteboard markers on the floor and said to Caitlin, "Do you mind if I help him?"

"By all means. But just show him where the error occurs. He wouldn't want you to finish the whole problem."

"Oh, sure." I struggled in geometry but algebra happened naturally for me. I drew my own arrow and wrote a short explanation with my own equation. "There."

"I'm sure Byron will be grateful," she said. "Only one stop left on the tour."

We took the next left and pushed through a set of double doors into another hallway covered in quotations. At the opposite end were two massive old oak doors with a quotation carved into each one. On the left: *Real knowledge is to know the extent of one's ignorance. – Confucius.* And the right: *The natural desire of good men is knowledge – Leonardo DaVinci.*

Above the doors was a metallic sign that read, The Breanna J. Waits Library.

CHAPTER TWENTY-TWO

Why do I know that name, Breanna J. Waits? "Who is she?" I asked, pointing at the sign.

The fun atmosphere suddenly disappeared. Nobody wanted to talk and they'd all bowed their heads, almost like they were praying. Finally Caitlin said, "Char says Breanna was the first student, even though she never came to Tabula Rasa."

I nodded. "She mentioned her to me once. I got the feeling she died."

"She did," Jamison said.

"She was a student Char knew when she was a principal, right after she won the lottery. Char's never stopped grieving her death and what she might have done to prevent it. Breanna's death focused Char on what she wanted to do with her money and her life choices. This whole place was kinda inspired by Breanna Waits."

"Oh," I said. "That's so wonderful and yet so tragic."

Caitlin grasped the large metal handle but didn't open it. She took a deep breath, smiled, and we all smiled back. "Okay. I think you're going to like this."

In that split-second Caitlin seemed like Willie Wonka right before he showed all the visitors his Chocolate Room. It was weird seeing students excited about a library.

She slowly opened the door. A dozen kids covered the couches, armchairs, and settees, reading paperback books or tablets. One girl lay on her back on the floor, her feet up against a wall. A few smiled when they saw us. Caitlin offered a little wave before leading us to a wide circulation desk. A woman in a wheelchair was speaking into a small microphone attached to her headset. I guessed she was in her late thirties with straight brown hair that flowed down her back. Her face was white as a doll's and she peered over her glasses at Caitlin before her beautiful eyes noticed me.

"Whom do we have here?" she asked with a British accent.

"Story, please meet our resident librarian, Ms. Mary Endicott. Mary, this is Story."

She met my handshake with a metal prosthetic, and I saw she didn't have hands, only claws. I smiled and hoped I didn't look too surprised.

"Is your name really Story or is that a nickname?" she asked.

"No, it's my real name."

"Perfect, I'll consider you just because of your name. When can you interview?"

I blinked and looked from her to Caitlin. "I…"

"Story's not a student. We're just taking a little tour right now." Caitlin looked at me and added, "Mary is waiting for a student helper to join her in the library."

"Not just any student. The *right* student."

I laughed and Mary laughed too—loudly. A few of the students looked up but nobody shushed us.

"Do you like books, Story, or is that a rhetorical question?"

"I love books."

"Then you need to see this place."

She wheeled out from behind the counter and we followed her to the other side of the library. Mary stopped in front of a large open space with bleacher seating that faced a small stage with a screen.

"This is where students give their own TED talks and other presentations."

"I hate that part," Jamison whispered.

"I think it would be hard for me too," I replied.

She made a left and went wheeling down a dark corridor. In front of us was another pair of wooden doors with the words READING ROOM printed in large letters.

She pressed the button for handi-capable access and the doors swung open. We stepped inside a cavernous space filled with bookshelves from the floor to the high ceiling. Students studied at long wooden tables that divided the room into two halves while others retrieved books from high shelves on moveable ladders.

The room reminded me of the New York City Library reading room. Mom had shown me pictures of it and said, "Story, when I die you sell off our crap and use the money for a plane ticket to New York. Scatter my ashes around this library." I wasn't really sure how that would work so whenever she mentioned it, I said nothing.

I stepped to the closest shelf and noticed every book was hardbound and some were incredibly old. I read a few of the spines—Kant, Descartes, Aristotle. The philosophy section. My gaze slid down the shelves and I inhaled their heavenly smell.

"May I touch them?" I asked meekly.

"Of course," Mary said. "That's what they're here for. This is the most complete high school collection *in the world.* If you are enrolled in this school, you will be expected to become a research expert. Life is nothing but the ongoing pursuit of knowledge. You will—"

Hector cleared his throat and Mary shook her head. "I'm very passionate about the library and could talk all day about it."

Mary led us out but I lingered in the doorway for a few extra seconds. I took one more deep breath, hoping I could imprint the Reading Room's beauty and smell on my brain forever. I couldn't help but think how much my mother would love this room.

"Thank you for the tour," I said.

"You're very welcome, Story, and you seem like exactly the right student for me to have as an assistant. However, you're not a student here, and I've never, *ever*, heard of a *tour.*" She scanned the students, her gaze settling on Caitlin. "What's going on?"

Everyone shuffled their feet. We were busted.

"It's not their fault," I said. "I've had a very hard time deciding whether to come here or not. Not because of the school," I quickly added. "Because of me. Because of my mom."

"Her mom is the force," Wen clarified.

"Oh," Mary said. "That was *your* mother at the Convincing Hour. I see." She sighed and picked up the phone. "Well, my darlings, I must end your ruse." Everyone protested and whined but Mary would have none of it. "Say your goodbyes outside because the cavalry will arrive shortly."

We made our way back to the green area Caitlin called "The Quad." I watched the chess players slide the life-size pieces across the board. I nodded when I saw the French defense. Seemed like the right choice.

Everybody just hung out, waiting for the adults to show up. I thought they all might just ditch me to escape punishment but they didn't. I turned in a circle, gazing at the buildings, the beautiful quad and the tree. Maybe I could just turn and run— or climb the tree to the highest branches. Dr. Baxter or maybe Tyrese would have to climb up and drag me down. I couldn't imagine Char would do it.

You know what you need to do.

I sensed Jamison next to me. She smelled distinctly of musk. "So, what did you think of the school?" she asked.

"It's as amazing as I imagined. Just seeing the library was worth going to detention."

"Would you like to go to school here?"

"Rhetorical question, right?"

We both laughed and she pointed her chin toward Hector, Wen, and Caitlin. "So, we're all taking bets on how long it takes you to get here."

"Oh, what are the odds?"

"Well, Wen, the eternal optimist, believes you're not going home today. Hector thinks it'll be tomorrow, and Caitlin's going for two days."

I cocked my head to the side. "And what do you think?"

Jamison bit her lip. "I'm thinking a week…if ever."

I knew I looked a little stunned and I didn't know what to say. A part of me wanted to cry.

Jamison took my hand. "Hey, it's not that I doubt you. You asked me about my story. It's similar to yours. Here, they call it push and pull factors. Push factors make students leave their environment and pull factors make it *impossible* to leave. I had both and I know you do too."

I nodded and felt myself tearing up. "I get it."

"But I'm holding strong at a week. I think you need to spend a little more time at Franklin High and then…then I think you'll come here."

She winked and it made me blush. And she hadn't dropped my hand yet. She looked over my shoulder and said, "O…kay."

I turned to see Dr. Baxter marching toward us—with Char. Even though it was Sunday, Dr. Baxter still wore a suit and a red bowtie. Char looked the same as the day she'd interviewed me in detention—tight jeans, a T-shirt under her leather jacket and those cool boots.

"Wow," Caitlin said. "You rate if the boss is here."

Dr. Baxter looked a little angry but Char's expression was impassive. All four of the students looked properly penitent.

"Hello, Story," Dr. Baxter said.

"Hi, Dr. Baxter. Hi, Char."

"Hi, Story."

Nobody else said anything and I felt like I had to keep my new friends out of trouble. "I'm sorry if being here today caused a problem. I think everyone was just trying to help me make the decision." I turned to the four of them. "Thank you. It means a lot that you bent—or broke—the rules for me. If I come here, will you be my friends?"

They all smiled and nodded and I felt a rush of excitement… and hope? Maybe it was hope? Jamison winked at me and I winked back. Then a different feeling overcame me, one that I smothered by looking at Dr. Baxter. He still wasn't smiling.

"Well, Story," Char said, "it's time to go back. As you might imagine, your mother has been phoning me, or rather she's been phoning my new assistant, constantly." She pointed at the four students. "I'm leaving your consequences with Dr. Baxter."

I waved goodbye and headed toward the tunnel with Char. "Are they in a lot of trouble?"

She shook her head. "They'll be okay. At Tabula Rasa we teach students that standing up for what you believe is right means something." She paused and asked, "So what did you think?"

"It's everything I thought it would be."

As we drove through the tunnel, the school behind us, I felt the tears come. I quickly wiped my face, banishing my self-pity.

"Do you know what you want to do?"

"Absolutely. I just don't know if I can do it." I gasped, "Why can't she be normal? Why can't she just do what's right for me?"

Char put an arm around me. "If she were normal in every sense of the word, she wouldn't be a meth user selling term papers and you wouldn't be living in a broken-down trailer. She'd be a genius making millions, working on the Human Genome Project."

"And I might not exist."

"Yes, that's the other side of that coin."

We got into the Beemer but she didn't start the car. "There's a great piece by Emerson about learning to work the ground you're given. You can curse it at first, but at some point you have to just accept what you have and take the opportunities that come your way."

I looked longingly at the school. "The opportunities…"

She pulled back onto the highway. Desperate for a new topic I asked, "Who's your new assistant? I didn't realize you had an old assistant."

"Well, I didn't, but actually, it's someone you know."

"Who?"

"Your friend Amblin' Amber."

"No kidding? And she accepted?"

"You won't recognize her when you see her."

"Wow. She's your assistant? You know she was an attorney."

"Yes, you told me that day we took our drive. You said a lot about her and she sounded like someone I should meet. So Elle and I went and found her. For now, all she wants is to be my assistant. She's changing her life slowly. But I think she'll become the Vice President of Housing Development and grapple with the homeless situation in Lakeview."

"Wow, she'd be perfect." I smiled. "I can't believe it. Thank you for helping her!" I reached over and gave her a one-arm hug. "That's great."

"I'm glad you think so. I try to help…when I have the chance." She said the last part softly, like it wasn't for me to hear.

"Um, can I ask you about something…about someone?"

"Sure. I might not answer but you can ask."

"Will you tell me more about Breanna J. Waits?"

CHAPTER TWENTY-THREE

The ride home seemed to go by in an instant. The only evidence of our nearly three hours in Char's Beemer were the wrappers and cups from our stop at a drive-thru and the wadded tissues from our mutual cry over Breanna J. Waits. Jamison had told me that Char recounted Breanna's story to new students, and with her telling it to me, I figured she was still counting on me to go to Tabula Rasa—or she thought it would nudge to do the right thing for myself, the thing Breanna never got the chance to do.

We pulled up to the trailer park and Char made no effort to get out or leave. I stared at the front light of our trailer just past the common area. It seemed like a really long walk.

"I hope she's not high," I said, thinking about our last trip to the trailer in the Beemer. "You might want to get out of here before she sees me."

"No, it's okay. Amber's in there with her."

"Oh," I said, relief washing through me. In an instant my blood pressure decreased. I exhaled and got out of the car.

"I'm glad you enjoyed your tour," Char called.

I stopped. I got it. I turned to her, chuckling and shaking my head. "You knew. Did you plan it?"

"No," she said emphatically. "I did not. Your new friend Jamison did. But I approved it."

"What about Dr. Baxter?" I asked hesitantly, making a face. "He didn't look happy."

"He wasn't. He was thinking of Jack, the boy we had to turn away because of his family's needs."

"I get it."

She leaned over the passenger seat and said, "Story, life's greatest choices will never come without a price. There are positive and negative consequences to everything worth experiencing. Just be sure you can live with your choice."

I nodded. I'd been weighing the pros and cons for days. "Goodnight," I said.

"Goodnight, Story."

I had a choice, a choice Breanna J. Waits never got.

When I opened the front door, my mother and a stranger sat on the couch reading. It took me a second to realize it was Amblin' Amber.

"Oh, my gosh!"

Her greasy long hair was cut into a stylish bob, she wore a fashionable mauve suit and her makeup accentuated her gorgeous face. I couldn't stop looking at her. She was beautiful. Then she smiled and flashed beautiful white teeth before she stood and pulled me into a crushing hug. "Oh, it's so good to see you, Story."

"I just don't believe…it's you," I said. "You look amazing."

"Thank you," she beamed. "Char out there?"

"Yeah."

I glanced at Mom who was still immersed in her book or pretending not to care that I'd gone missing for ten hours. Amber pulled me into another hug and whispered, "You need to hear her out but you need to do what's right for you."

She stepped away and said to Mom, "Patty, I'll be checking on you."

"Roger," Mom replied, never looking up from her book.

We exchanged a smile and she strolled out, her bag on her arm, a little sway of her hips. She'd never be Amblin' Amber ever again. She'd made her choice.

I shut the front door and said, "I'm sorry if I worried you. I didn't know what Jamison had planned and then my crappy phone didn't have service…"

I knew that part was true—I did have crappy service—but I'd also never bothered to check, too involved with the students.

She plucked her bookmark from the table, cradled it between the pages, gently shut the book and set it on the end table. *Now comes the screaming.* It never happened until after she'd handled her book like it was a newborn baby.

But she didn't explode. She pointed to the seat next to her and I timidly slid onto the sofa. She reached down and hefted the can with the burned chess pieces onto the coffee table. She pulled out the partially disintegrated black queen and held it up.

It's always about the queen.

"I've defined people's intelligence by how they play chess, how well they play chess against me. Since I taught you, you've always stood head and shoulders above everyone else."

She looked at me but I didn't know what to say. "Thanks, I guess."

"Amber taught me a few things today and now I'm going to share some things with you, if you'd like to hear them."

"Sure."

She fingered the queen and looked away. "I know you heard Char mention Hayden Runyon that night outside."

"Uh-huh."

"She was my lover."

I blinked. "What?"

"That's part of the story. Sure you still want to hear it?"

I nodded.

"My mother, your gran, sent me to the Willoughby School when Rich Husband Number Three joined our family. Me going away was one of his stipulations for marrying her, that and the prenup," she said sarcastically. "That was the school that named me the Renaissance woman and gave me the plaque."

"I remember."

She looked at me. "I should tell you before this little tale goes too far that you're not going to like your gran in it. You have her on a pedestal that reaches the clouds. Well, she's proof that people can change because she was barely civil to me. I was happy to get away. I loved boarding school. Then during my junior year, I met Hayden Runyon, my British literature teacher and the sponsor of the chess club."

She waved the queen at me. "Smart, funny, attractive, a snazzy dresser, only twenty-three and equally smitten with me. Hayden offered me private coaching, which I gladly accepted. It started innocently enough but…it progressed. We were mental and physical equals and we were in love. I know it sounds scandalous, but she was only a few years older than me."

I blinked several times, stunned. "*She?* Mom, you were involved with a *woman*? Why didn't you ever tell me that, like when I came out to you?"

Mom shrugged. "Not important."

I could only shake my head with my usual frustration. But still, it explained a lot. Mom had never married or had a serious boyfriend. She had no problem with me being a lesbian, hadn't even mentioned it.

Mom turned inward and her gaze dropped to the floor. "By the third trimester, neither of us was being as careful as we should have. Other girls had a crush on her but I was her lover. One girl in particular, Janae, figured it out. One day I was headed to Hayden's house and Janae stopped me on a street corner and said, 'Stop it right now. End it.' She walked away before I could respond. I knew what she meant but there was no way she could know what was between me and Hayden. How much we loved each other. I dismissed what she said and didn't think about it again."

Mom wiped sweat from her brow and reached for her tea on the end table. "One thing I should also mention is that Hayden was a graduate of the school and a legacy. Runyons had attended Willoughby School for nearly a century. Well, word reached the chancellor that we were having an affair. I'm rather certain Janae was the one who told him."

Mom's hands shook as she lit a cigarette. "Chancellor had me followed to Hayden's house. It was a cute little cottage at the end of the street, not too many neighbors, private. It backed up to a ravine with lots of trees, perfect cover for someone with a camera.

"In early May I was summoned to the chancellor's office. I found my mother, Rich Husband Number Three, and Hayden huddled around a conference table with the chancellor. Hayden was a mess. It looked like they'd pulled her out of bed. Her hair was everywhere and she was wearing sweats, which she never wore outside the house. And her eyes were blotchy from crying. There were all these eight by ten black and white photos spread across the conference table like trash. You can guess what the pictures showed.

"I wanted to scream at Hayden, 'Run!' Then I'd scoop up all those pictures, grab her hand and leave forever. But that didn't happen," she whispered.

"What did?"

Mom shrugged. "Not much else to say. They'd packed my things and the chancellor had already told them I was expelled. I had just enough time to look at all the photos on the table before my damn stepfather, whose name I can't remember, grabbed my bags and stormed out. My mother looked at me as if I were trash. She told the chancellor, 'I didn't raise my child to be this way,' and then she took my hand and pulled me to the door."

"I don't believe it," I said. "I can't believe Gran—"

"Believe it, Story," Mom barked. She took a breath and said calmly, "Look, I don't know why your grandmother did so much better with you than me. Maybe she got wiser."

I'd said almost the exact same thing to Char during my interview. Why indeed had Gran done so much better with me?

Mom stubbed out her cigarette. "Anyway, as they were pulling me out of the chancellor's office, I looked over at Hayden. She was watching me through her tears." Mom wiped her own tears with her sleeve. "That means something, right? I've thought about our last look thousands of times. She looked at me. She didn't turn away like she was ashamed. She didn't put her hands over her face. She looked at *me*. She still loved me. I know it."

"Is that the end of the story?"

"No," Mom said as she picked up the black queen again. "I doubt Ms. Billionaire found anything concrete in the records about my junior year in high school. My transcripts showed I entered Palmer High School but I'll bet she never found any yearbook photos or mentions of awards, anything like that."

"Why? What happened?" I really wasn't sure if I wanted to know but I couldn't end the conversation. This was by far the most Mom had ever told me about herself.

She lit another cigarette and I waited. After she took a drag she said, "We got in the car and drove straight to the Phoenix Airport and got on a plane bound for Tennessee. I kept asking where we were going, but they wouldn't say a word to me. I remember I was starving but they wouldn't let me get anything to eat. They wouldn't even let me eat the airplane dinner. It was late when we landed. We had a rental car and drove for a long while, deep into the Smoky Mountains. We wound up on a dirt road. Rich Husband Number Three drove while Mom navigated with a flashlight. I'd begun to think they were just going to push me out of the car and expect me to live on berries and twigs. That might've been better than what actually happened." She took another drag and closed her eyes.

"We drove for so long. I was light-headed from hunger and my mouth was dry. I'd stuck my mouth under the faucet in the airport bathroom while we waited for the plane, so at least I'd hydrated a little. But the fatigue was unreal. I couldn't keep my eyes open.

"We came to this electrified fence with a big wooden sign over it that read, Camp Positivity. Rich Husband Number Three hit the intercom and explained who we were and the gate opened. We drove down to the office and a clean-cut young guy greeted us. Number Three growled, 'Get out.' I said, 'Mom, what's going on?' She wouldn't look at me. She said, 'Just do as your father says.' She referred to all of the husbands as my father and I didn't have the strength to be angry as usual or even argue. I got out. Husband Number Three got back in and floored the gas. I tried to reach for the car handle but the young guy pulled me into a bear hug. He kept saying it was going to be okay while I fought him, but I was too weak and totally drained. I'd just lost my life. I gave up. It—"

"Wait," I commanded. "You're telling me that Gran abandoned you at some camp?"

"Yeah."

She knew her story was destroying my world. I shook my head, tears streaming down my face. "This is so wrong."

She reached over and took my hand. "I'm truly sorry to share this with you, Story, but you're almost an adult now. I'm glad your grandmother was there for you when I wasn't, but you deserve to know a little about why I am the way I am. Do you want to hear the rest?"

I nodded.

"It was pitch dark and I was in the middle of the woods. I stopped struggling and he walked me into the office. There was a pegboard with keys and he took number seven from a hook and faced me. He said his name was Troy and he was my camp counselor. He asked if I was hungry and I said yes. He grabbed my bags and led me to number seven. There wasn't anyone else in the room but there was a big turkey sandwich with chips and a Coke, my absolute favorite lunch." She paused and blinked. "You know, it took me years to realize it wasn't a coincidence that my favorite sandwich was there."

"Food deprivation. I've read about it. What did you have to do before he let you eat the sandwich?"

She looked away. "He sat on the bed with the sandwich in his lap. He patted the bed and I sat next to him. He told me this was a camp that would straighten me out, literally. He laughed at his joke and told me that each bite would cost me a kiss, not like a brother kiss, but like a boyfriend kiss. I told him that wasn't happening." She laughed. "God, I was stubborn. He sat there for two hours. Even started eating the damn sandwich while I watched. But I wouldn't kiss him. Finally he left with the sandwich and locked the door behind him."

"How long did you hold out?"

"Three days. He came in every few hours with that same damn sandwich and it looked pretty unappetizing by the third day. I was also going stir-crazy. I could hear people outside, having fun and talking. I had nothing in the room to read or do. I kept thinking about my parents and Hayden. God, I missed her so much. But I knew nothing would move forward if I didn't give in. By that evening, I couldn't go any longer. He came in and I said I'd kiss him. We sat on the bed. I gave him a nice kiss and he gave me a bite of sandwich.

"We went back and forth, exchanging kisses for sandwich and a drink of soda until the sandwich was gone. He told me that was practice. If I wanted to get out of the room and start participating in the fun activities I heard outside, I had to kiss him, touch him and let him touch me."

She looked at me. I was ready to explode. I jumped up and she said, "Hey it's okay. It was a long time ago."

"It's not okay," I growled. "Not at all."

"I know. I appreciate your feelings." She sighed. "Things went on from there. You can guess. I left that place nearly a year later, completely changed."

I held up a hand. "Wait, are you telling me they turned you straight?"

She shrugged. "No...I don't know. I was a kid, alone and abandoned. Since then I've always thought of myself as bisexual."

"And brainwashed," I added.

"I won't disagree with that." Mom took a deep breath. "Eleven months later Mom came to get me. Number Three was gone but she was dating someone nice. He'd turn out to be Number Four, the last of the marriages. Troy put my little suitcases in the car and gave me this big kiss. A part of me was sorry to lose him. I got in the car and he squatted at the driver's side window. My mom thanked him profusely and slipped him a hundred-dollar bill. We drove away and she babbled on for hours about everything I'd missed but we never talked about that place. Not until she was on her deathbed. Then she apologized.

"I started next year at Palmer High School but Mom paid off the records clerk to change my entry dates and create fake grades like I'd already been there a year. That way I'd graduate on time. When the scholarship people inquired, I'd have all my credits. Mom certainly couldn't tell them I'd spent a year at a sexual deviant camp. Nobody asked. It was a big school." Mom waved a hand. "And I knew everything. It's not like I would've learned anything in high school." She dropped her hands onto the table. "Okay, I'm done. Now you know everything worth knowing about me, including the mystery of Hayden Runyon. All the rest, as Ms. Billionaire has insisted, was predictable."

Mom's childhood was one of the most awful I'd ever heard. She hadn't said it but it sounded like she never recovered from the trauma of the camp. Even though she got into a university on a scholarship, she threw it all away for drugs and my father. And Gran… *Why, Gran? Why?*

Mom broke the silence and asked me, "Are you okay?"

"No," I whispered, my gaze downcast. "Can I ask you one more question?"

"Sure."

"Did the camp make you forget Hayden or have you thought about her over the years, maybe looked her up?"

She shook her head. "It just wasn't in the cards."

I raked my hands through my hair. It felt like everything was upside down. Inside out. I realized I was about to be violently ill and ran to the bathroom. Purging my dinner felt like I was purging the whole day.

"Are you okay?" Mom called from the other side of the door.

I brushed my teeth and splashed water over my face. I thought I might cry…but I didn't. I couldn't land on an emotion. I just had more questions.

I came out and found her back on the sofa, smoking.

"Why? Why didn't you ever tell me any of this? We've spent years living together! I came out to you. Don't you think that might've been a logical comment to make at the time? A moment when you could've said, 'Oh, by the way, the love of my life was a woman?'"

Out of habit, I bolted to the kitchen and closed the window. I rarely shouted in our trailer, but I was always conscious that Ms. Finnerly might hear our fights. While I was at the sink, I drank an entire glass of water. I thought about lecherous Troy at the gay brainwashing camp. I wanted to kill him.

Mom rose from the sofa and came to the counter. "Story, you seem to think knowing all that stuff about my past would've brought us closer but it would've done exactly the opposite."

I set the glass in the sink and faced her. "How can you be so sure?"

"Because in your eyes, Gran was perfect."

"I never thought she was perfect."

"Ha!" Mom laughed. "Pretty damn close! The pedestal you had her on was higher than a cloud in summer. She could do no wrong. And compared to me, yeah, she was a saint."

"So you don't think I would've believed you since your story made Gran look bad."

"Not a *story*. The *truth* is Gran *was* bad, at least to me. I wanted to go to college just to get away from her but I hated myself. I knew I was smart and that meant I should know what to do with my life but I was directionless. I was just starting to put everything together when I met your father. He seemed to fit but that might've been the drugs. Then you came into the picture—"

"And ruined your life."

"No. But you were no match for the drugs. And the older you got, I saw how smart you were, how kind you were—are. You're a far better person than me. I've always been so proud of you…but…"

I closed my eyes and hung my head, so afraid of what she'd say next. There was always a *but*. I couldn't look at her. I heard her sniffling. I knew she was crying. Whatever she said next was probably going to change our relationship forever. It was probably going to be a reason I couldn't forgive. I'd always resented her, but I'd never hated her. *Please don't say anything to make me hate you.*

"I've always been so proud of you," she started again, "but… I've never felt worthy of you. To be your mom. To be anything to you."

Not what I expected her to say. Not at all.

She sighed. "And your grandmother didn't help."

I shook my head. "She didn't make you take drugs."

"That's absolutely true. But she didn't help. She gave up on me and did everything she could to be a wedge between us. I know she felt guilty about what she'd done and every time she looked at me, she felt her shame. She told me that on her deathbed so I know it's true. You have your memories and I respect that, but I have mine."

She shuffled away, no doubt headed for the couch and her stack of books where she'd escape into the world created by George Orwell, the topic of her latest term paper. I retreated to my room, dazed and confused. Bertie's letter was on my bed and I retrieved the emancipation petition from my desk and put them side by side. My phone suddenly pinged. I hoped it might be Bertie but it was Jamison. A part of me was relieved.

R u mad at me? Had to ask Char. Didn't want 2 let her down.

I replied, *Ok. Not mad. Totally get it. Was a gr8 day.*

She replied: *Text when you decide.*

Ok

I was still sitting on my bed an hour later. If it were possible for emotions to wage war on a person, it was happening to me. The day was a roller coaster. Losing Bertie, visiting Tabula Rasa, hanging with Jamison, talking with Char about Breanna, seeing Amber, and…Mom's story. Why did she tell me that? I guessed it was because she hoped I'd feel sorry for her and decide to stay. That had to be it. She wanted my sympathy.

Then I remembered what Amber had said. *Hear her out but make your own choice.*

I guessed Mom had told her that story as well. I wondered whether Char had solved the mystery of Hayden Runyon or if Amber would share it. I didn't think so and I wouldn't be the one sharing it either. Besides, it didn't matter.

"It wasn't really her story," I muttered. "It was *Gran's* story. She let Gran run her life. That's why she told me. She is who she is."

Suddenly, I wanted—needed—to know something, something from the smartest person I'd ever met. I raced into the living room. Mom was still on the sofa reading.

"I have a question and I want the truth. Do you promise to tell me the truth?"

She looked at me strangely, almost concerned. "Yes."

"Forget me for a minute. When you think about all of the other kids you know, all the other people you know, when it's not about me, do you agree with Char's mission at Tabula Rasa? Seriously. Honestly."

Mom looked at me thoughtfully and laid her book across her chest. She took a deep breath and said, "Do you remember Rey Ruiz? A few years younger than you?"

I nodded. "He was brilliant. He was in a bunch of my classes in eighth grade. They skipped him two or three grades because he was so smart."

"And then?"

I thought about it and shook my head. "I don't know. He didn't go to Franklin. He...he's at Tabula Rasa, isn't he?"

"Rey's mom, Julieta, was my dealer."

"She was?"

"And Char locked her up to get the leverage she needed with Rey."

"Okay."

Mom sat up and leaned forward. "Julieta had two rules for all her customers: no swearing in her presence and no coming into the house. All transactions were at the door. One day I arrived, hungry for my fix. I was shaking bad. She needed to get more product so she leaves me at the door and Rey comes up. He was probably five. It was late and he's wearing pajamas with fire engines on them. He holds up this pad of paper and says, 'I'm doing *dision*.' He couldn't say the word correctly but I knew he meant di-vi-sion because he had this division problem with decimal points. He couldn't say the word, but he was dividing decimals. At *five*."

That sounded like Rey. "What happened when Julieta came back to the door?"

Mom shrugged and returned her gaze to the board. "Nothing. She knew I was cool and had a kid too. After that she always let me inside. Sometimes I helped Rey with whatever math he was doing, if I didn't have the shakes too bad. Sometimes I just needed my fix. No, I wasn't the problem. It was the animals that came to her door, *those* guys were the problem. When Rey was about eight, a tweaker burst into the apartment and held a gun to his head."

"That's horrible."

"Yeah, the guy told Julieta to give him all the product she had or he'd shoot Rey. So she gave it to him and he left. After that, Rey was banished to his room and Julieta bought a gun. She also had her brother Gustavo move in. He became the guy who *held* the gun during a transaction."

"Mom, I appreciate the story but you didn't answer my question."

"I am, in my way," Mom disagreed. "When I think about what Ms. Billionaire is doing and I think about Rey, and I think about that night he showed me his *dision*, I'm okay with it." She swallowed and shook her head. "No, I'm more than okay with it." She sighed. "And I have my selfish reasons for being grateful that she locked up my regular dealer."

I closed my eyes. "Why did you tell me that story tonight? Of all nights, why tonight?"

She rubbed her hands together but she couldn't look at me. She shrugged. "I don't know."

I actually laughed and she looked up, hurt.

"What's so funny?"

"You have *never*, in my entire life, uttered those words to me. You know exactly why you do everything. There's always a reason. Even if it's zugzwang."

She shook her head. "Then tonight's a first."

I crossed my arms. "No, I don't believe it. I can't believe it. Did you tell me that story so I'd stay with you? Did you reach out so I could find some way to trust you? After everything?"

She covered her face with her hands. "Maybe?" She looked at me, lost. "I really don't know, Story."

I thought of the woman in Walmart. I knew who I was in the story. Then there was Gran. And Mom. Stuck.

We stared at each other and I finally said, "Gran never changed with you. Not really."

"No."

I had to take a deep breath before I said, "And you're not going to change with me. You'll never *let* me go."

She closed her eyes but the tears still leaked out. "No," she whispered. "Probably not."

I started to cry...but it was different. I thought about all the times since I'd met Char that I'd cried. The sobbing. The weeping. I felt like such a baby. But not now.

I nodded and my whole body started to move. I clapped my hands together. I thought I might dance. She was still staring at me.

"I'm filing for emancipation and I'm going to Tabula Rasa."

As I bolted down our short hall, over the rumble of the fridge and the always-running toilet, I thought I heard her say, "Good," but it might've just been in my mind.

It didn't matter. I was making my choice.

I grabbed my phone and started to text Jamison, but then I realized who I really wanted to text first was Char and J.B. It was super late and I wasn't sure it was a good idea, but I did it anyway. *I'm filling out the emancipation paperwork now. Do you think I can be a student assistant with Mrs. Endicott in the library?* I tapped my foot like crazy until the text dots appeared.

It was J.B. who answered. *It is not in the stars to hold our destiny but in ourselves.* Julius Caesar, Act I, Scene III.

Before I texted Jamison, I wanted to reach out to Bertie. I didn't know if she'd reply, but... *I'm living my own life. Going to Tabula Rasa.*

It only took a few seconds for the reply. *So happy for you!*

I sighed. She didn't say anything else like "Let's talk soon," but that was okay.

I smiled and started my text to Jamison, thinking about the engineering program, the library, the life-size chess set and the motto above the tunnel, *Learn-Live-Renew.*

I knew I had a lot of shit to work through but I was taking my chance.

My chance.

It was right on the other side of that tunnel.

About the Author

Award-winning author Ann Roberts has penned twenty-one books and a handful of short stories. A lifelong educator, Ann retired to focus on her writing. She also edits and coaches other authors. She and her partner (now wife) of nearly twenty-seven years moved from the dry desert of Arizona to the ocean and tall firs of Oregon in 2017. She loves to hear from readers and can be reached through her website annroberts.net.

Acknowledgments

I was incredibly fortunate to spend twenty-eight years in a profession I loved, working with amazing colleagues, doing work that was important, and engaging with kids from pre-school to 12th grade. I cared *for* and *about* all of my students, even the ones who didn't like English class or weren't happy when I, as a principal, had to give them consequences for poor choices. Through Facebook and chance encounters, I've delighted in hearing about the wonderful lives they've made for themselves, admired their grit and tenacity when faced with adversity, and wept at the loss of those who died far too soon, sometimes because they couldn't overcome their circumstances. I think of those students often.

While none of the characters in this book is modeled after a particular person, the students are composites of many. I've known dozens of Storys and Breannas. A part of each of them is in this book.

I am forever grateful to Mr. Frank Burnsed and Ms. Ximena Doyle, former Instructional Leaders with the Maricopa County Regional School District (MCRSD), and the teachers at Durango Transitional Learning Center and Mesa Transitional Learning Center. They welcomed me into their schools and classrooms. Their vast experience with alternative populations ensured I created a genuine and realistic backdrop of juvenile detention. Whatever isn't accurately portrayed is either my literary license or my own error.

Bella Books is a place of collegiality and friendship. I'm forever grateful to Linda and Jessica Hill for their unwavering support these past fifteen years. Authors Marie Castle, Erica Abbott, Cindy Rizzo, and Catherine Maiorisi provided key feedback that helped develop the characters and plot. Award-winning YA author Rachel Gold pushed me in all the right ways to make Story Black a strong heroine. And speaking of pushing, my editor Katherine V. Forrest always knows the direction a book should take and what I need to do to get there. Thanks for being such a terrific guide, Katherine.

Along the way there were my beta readers Susan and Patricia, my high school neighbor Carsen who helped with texting lingo, and my wife, Amy. No one believed more in this story than she did. I couldn't have a better partner in life, especially during a pandemic.

Bella Books, Inc.

Women. Books. Even Better Together.

P.O. Box 10543
Tallahassee, FL 32302

Phone: 800-729-4992
www.bellabooks.com